"I D[...]
I DON'T [...]

Then as if to prov[...]
and stared at me. Searchingly. For a long,
long moment.

I was taken off guard. Otherwise, I certainly
wouldn't have remained mute, staring into
Matthias Cross's eyes, suddenly aware that he
was wearing Aramis aftershave, a scent that
has been known to make me a little dizzy when
worn by the right person.

Matthias Cross was not, however, the right
person. Let us not forget that this was the same
man who had just finished showing my bikini
photo all over the office, totally ignoring my
objections. *And* this was the same man who
not an hour ago had all but accused me of
murdering his father. Call me pessimistic, but
I don't think these things portend a promising
relationship. While it was true it had been
months since I'd met a really interesting man,
I didn't think I was so desperate that I needed
to start considering as a possibility the one
man in the world who might most want to see
me on Death Row....

HEIR CONDITION

HEIR
CONDITION

Tierney McClellan

A SIGNET BOOK

SIGNET
Published by the Penguin Group
Penguin Books USA Inc., 375 Hudson Street,
New York, New York 10014, U.S.A.
Penguin Books Ltd, 27 Wrights Lane,
London W8 5TZ, England
Penguin Books Australia Ltd, Ringwood,
Victoria, Australia
Penguin Books Canada Ltd, 10 Alcorn Avenue,
Toronto, Ontario, Canada M4V 3B2
Penguin Books (N.Z.) Ltd, 182–190 Wairau Road,
Auckland 10, New Zealand

Penguin Books Ltd, Registered Offices:
Harmondsworth, Middlesex, England

First published by Signet,
an imprint of Dutton Signet,
a division of Penguin Books USA Inc.

First Printing, January, 1995
10 9 8 7 6 5 4 3 2 1

Cover art by Robert Crawford

REGISTERED TRADEMARK—MARCA REGISTRADA

Printed in the United States of America

PUBLISHER'S NOTE
This is a work of fiction. Names, characters, places, and incidents either
are the product of the author's imagination or are used fictitiously,
and any resemblance to actual persons, living or dead, events, or locales
is entirely coincidental.

BOOKS ARE AVAILABLE AT QUANTITY DISCOUNTS WHEN USED TO PROMOTE
PRODUCTS OR SERVICES. FOR INFORMATION PLEASE WRITE TO PREMIUM
MARKETING DIVISION, PENGUIN BOOKS USA INC., 375 HUDSON STREET, NEW
YORK, NEW YORK 10014.

To my three heirs,
Geoff, Chris, and Rachael,
with much love

ACKNOWLEDGMENTS

I would like to thank the following for their assistance: Sergeant Fraction of the Louisville Police Department; Bill Russell, Sharon Leaman, and especially, Laurie Birnsteel, of Cherokee Realty in Lousville, Kentucky; and all the kind people at Ridgway Memorial Library in Shepherdsville, Kentucky. I would also like to especially thank my twin sister, Beverly Herald, for serving as my first reader.

Chapter 1

When the doorbell rang that Saturday morning in early June, I was thinking about murder, appropriately enough.

The murder I was thinking about was the one I always go over in my mind while I do my exercises. While I twist and turn and bounce sweatily to Jane Fonda's latest video, I always dull the pain by trying to come up with the most appropriate way to bump Jane off. Months ago, it had taken me only one twenty-minute session of exercising to her latest relentlessly cheerful video to decide that Jane deserved it. For one thing, if it wasn't for Jane Fonda looking so great in her *fifties*, for God's sake, I no doubt would've been perfectly happy to slip into the chubby, misshapen lump I was meant to be once I passed the big Four-O.

For another thing, any woman who would keep producing these exercise tapes has got to be a sadist. In fact, you only have to watch one minute of any of Jane's videos, to see her thin, excessively healthy body cavorting happily across the screen, silently mocking the rest of us, to realize that Jane is one sick puppy. She must particularly hate women my age, because she keeps giving us these idiot exercises that even a school kid would have trouble doing.

I'd been exercising to Jane's latest torture-tape for almost three months, and I still hadn't even come close to being able to touch my toes. Moreover, even *waving* at my toes still caused me considerable pain. It wasn't as if I were overweight, either. By cutting out ice cream and potato chips—a monumental sacrifice, I might add—I'd finally gotten down to what my doctor calls the "optimum" weight for my 5'6" frame—130 pounds. Nevertheless, my toes still remained painfully out of reach.

I knew, of course, what Jane would say about that. No pain, no gain. She'd probably also mention that, perhaps, I should've started exercising regularly some time before I turned forty-one. Fact was, being out of condition really hadn't bothered me until about three months ago when I noticed that I was actually getting out of breath just walking briskly from room to room through a small ranch-type house. Since I'm a real estate agent, and since this particular ranch happened to be a new listing of mine, I was getting out of breath on a fairly regular basis.

That's when I went out and bought the Jane Fonda video. Personally, I think Jane should be glad that there is *anybody* out here in video land who is willing to tie herself into a human pretzel—and pay $29.95 plus tax for Jane to show her how to do it.

Anyway, that Saturday morning I'd been doing pretzel imitations for twenty grueling minutes, and I'd pretty much decided that throwing Jane into a vat of chocolate syrup and then pummeling her with maraschino cherries until she went under would be a fitting end. The doorbell, as I mentioned before, interrupted my exercising and my murderous impulses.

For a second, even though the doorbell kept ringing, I actually considered not answering it. I was dressed in a purple leotard and purple tights that I'd found on a clearance table the day I'd bought the videotape. At the time, it hadn't occurred to me to question why this particular outfit was on sale, and having just spent the aforementioned $29.95 plus tax on the video, I'd leaped at the chance to get the leotard and tights dirt cheap. Once I'd gotten them home, however, it hadn't taken me long to realize why this get-up had been marked down. It made you look like an overripe grape. Also, the color was the exact shade of your face after you'd been exercising with Jane for any time longer than thirty seconds.

From where I stood in my living room, however, I could clearly see the figure out on my front porch, peering through the semisheer curtains covering one of the long, narrow windows on either side of my front door out in the foyer. It was obvious that if I could see him, he could see me—the sweaty grape in the middle of the room. And he'd have to be deaf not to hear Jane glee-fully barking out her instructions.

I sighed, turned Jane off, and went to the door.

"Certified letter for Schuyler Ridgway," the mailman said. His eyes, I noticed, did not meet mine. I knew the guy, too. At least, I knew him as much as you can know the man who has brought you your mail for the last ten years or so. Generally, on the rare occasions when he gives me my mail personally, the mailman calls me "Mrs. Ridgway." This time, however, he apparently refused to recognize me in my grape disguise. He handed me a receipt to sign, a pen to sign it with, and with a look of relief, was gone.

I said, "Thank you," to his hastily retreating back, and opened the envelope. Maybe the next time I ought to put on a robe before I go to the door. So as not to scare anybody.

The letter was short and to the point. "Dear Ms. Ridgway: You have been named as an heir in the estate of Ephraim Benjamin Cross, and are hereby requested to attend a formal reading of Mr. Cross's Last Will and Testament in the offices of Bentley, Stern, and Glassner, 2300A Citizens Plaza, Louisville." The reading was scheduled for the following Monday at 2:30 in the afternoon.

I read the letter through twice, and I could actually feel some of the purple fading from my face. I even found myself just staring at the body of the letter like some fool. As if maybe I expected the words to change even as I read them. Turning over the envelope, I reread the address on the front. Schuyler Ridgway, 17443 Harvard Drive, Louisville, Kentucky 40205. It was my name and my address, all right. I scratched my damp head. Now, why on earth would Ephraim Cross, of all people, have left me anything? I didn't even know the man.

I did know *of* him, of course. There weren't many people in Louisville who did not know *of* Ephraim

Cross. As the CEO of CareGivers, Inc.—a lucrative company that owns and manages a chain of nursing homes throughout Kentucky and Tennessee—Ephraim Cross was, if not the richest man in Kentucky, at least in the top ten. The man had often had his photo featured in the Louisville *Courier-Journal,* mostly in the business section, but occasionally in society layouts. Around Derby time, he'd always been shown hobnobbing with the great and the wealthy at various posh parties, and the Sunday after Derby his photo had always been displayed prominently with all the others who'd showed up on Millionaires' Row at Churchill Downs on Derby Day.

I guess most everybody in Louisville knew *of* Ephraim Cross. And if they'd been reading their *Courier-Journal* the day before yesterday, they also knew how he'd died. According to the headlines, on Wednesday evening the body of Ephraim Cross had been found in his BMW, which had been pulled off to the side of the road in a remote area of Cherokee Park. He'd been shot in the head.

Standing there, holding that envelope, I remembered reading about Cross's death and, at the time, feeling a distinct chill. Cherokee Park is a heavily wooded community park not far from the Highlands, the section of Louisville where I live. In the midst of reading the *Courier*'s lead article Thursday night just after I got home from work, I'd gotten up and made sure that both my back door *and* my front door were locked.

It hadn't helped any to continue reading and find out that Ephraim Cross's body had been found with a flower laying across his lap. The police had identified the flower as a buttercup, of all innocuous things, and according to the *Courier,* the authorities had surmised that either Cross himself had brought the flower along to give to the person he was meeting—or it had been left behind by his murderer. Somehow, that little yellow buttercup being found there at the scene of a murder had made the whole thing seem even more gruesome. I guess that's why I could still remember it two days later.

Nevertheless, being able to actually recognize the man and remembering how he'd died surely didn't qualify me as an heir. Why would the man have left *me* anything? It seemed unlikely that Ephraim Cross had just picked a few heirs out of the phone book. Not to mention, I wasn't even *in* the phone book. I'd had an unlisted number for over three years now, ever since I started getting obscene phone calls in the middle of the night. At the time I hadn't minded what the obscene caller had said to me so much as his having the gall to wake me up in the middle of the night to hear it. *That* had added injury to insult.

The phone book eliminated, though, how exactly had Cross come up with my name? The only time I could recall our paths had even come close to crossing was about six weeks ago when the real estate firm I work for—Jarvis Arndoerfer Realty—had negotiated the sale of one of Cross's rental properties. I myself, however, had not handled the listing.

Not that I wasn't perfectly qualified to handle it. I've had my real estate license for over nine years now, and I've negotiated far more complicated sales on far more expensive properties than the Cross building.

No, I believe I can say without fear of contradiction that the reason neither I—nor any other Arndoerfer agent, for that matter—had handled the Cross sale was that Jarvis Arndoerfer, broker and, not incidentally, *owner* of Jarvis Arndoerfer Realty, wasn't about to let anybody else deal with somebody as important as Ephraim Cross. Old Jarvis, bless his greedy little soul, had insisted on handling the sale personally.

As I recalled, the closest I'd come to actually speaking with Ephraim Cross was when he'd walked past my desk on his way into Jarvis's office. Now that I thought about it, I was pretty sure Cross had not even glanced my way.

And *now* he'd mentioned me in his will?

I realized suddenly that I'd been standing there in the middle of my foyer, unmoving, staring at the letter, like some purple mannequin, for several minutes. I was that amazed by the whole thing. Then it occurred to me. Maybe Cross had left something for everybody who worked at Jarvis Arndoerfer Realty. Maybe, for him, it was like leaving a tip. Maybe he'd been so happy with the way the sale of his building had gone that he'd decided to leave a little something to every member of Jarvis's faithful staff.

I was pretty much convinced that this had to be the explanation, but I decided to give the law firm Bentley, Stern, and Glassner, a phone call anyway. Just to check out my theory. It was only about eleven, and even though it was a Saturday, there was a possibility that someone might be in. I'd worked as a secretary for a downtown law firm one summer between high school and college, and my former employer had always been in on Saturday mornings. And unfortunately, they had expected *me* to be there, too.

Sure enough, Bentley, Stern, and Glassner was in, too. Their phone was answered on the second ring. A breathy female voice said, "Bentley, Stern, and Glassner," running the words together so that if, before you called, you hadn't been sure what the name of the firm was, calling them up wasn't going to help.

I identified myself and explained why I was calling. Oddly enough, the breathy voice immediately frosted up. For a second, I thought maybe she was just terribly irritated at having to be in the office on Saturdays. Then I realized her hostility was a little more specific than that. It was definitely aimed at me. "I'm not at liberty to divulge the names of the other heirs," she said. If I'd been standing in front of her, I'm sure I would've seen her breath icing the air between us.

"Oh, I don't want to know their names," I said. "I just want to know if there are other people mentioned in the will who also worked at Jarvis Arndoerfer Realty."

Ice Breath hesitated. "Well, I probably shouldn't tell you this, but I don't suppose there's any harm. You will be finding it out on Monday, anyway. I myself typed the will, so I know for a fact that *you*, Ms. Ridgway, are the only person—other than family—named in it." Ice Breath made it sound as if being in Cross's will was not something I should take as a compliment.

I, however, was too busy digesting what she'd just told me to worry about her tone. "This can't be right," I said. "I didn't even know the man."

Ice Breath made a noise in the back of her throat. It managed to convey disbelief and contempt in a single sound. I could hardly blame her for being skeptical. If roles were reversed, *I* probably wouldn't have believed me, either. "Ms. Ridgway—" Ice Breath started to say.

I couldn't help it, I had to interrupt her. I can excuse Ice Breath calling me "Ms." once, but *twice*? I have never called myself "Ms." in my life. Even in the mid-seventies, at the height of the women's lib movement, I couldn't bring myself to do it. I wore my hair in braids, went braless, and made macramé hangings, but "Ms." seemed a bit much. I know, I know, it's supposed to be a political statement or some such thing, but to me, "Ms." just sounds too vague, like maybe you've been married so many times, you can't remember if you're single this year or not. It also sounds too Southern. Every time I hear it, I always think of *Miz* Scarlett and *Gone with the Wind* and all those Southern women who laced themselves into corsets so tight, they kept swooning all the time. Since it's not likely that I'm going to be doing any swooning any time soon—or lacing myself into a corset, either, for that matter—I always draw the line at "Ms." "It's *Mrs.* Ridgway," I said. To be exact, it was ex-Mrs. Ridgway, but that seemed to be cutting it too fine.

Ice breath drew a quick breath. You could've thought I'd slapped her. "*Mrs.* Ridgway, then," she said, emphasizing the first word. "As I was saying, there has been no mistake. Mr. Cross's instructions were very specific."

I sighed. Apparently, I was not getting through to the woman. "Well, your office must've mixed me up with some other Schuyler Ridgway, because I've never even met Ephraim Cross."

There was a long silence. I thought maybe I'd actually made a dent, and Ice Breath was weighing the possibility in her mind of there being another woman in Louisville with the exact same name as mine. Of course, even *I* had to admit the odds didn't look good. My name isn't exactly a common one. My mother had named me after a great-great-grandmother.

Sometimes, I wonder if this great-great-grandmother of mine had had as many problems with the name as I do. People never know how to spell it, and whenever they see it written down, they usually mispronounce it. "Shuler," is what they generally come up with. If I had a dollar for every time in my life I've had to say, "No, not *Shoo*-ler, *Sky*-ler," I'd be a rich woman today.

Still, couldn't there be another woman out there with an odd, frequently mispronounced name? Stranger things *have* happened, I suppose. Ice Breath, however, wasn't supposing at all. Apparently, she was going through her desk, looking for documentation, because finally she said in a bored, but still very cold, tone, "I'm looking at the file now. Is your Social Security number 402-65-5393?"

I hated to answer. It was like admitting I was wrong. "Yes, but—"

Ice Breath evidently didn't want to discuss it any further. "That's the number Mr. Cross gave us." Her voice was now not only icy, but brisk. "You're expected to attend the reading of the will on Monday at two-thirty," she finished. As if I'd asked.

"Why, thank you *so* much," I said. "I *certainly* appreciate your help."

Ice Breath must not have appreciated sarcasm. She hung up.

Needless to say, after that warm reception over the phone, I was really looking forward to the reading of the will. In fact, I think it was a toss-up between going to that and having a root canal. Fortunately, however, I had the never-ending excitement of a career in real estate to distract me. Meaning I had an open house from 1 to 4 on that Saturday afternoon and another one on Sunday from 2 to 5. After I'd spent several hours herding about a hundred people through two outrageously overpriced houses in the East End, and had managed to tell each one of them what the owners were asking— with a straight face, mind you—I'd almost, but not quite, put a little thing like having to go to the reading of the will of a murder victim right out of my mind.

By Sunday evening, I was also starting to think, what

was my problem? If a wealthy dead man wanted to leave me a little something, who was I to object?

I was still a little uneasy about one thing, though. How had Ephraim Cross gotten hold of my Social Security number?"

Chapter 2

In many cities, such as Chicago or Atlanta or New York, the Citizens Plaza building wouldn't even come close to being called a skyscraper. It's only got a piddling thirty floors. In Louisville, though, the sleek gray building stands out in the crowd, towering over the older office buildings around it. In Louisville Citizens Plaza is a skyscraper *par excellence*.

A lot of my neighbors in the Highlands would have no idea where the Citizens Plaza building was. However, most of my neighbors are elderly—they look at going into downtown Louisville a lot like a mouse probably looks at going into a maze. I myself don't mind driving downtown, even if the one-way streets do get a bit confusing. I've been to Citizens Plaza quite a few times, though, since several of my closings have been held in one of the many law offices located on its thirty floors.

I probably wouldn't have minded going downtown at all on Monday, if that particular day hadn't been one of the typical summer days we get a lot of here in Louisville. Even though it was only early June, the weatherman on Channel 3 was saying that the temperature was aiming for 100 that day, and—judging from how heavy the air already felt when I got up at seven o'clock—I was betting it would make it.

Louisville in the summertime doesn't limit itself to just getting hot. That would be too easy. I've lived here all my life, and every year the city apparently goes for the record. Worst Humidity Ever Experienced This Century. Louisville goes for air you can sink your teeth into. And chew.

By one-thirty that afternoon, having spent the morning showing a house way out in Shelby County, with the air conditioner in my seven-year-old Toyota Tercel giving off death rattles, I had no doubt I was going to have to change clothes before I went to the will reading. The air outside was the consistency of custard, and the back of my navy blue linen dress felt clammily damp by the time I finally drove back into the parking lot at Jarvis Arndoerfer Reality with my clients. I wasn't at all certain that the reason they didn't make an offer on the house I'd just showed them was that they couldn't stand being near me a minute longer. So, it was either go back to my house and change—or douse myself in so much perfume, I'd probably be attracting bees. Indoors.

I decided changing would be safer. I went home and dressed this time in a dark gray pinstripe suit, with low-heeled dark gray pumps and dark gray hose—what, no doubt, all the best-dressed heirs were wearing this season. I kind of hated to do it—the suit wasn't going to be any too cool, but the only thing else I had that wasn't still in the cleaners was a sleeveless, full-skirted white dress with bright red polka dots that I'd bought one day when I was feeling old. The dress had not helped. It had only made me feel old—and silly.

For a will reading, the suit seemed the better choice. It was appropriately somber. I was also fairly certain I couldn't have gotten any more conservative—unless I'd dressed in a nun's habit. Which was a thought.

Apparently, however, it didn't matter what I wore. As soon as I walked through the huge mahogany double doors of Bentley, Stern, and Glassner on the twenty-third floor of the Citizen Plaza building, several men and women poked their heads out of offices down the hall and gave me the once-over. It might have been my imagination, but it seemed to me that none of these glances looked approving.

"May I help you?" The voice was unmistakable. It was Ice Breath sitting behind the receptionist's desk. Ice Breath looked to be about thirty, with dark brown hair, dark brown eyes, and wearing a dark brown dress. She looked as if she'd dipped her frosty self in chocolate.

"I'm Schuyler Ridgway, and I'm—"

Ice Breath didn't wait for me to finish. She gave me a look of total disdain, got immediately to her feet, and said, "If you'll follow me—" Then, without checking once to see if I was still behind her, she walked briskly down the hall. I had to hurry to catch up, but before I moved down the hall after her, I noticed the nameplate on her desk. It said, "Flossy Fenwick." Really. No joke. This woman was giving *me* superior looks, and she had a name like Flossy Fenwick. I stared after her. Who in the world did she think she was kidding?

Frosty Flossy stopped in front of a large mahogany door at the end of the hall. In the middle of the door, at eye level so that you couldn't possibly miss it even if you wanted to, was a wide brass plate that read, ADDISON GLASSNER, ATTORNEY AT LAW.

I started to step past Flossy and go on in, but evidently, Flossy had other ideas. As I moved toward the door, Flossy held up her hand as if to stop me and said, "You know, we've all known Mrs. Cross for years. We're all friends of hers here."

I stared at her, not sure what she was getting at. "How nice," I said. I didn't mean anything by it. In fact, I was thinking that the poor woman, no doubt, needed all the friends she could get, having just lost her husband in such a horrible way. Flossy, however, looked as if I'd cursed at her. She pressed her thin lips together, squared her padded brown shoulders and stalked back toward her desk.

I watched her go. This was one extremely touchy woman.

If, however, I thought that Flossy was touchy, I'd seen nothing yet. The second I walked through the door of Addison Glassner's office, every head in the room swiveled toward me. It was as if they were all powered by the same motor.

There were quite a few heads being powered, too. Glancing around the room, feeling about as inconspicuous as a doorknob, I recognized several of the faces from newspaper photos that had appeared with the article Thursday.

The lady with the high cheekbones and the regal bearing was Mrs. Ephraim Cross herself, widow of the deceased. With a long, straight nose and upswept short silver hair, she looked even more beautiful in person than she had in the paper. Apparently, like me, Mrs. Cross had also decided that gray was the color of the day. Seated in the front row of wooden chairs facing the massive oak desk that dominated the room, she was dressed in a simple gray silk that was obviously designer-made. In fact, Mrs. Cross's gray silk dress looked as if it had probably cost what my Toyota was currently worth. Her eyes bored into mine.

I glanced away.

Seated next to Mrs. Cross was her son, Matthias Cross, who was also wearing the color of the day. A gray pinstripe suit, not unlike mine, except, of course, mine had a skirt. If he had not had that scowl on his face, Matthias might've been very handsome. I guessed him to be in his early forties. With unruly dark brown hair that almost touched his shoulders and a full beard to match, he looked distinctly uncomfortable in a suit. He also looked uncomfortable with me in the room. His eyes, like his mother's, bored into mine.

I glanced away again.

On Matthias's left sat his sister, Tiffany, who looked to be about sixteen. In the *Courier* Matthias and Tiffany had been pictured together, clearly in happier times, both of them laughing into each other's eyes. I remembered, right after I'd read the article on their father, I'd studied the picture of Matthias and Tiffany, thinking how *immune* the two of them looked—totally immune to any unpleasantness. As if wealth might be a kind of lifetime inoculation.

Their father's death must've been an awful shock.

That Thursday I'd also stared at the photo of the laughing brother and sister and thought that surely the *Courier* could've found a more appropriate picture of Cross's kids in the *Courier*'s photo files. This particular photo made the children of the deceased look as if they thought their father's demise was a hoot.

Tiffany may have been about sixteen, but today she was dressed as if she were even younger. Her limp brown hair was pulled over to one side with a barrette, and she was wearing a cranberry dress with puffed sleeves, a lace collar and covered buttons all down the front. It was my guess that Tiffany had gained some weight since she'd bought this little number. Every button seemed to be holding on for dear life. The girl's eyes were—you guessed it—boring holes into me, just like her brother's and mother's.

I stood there just inside the door, beginning to identify with Swiss cheese.

"Ms. Ridgway?" It was a big-boned man in his late fifties, wearing a navy blue suit and what looked to be a diamond stickpin in his lapel. Square-jawed and good-looking in a rugged sort of way, his silver-streaked hair obviously professionally styled, he was seated behind the huge oak desk, in front of a matching credenza. This had to be Addison Glassner, Esquire.

"*Mrs.* Ridgway," I corrected him. As soon as I spoke, Mrs. Cross did a noticeable intake of breath. I glanced back over at her, puzzled. Why would just saying my name get that kind of reaction?

Addison Glassner, however, smiled, revealing bright white teeth so even it made you wonder if they were false. "Come in, Mrs. Ridgway," he said. "We're just about to start."

I took a seat in the last row as far away from the others as possible. There, I started looking at the walls around me to avoid looking at the motorized heads who were all still looking at me.

The large room was done in Basic Law Office. Sometimes, I suspect these things come in a kit. For one price, you get dark mahogany paneling to put on the walls, deep plush carpeting in a noncommittal beige to put on the floors, and about twenty official-looking certificates of one kind or another to hang on the paneling. You also get a stack of bound navy blue leather books and a bookcase to display them in. Addison Glassner's books looked as if they'd never been opened. Or maybe you couldn't open them. Maybe they were just leather-bound cardboard props.

Just what you'd expect from a kit.

I moved so that my back was resting more comfortably against the wooden back of my chair, and I tried—without success—to relax. I noticed that seated in my row, over next to the wall, were two other men. These two were dressed in identical tan suits, but where one was very dark, almost swarthy, the other was so blond, his hair was nearly white. I gave them just the briefest of glances, but it didn't take any more than that to guess who these two were. Louisville's Finest. Both men had the same "I've-Seen-It-All-and-It's-Pissed-Me-Off" look that you see on a lot of policemen's faces. I can't say I blame them. I guess if I had to face what they faced every day, I wouldn't be in any too good a mood, either.

Both men looked me over as I sat down, but that was the extent of it. Maybe the somber gray suit had been the right attire, after all. It made me nondescript.

At least, it made me nondescript for a while. Right up until the attorney got to the part in the will that mentioned my name. Up until then, the will had been fairly run-of-the-mill, as best as I could tell. Even the attorney, Glassner, looked a little bored as he read, "The Last Will and Testament of Ephraim Benjamin Cross. I, Ephraim Benjamin Cross, of the City of Louisville, County of Jefferson, State of Kentucky, declare this to be my Will and revoke all of my former Wills and Codicils. Article One. I direct that my debts, expenses, memorial service and the administration of my estate be paid by my Executor, Addison Glassner—"

Oh, yes, for a while, the will was definitely a yawner. Apparently, Cross had left his entire estate to his beloved wife, Harriet Schackelford Cross. In the event that she did not survive him by thirty days, his estate was to be divided between his two beloved children, Matthias and Tiffany. This must've been what everybody in the room expected, because nobody looked upset.

At least, nobody looked upset until Addison Glassner cleared his throat and, with a quick glance around the room, as if to make sure that nobody missed this next part, he said, "I also make the following cash gift: I give to my beloved friend, Schuyler Ridgway, who has given

me passion and joy and a "raison d'être," the amount
of $107,560 and my eternal love."

Under other circumstances, it might've been a touching moment. The deceased lover reaching out from beyond the grave to say goodbye to the woman he loved.
Unfortunately, this particular moment was pretty much
wasted on those present. There *was* a dry eye in the
house. In fact, every single one was dry, including mine.

Dry-eyed, all those motorized heads whirred into action and once again swiveled in my direction. Mrs.
Cross's face had gone so white, even her mouth looked
pale. I was fairly certain that the look she gave me at
that moment could've been classified a lethal weapon.
Beside Mrs. Cross, her son Matthias didn't look as if
he would be adding me to his Christmas card list any
time soon, either. And beside *me,* the two policemen
were now looking in my direction pretty much, I believe,
the way two hungry dogs look at a fresh cut slab of
sirloin.

Other than Glassner who had now taken a sip of water
and was continuing to read, Tiffany was the only one in
the room who was not looking at me with open suspicion. She, however, was looking at her lap.

Me, I was so flabbergasted that at first I just stared,
openmouthed, at Glassner. I even thought fleetingly of
saying, "Hey, wait a minute. Hold the phone. This has
got to be some kind of mistake." I wanted to point out
to all those present that Ephraim Cross and I had not
even *met,* for God's sake. But then, I thought better of it.

I don't know, maybe it was all that wood paneling on
the walls, and everybody being so somber and all. It was
a lot like being in church. In church, even if you don't
exactly agree with everything that's being said up there
on the pulpit, you don't really feel as if you can raise
your hand and object. I decided it would be a better
idea to just go up after the reading and discuss the matter with Glassner in private.

As I became all too uncomfortably aware that all the
motorized heads were continuing to stare, I decided to
take a cue from Tiffany. I can't say my lap was all that

interesting to look at, but it sure beat looking at anything else in the room.

While I looked as if I were concentrating on the wrinkles in my skirt, however, my mind was going like sixty. Glassner had actually said, a hundred and seven *thousand* dollars and some change. Holy Christmas. That was a *lot* of money. And yet, it couldn't really belong to me, could it? For one thing, what on earth was all this "passion and joy" stuff? Surely, if I'd been making that kind of impression on somebody, I would've remembered it. Wouldn't I? For a second, I actually wondered if maybe I had some kind of split personality—and if, judging from what I'd just heard, my other personality was having a lot better time than I was.

The last guy *I* remembered dating for any length of time was a CPA about three months ago. I'd gone out with him twice before I'd discovered that all his previous girlfriends—and every one of his four ex-wives—had first names that began with S. It apparently had been a requirement for him. Now I don't know, maybe I'm just picky, but I find that kind of requirement more than a little strange—with a capital S. After I found out that tiny bit of information, I came up with an "S" word of my own—sayonara.

Since then, there had been nobody. Unless, of course, like I said, my other personality was having the time of my life, and I didn't know a thing about it. I discounted this theory immediately, though. I think if you're a split personality, you're supposed to have some holes in your memory. Unfortunately, I could remember every second of my totally boring romantic life. Lately, it had mainly consisted of watching cable on Friday and Saturday nights. Some of those movies had been love stories, but I don't think my *watching* other people have a love life would've moved Ephraim Cross to leave me in excess of a hundred thousand dollars.

Unless it was out of pity. Which seemed unlikely.

So why was a dead man trying to make people believe that he and I had been a thing? Was he just trying to hurt his wife one last time while he still had the chance? It did seem an unbelievably cruel thing to do. Glancing over at Mrs. Cross's pinched face, now almost as gray as her dress, I couldn't help but feel sorry for her. Her husband was rubbing her nose in it from the grave. And "it" wasn't even true.

Not to speak ill of the dead, but I might as well say it. What an asshole. It made you feel not terribly surprised that somebody had seen fit to murder this guy.

The thought made me feel instantly cold. Because here, for crying out loud, was yet another problem for me to deal with. I didn't even have to glance to my left to feel all four eyes of the two cops beside me. It didn't take a genius to figure out what *they* were thinking.

Ephraim Cross's will had just given me over a hundred thousand motives for murder.

Chapter 3

Once my name had been mentioned, it seemed to take forever for Glassner to finish reading the will. He droned on and on in legalese, about residuary estates and surviving beneficiaries and the like. The bottom line, as best as I could make out through the jargon jungle, was that if I should die, Mrs. Cross—who, at that very moment, looked as if my demise might be a terrific idea—would get to keep the $100,000 plus that was going to me. And if Mrs. Cross died *after* I died, her kids would get to split what was left.

I'd read in the paper that Ephraim Cross's estate numbered in the millions, so in all probability, my walking away with a little over a hundred thousand dollars was not going to cause Mrs. Cross any financial hardship by any stretch of the imagination. However, judging from the expression on her face whenever she looked my way, it was no doubt the principle of the thing that bothered her. Mrs. Cross obviously did not consider it a good idea if she had to pay anything at all to the person who had apparently been her late husband's mistress.

I could see her viewpoint. Maybe if I had actually *been* her husband's mistress, I would've looked at it a little differently. But since I didn't even know the man, I could see Mrs. Cross's viewpoint perfectly. If my ex-husband had wanted me to hand over ten cents to his latest Girlfriend-of-the-Month, I definitely would've balked.

Glassner finally finished with his reading, looked over at the rest of us and said, "That about does it. Are there any questions?"

No one in the room said anything. Glassner apparently took that as a resounding "no," because he nodded curtly and stood up, his signal that the meeting was over.

Glassner, however, had apparently leaped a little too fast to his conclusion because Matthias Cross clearly did have a question. He moved immediately over to the oak desk, and leaning forward, asked something that, from where I was sitting in the last row, I couldn't make out. You didn't have to hear it, however, to figure out what Matthias had just asked. Glassner's reply boomed around us. "Well, you could try, of course. But I think it would be thrown out of court. Ephraim signed the new will, not five days ago, right here in this office. It was duly witnessed, and—"

Matthias interrupted, again mumbling something I couldn't hear.

Glassner shook his coiffed head. "You'd need a psychiatrist's statement to prove that. Otherwise—"

I got to my feet, feeling tired. Obviously, Matthias felt that you'd have to be crazy to leave me this much money. I could've been wrong, but I was pretty sure I could take that as an insult.

I'd been concentrating so heavily on eavesdropping on the conversation between Matthias and Glassner that I hadn't paid all that much attention to the others in the room. I had, of course, noticed out of the corner of my eye that the two tan suits beside me had gotten up from their seats right after Glassner finished reading, and that both of them had made for the door, apparently having heard all they needed to. Now, as I stood there, waiting for Matthias to get finished with Glassner so that I myself could have a little talk with the attorney, I realized that Mrs. Cross had positioned herself right in front of me.

Behind her mother, plump Tiffany stared fixedly at the floor.

For a long moment Harriet Cross just looked at me. The way you might a roach.

I stared back at her at a complete loss for words.

I'm usually not at all tongue-tied. In my line of work, you get accustomed to dealing with sticky situations. Situations like houses being put on the market because the owners are divorcing. So that, when you bring in an offer which actually exceeds their asking price, instead of being happy, the woman bursts into tears.

I've also had situations in which I've had to tell people point-blank that they can't possibly afford the house they've been insisting I show them. Once I even had to tell a couple that the huge posters of Miss January, Miss August, and Miss October featured prominently in their teenage son's bedroom really should come down before their open house.

Some of the real estate courses you take, and quite a few of the manuals, give you helpful tips on how to handle uncomfortable situations with tact and diplomacy. I'm fairly certain, however, that no course I've taken and no manual I've read has ever covered this particular situation: What to Say to the Woman Who Thinks You've Been Sleeping with Her Husband, and, Incidentally, Who Also Might Suspect You of Killing Him.

I was going through possible things to say—"So sorry to hear about your loss—," and then discarding them—in this case, because she might think I was talking about the money, and not about her husband—when Mrs. Cross said, "I'm Harriet Schackelford Cross." Flossy Fenwick, Ice Breath herself, could take lessons from this woman. Harriet's voice had passed "icy," and was now working on "arctic." It made you think of Jack London and *White Fang*.

"I'm—" I started to say, introducing myself, but apparently, Harriet already knew who I was, and she didn't feel she needed to hear it again.

Harriet immediately interrupted, her white fangs showing. "How old are you? Early thirties?"

Under other circumstances, I would've been flattered. In this case, however, I believe I could assume that Harriet was not trying to boost my ego. I, however, have never been one of those women who are secretive about their age. The way I look at it, it's taken me a long time to get this old, so I probably ought to treat it as some kind of accomplishment. "No," I said, "as a matter of fact, I'm forty-one."

Up close, Harriet didn't look quite as beautiful as she had when she'd been sitting across the room. Up close, you could plainly see the vertical lines etched between her eyebrows and at the sides of her mouth. It made you realize that this was, in all probability, not the first time she'd been in a bad mood.

"Forty-one," she repeated. From the tone in which she said it, you might've thought I'd just told her I was fourteen. She blinked. Her eyes really were beautiful, large and gray and slightly uptilted at the corners. "Did you know that Ephraim was sixty-four?"

My answer was very quick. "No, I—"

Harriet's interruption was even quicker. "I didn't think so." Harriet's lips were a thin, pale line. "You weren't at Ephraim's memorial service, were you?"

I swallowed. Memorial service? I hadn't even known there had been one. Furthermore, I really did have a great excuse for not attending. I made it a point not to go to funerals or memorial services of people I don't know. Call me callous.

I opened my mouth to explain. "No, I didn't attend, but—"

Harriet gave her silver head the briefest of nods. "Pity," she said, cutting me off again, her gray eyes now slits. "*Everyone* who truly loved Ephraim was there."

Before I had a chance to reply—or, say, to defend myself—Harriet abruptly turned away, moving out of the mahogany door so fast, you might've thought I was chasing her.

Her eyes still on the floor, Tiffany shambled along in the wake of her mother. When Tiffany got to the door, I half expected her to walk right into it since she wasn't watching where she was going. But no, Tiffany managed to negotiate the thing perfectly, neatly sidestepping at the last minute so that she sailed right into the hall without pausing even a fraction of a second. That girl must be accustomed to walking around looking down.

There didn't seem anything else to do after that, but to move forward to the oak desk where Glassner was, no doubt, going to be delighted to hear what I had to say. Unfortunately, this put me on a collision course with

Matthias Cross who evidently had asked all the questions he intended to, and had himself just started toward the door.

Actually, collision course is probably a slight exaggeration. We didn't exactly collide. At least, not physically. Matthias simply stood in the aisle, blocking my way. This close he, like his mother, also looked very different than he had across the room. He was a lot bigger—at least six three, very muscular, with very broad shoulders. With that build and that dark beard shot through here and there with gray, Matthias Cross looked a lot more like a blacksmith than the son of a millionaire.

I would've just stepped wordlessly around him, eyes on the ground—Tiffany continued to be my role model—but evidently, Matthias wasn't about to let me get away that easy. He said, his voice surprisingly soft, "I'm Matthias Cross, Ephraim Cross's son."

I had to look up at him. "I know," I said lamely. Surprisingly, his eyes were a deep shade of emerald green. Not surprisingly, they didn't look friendly. "I'm Schuyler Ridgway," I said. As I spoke, I put out my hand as if to shake his.

Matthias did not put out his hand. "I already know who you are. You're the woman who killed my father," he said.

I'd been just getting ready to say "Glad to meet you." It was on the tip of my tongue, but thank God, I managed to stop myself in time. Instead, I dropped my hand and said, "Now, wait a minute, I didn't even know your dad. I have never met Ephraim Cross in my life."

Matthias did not look moved by my honesty. His green eyes narrowed. "Do you really expect me to believe that?" His tone implied that he thought that *I* thought he was a moron.

It was an idea worth considering.

I shrugged, as if I couldn't care less what he believed. My shrug, however, was lying. "It's the truth," I said. "This is all some kind of a mistake."

Matthias looked as skeptical as Flossy Fenwick had sounded yesterday over the phone. "I'll say it was a mistake. A mistake that's made you over a hundred thousand dollars richer," he said, and moving quickly past me, followed his mother and sister out the door.

After that, I could pretty much guess how the conversation with Addison Glassner was going to go. But, no doubt because I have masochistic tendencies, I decided I'd still go forward and talk to him.

Predictably, Glassner was not any more moved by my honesty than Matthias Cross had been. "Are you trying to tell me that you didn't know Ephraim Cross *at all*?" he asked.

I shook my head. Emphatically. "I've never even *met* Ephraim Cross. I believe that the real estate firm I work for did negotiate the sale of an apartment building for him a few weeks ago, but other than seeing him once in the office, I've never been in the same room with the man. Ever."

The entire time I was telling him this, Glassner was looking me up and down. It's very irritating to be talking to someone whose attention is so obviously diverted.

I took a deep breath. "Mr. Glassner," I said, "my face is up here."

All right, all right, maybe I *was* being a little touchy. I was definitely not in my best mood by that time. Having just been accused of being a murderer and all. Glassner did not, however, look the least bit embarrassed or nonplussed or whatever he should've looked like. Instead, he looked as if he'd just given me a monumental compliment. Apparently, at my age, having a man's eyes wander up and down my body was something I ought to be grateful for.

"You really are a very attractive woman," Glassner said. He smiled, revealing those amazingly white, terribly even teeth. Maybe he'd had them all capped. "With that lovely chestnut hair and those liquid brown eyes, it's no wonder Ephraim was so taken with you," Glassner added.

I blinked my liquid brown eyes. "Ephraim was *not* taken with me!" I said. "He'd never even met me!"

Glassner smiled at me even wider. "Hmm," he said. Really. That's what he said. Hmm. The man was a lawyer, and the best he could do to sum up this entire case was to make a sound that's not even a word. Hmm.

"I can see how you might want to continue to be discreet, Mrs. Ridgway," he said, spreading his hands out in a conciliatory gesture, "but that is hardly necessary at this point. Mr. Cross chose to leave you this money, and there's really no reason why you shouldn't—"

I had to interrupt. "There is a reason! It's not mine. Not that I wouldn't love the money, but there really has been some kind of mistake, I'm telling you. Ephraim Cross and I did not *know* each other."

Glassner was starting to look sorry for me. Sort of the way you might look at someone who keeps telling you that they really, really, really were picked up by aliens a couple of nights ago. "Mrs. Ridgway, Ephraim gave us your Social Security number, your address—he even told us where you worked. He was very specific, and you can be sure that this firm will be carrying out his wishes with all due haste. You'll be receiving a check by registered mail very shortly." Glassner paused here, his eyes now glowing almost as brightly as his teeth, and added, "Ephraim told me quite a few things about you. About your, ah, *appetites.*"

I believe that I could assume here that Addison Glassner was not referring to the gusto with which I consumed meals.

I gave him a level stare. "Mr. Glassner—"

"Call me Addison," Glassner said. With the white teeth again. This man should sell used cars. "Up until five days before his death, Ephraim Cross had left his entire estate to his beloved wife. That was how his will read. After meeting you, however, he was simply—well, shall we say?—*mesmerized.* Ephraim insisted on making this change." Glassner leaned forward. "I gather that you made quite an impression."

I stared at Glassner. The expression on his face was definitely a leer. I wasn't sure whether he expected me to beam with pride at having achieved such a thing, or to be outraged. Personally, I leaned toward the latter.

"Ephraim also told me that you were very aware that

this was being done," Glassner added. "He told me you knew he was leaving you this money."

I blinked again. "Me?" That was ridiculous. How could I know such a thing, if I'd never, ever talked to the man?

Glassner now rose from his leather chair. "You know, my dear," he said, white teeth still aglow, "we really should discuss this over dinner. How about it?"

I stared at him, my throat tightening. Could my current reputation as a rich man's plaything have anything at all to do with Addison Glassner's sudden inclination to break bread with me? Was that at all possible? Or was I just jumping to unjust conclusions?

Right.

Or was there a distinct possibility that Addison Glassner was jumping to some conclusions of his own? Perhaps Glassner had put it best himself. Hmm.

"Thanks, anyway," I said, "but I don't think so."

Glassner really was a good-looking man, particularly if nice teeth meant anything at all to you, and maybe because of this, he apparently was not at all accustomed to being refused. His mouth actually dropped open. He shut it right away, though, and reached for my hand. "You don't think we could find, well, *something* to talk about, over dinner?" He gave my hand what I think was supposed to be a meaningful squeeze.

Glancing down, I couldn't help but notice that the hand that was doing the squeezing was also wearing a wedding band on the third finger.

I don't know. Something happens to a woman when she reaches forty. It's as if, all of a sudden, there are quite a few things that you no longer put up with. Things like, say, slimy men holding onto your hand. I pulled away, resisting the urge to immediately wipe my hand on my skirt. Then I leaned forward and lowered my voice. "Let me make this very clear," I said. "I think that if you and I had the rest of our lives, we wouldn't be able to find a single thing to discuss. *Ever.*"

Glassner's eyes now looked a lot smaller. As if maybe they'd shrunk some even as I spoke. Then his eyes went back to normal, and he gave an idiotic little laugh. "Mrs.

Ridgway," he said, "I was *talking* about going to dinner to discuss the provisions of the will. Nothing more." He actually sounded offended.

That made two of us. I gave him a brief nod. Sure, that's all he meant, and I'm the queen of England. I headed for the door.

By the time I got to the parking garage and retrieved my Tercel, I wasn't feeling all that offended anymore. Mainly because every bit of my attention was suddenly diverted by the dark blue sedan that pulled into traffic right behind me. In the front seat were the two tan suits that had been seated next to me in Addison Glassner's office. They followed me, like two stray dogs you don't want to keep, all the way home.

Chapter 4

The Highlands area where I live is supposed to have gotten its name back in '37. That was the year the Ohio River overflowed its banks worse than it ever did before or since, and this area was one of the few places in Louisville elevated enough not to be under water.

Of course, Louisville hasn't flooded like that for some time. Not since they built up the dam or put in the locks or whatever it was they did to correct the problem. These days it doesn't really matter how high the land around here happens to be. In fact, I suspect the only reason this part of town is still called the Highlands is that this name today pretty accurately reflects the prices of the homes in this area.

Of course, back in the early seventies when Ed, my then-husband, and I bought my house, the prices had not yet begun to skyrocket. Otherwise, I'm sure I wouldn't be able to afford to be here today. Even back then, though, this neighborhood of stately brick homes on quiet, tree-lined streets already had an air of serene gentility. I remember the day we moved in, Ed took me aside and said, in his best condescending tone, "Look, Schuyler, I don't want you shaking your dust mop out the front door anymore. That simply isn't done in a neighborhood like this."

Ed had grown up in one of the most expensive subdivisions in Louisville's prestigious East End, whereas I, on the other hand, had been raised in Louisville's lowly South End. "Blue-Collar Country," as Ed so eloquently put it. During the eight years we were married, I don't think Ed ever missed a single opportunity to remind me how superior his social skills were compared to mine.

According to Ed, I was lucky if I knew which fork to use. Or even, to remember to use a fork at all.

On the day we moved to Harvard Drive, it did, of course, cross my mind to tell Ed what he could do with his dust mop. But I didn't. When you're in your twenties—unlike when you're in your *forties*—there are still a lot of things you put up with.

Then, too, there were the boys to consider. Daniel was not yet two, and Nathan was only months old. I was determined not to scar their little psyches by fighting in front of them.

And, if I need any more excuses for letting Ed talk to me as if I were his servant, I probably ought to mention that Ed's and my wedding ceremony not quite three years earlier had no doubt been one of the last ones in the country that still had the word "obey" in it. Today it's hard to believe, but back in the early seventies—before the women's movement really got rolling—I was still taking that one seriously.

Of course, had I known at the time that Ed himself was not taking seriously the part of the wedding ceremony that said "forsaking all others," I probably would have not only told him what he could do with his mop, but given him a little demonstration.

If mop shaking in public simply isn't "done" in this neighborhood, I believe having the cops follow you home wouldn't make the list of accepted behaviors, either.

I took a quick glance around as I approached my driveway. Mrs. Hollander and Mrs. Alta, the two widow ladies who occupy either side of the red brick duplex directly across from my house, were out on their porch, engaged in conversation. Two doors down, on my left, Henry Kramer was sitting out on his porch, reading. And right next door, not three feet away from my driveway, Mrs. Pettigrew was down on her knees, clipping the bayberry bushes separating my property from hers.

I took a deep breath. Wouldn't you know it? The one day I happen to show up with Louisville's Finest in tow, a random sampling of my neighbors *would* be on hand to witness the event.

I didn't mind so much Mrs. Hollander or Mrs. Alta or Mr. Kramer seeing me come home with the police. All three didn't do much more than just glance in my direction when I pulled into my driveway. Even after the blue sedan pulled in right in back of me, they still didn't take much notice. Mrs. Hollander and Mrs. Alta immediately went back to their jabbering, and Mr. Kramer turned back to his book. Either they all considered whatever they were doing far more interesting, or not one of them could see all that well at a distance. The last was a distinct possibility as Mrs. Alta was the baby of the group—at eighty-two.

Mrs. Pettigrew next door, however, was something else again.

Mrs. Pettigrew has been my next-door neighbor for all of the twenty years I've lived here, and it is probably a testament to her warm and giving nature that even after all this time, I still don't feel comfortable calling her by her first name. Fact is, I'm not sure I could tell you offhand what Mrs. Pettigrew's first name is. Or even if she has one.

The woman is in her late sixties, and even on a day as hot as this one—even when she's working out in her *yard,* for God's sake—she still wears housedresses with hemlines down to her ankles and ruffled necklines tickling her chin. Today's little number looked as if she'd picked it up at the convent dress shop.

Mrs. Pettigrew has gray hair that looks like silver wires sticking out at odd angles all over her head, a figure remarkably like a washing machine—squat and boxy—and gray eyes that do a slow burn when she thinks she's spotted something not quite up to her high moral standards. As I got out of my car, I couldn't help noticing that, at that moment, Mrs. Pettigrew's eyes looked as if they could grill steaks.

I decided long ago that it's a matter of pride with Mrs. Pettigrew to think the worst of everybody she knows. Last month the woman actually told me with a straight face that she was positive that Henry Kramer and Mrs. Alta were having an affair. This, even though Henry needs a walker these days to get around.

Mrs. Pettigrew's ember-eyes all but shot sparks when the two tan suits got out of their blue sedan. She didn't bother to even pretend she wasn't staring. I headed toward my front door, feeling faintly relieved that at least the policemen were not in uniform and their car was unmarked. My relief, however, lasted about ten seconds—just about the time for the tan suits to start up my walk. That's when it occurred to me that Mrs. Pettigrew not knowing that these guys were police probably wasn't all that great an idea. By nightfall, she'd probably have told everybody on the block that she was sure I'd given up the real estate business in order to pursue a more lucrative career in prostitution.

Or worse—a *less* lucrative career.

Mrs. Pettigrew put down her pruning shears so that she could devote all her energy to gawking at me and the tan suits. I gave her a cheery wave as I unlocked my front door. Mrs. Pettigrew lifted a listless hand, but her eyes were clearly riveted on the two men coming up my sidewalk.

I couldn't make up my mind which was worse. Her thinking that these guys were dropping by so that we could engage in God-knows-what lewd acts in the middle of the day, or her finding out that they were police.

As it turned out, I didn't have time to think about it. I'd no more than gotten my door open and turned around when the tan suit with the white-blond hair flashed his badge at me. Mrs. Pettigrew's eyes were no longer embers. They now looked like bonfires.

"Mrs. Ridgway," White Hair said, "I'm Murray Reed from the Louisville Police Department, and this is my partner, Tony Constello."

Reed and his partner could've been salt-and-pepper shakers. Reed—the salt—had a beefy, square-jawed face, a weight lifter's build, and white-blond hair cut in a flat top. He looked something like Arnold Schwarzenegger—only, with that hair, it would've had to be Arnold after he'd had a bad scare.

Constello—the pepper—was swarthy skinned, thin, very tall, with heavy-lidded black eyes. If I'd been casting the part of an Italian gangster in a movie, I'd have chosen Constello in a heartbeat. Constello's thick, black mustache added to the illusion.

I could've been wrong, but it looked to me as if quite a few of Constello's mustache hairs were sticking straight up into his nostrils. I fought off the impulse to scratch my own nose, and tried to smile at the two of them. "Glad to meet you," I lied.

"We'd like to talk to you for a few minutes," Reed said. He made no effort to keep his voice down.

Ever mindful of the bonfires next door, I nodded and tried to herd both men inside as quickly as I could. Constello, however, took the time to say, "Yep, we need to ask ya'll a few questions about the murder of Ephraim Cross—"

Constello may have looked like an Italian gangster, but he had the heavy, rural accent of someone who hailed from eastern Kentucky. A heavy, rural accent loud enough to echo off hills in the distance.

"—if'n y'all don't mind," Constello finished.

Somehow, I got the feeling that if'n I all *did* mind, it wasn't going to make much difference. I gave them another insincere smile. "Why, certainly," I said. "Won't you please come in?"

Ed would be amazed. Even under duress, this South End girl had not forgotten her manners. I couldn't resist taking a tiny peek at Mrs. Pettigrew as we all moved inside.

Mrs. Pettigrew's mouth was hanging open.

I went in and sat down on the rust and teal colonial print couch I've got positioned in front of the triple windows in my living room. This couch is one of my most prized possessions. It's Ethan Allen, I got it at an estate auction for about a tenth of its cost new, and every time I sit on it, I feel a lot wealthier than I really am. I settled back against the cushions. At least, if I were going to be grilled, I would do it in style.

Reed and Constello settled themselves into the two teal Queen Anne chairs flanking my fireplace. Unfortunately, one of their chairs came with a little bonus. I hadn't been expecting company, so in the chair Reed took, there was a big basket of laundry, waiting to be folded and put away.

The look Reed gave me when he picked up the laundry basket and put it down on the floor to his left was clearly critical of my housekeeping abilities.

I stared right back at him. Hadn't he heard? It was the nineties. Women weren't supposed to be judged solely on how well they maintained their homes anymore.

Reed obviously had not gotten the word. He took out a small notebook and immediately started writing. I wondered if he was listing my crimes. "1. First-Degree Murder. 2. Disorderly Housekeeping."

I was half expecting the two of them to go into that routine you see all the time on television. Bad Cop, Good Cop. With one of them playing the heavy, and the other acting sympathetic? On a lot of the made-for TV detective movies I'd been watching lately—usually, as I've mentioned before, on Friday and Saturday nights, more's the pity—the police do the Bad Cop, Good Cop routine so that the culprit will let down his guard with the sympathetic cop and blurt out all he knows.

Unfortunately, I couldn't think of a thing to blurt. It was just as well because these guys had apparently never seen any of these movies. Or maybe the two of them just couldn't agree on who would play which part. Because it was obvious right from the start the part they *both* wanted to play.

Bad Cop #1, Reed, started it off. "You know why we're here, Mrs. Ridgway. We need some answers." He tapped his notebook with his pencil, his flat, staccato monotone reminiscent of Joe Friday's of *Dragnet* fame. You'd think the one thing a cop wouldn't do was try to sound like Joe Friday. If Reed said, "We just want the facts, ma'am, nothing but the facts," it was going to be all I could do not to laugh in his face.

"Well, I probably don't have the answers you're looking for," I said in my best Good-Citizen-Eager-to-Cooperate voice. "I didn't even know Ephraim Cross."

My Good-Citizen voice must not be all that convincing. Bad Cop #2, Constello, just stared at me. "What?" he said.

"I never met Ephraim Cross," I said.

After that little pronouncement, for a long moment you couldn't hear anything in the room except the clock on my mantel ticking. While the clock ticked, Reed and Constello glanced first at each other and then back at me. Frowning.

Constello finally broke the silence. Smoothing down his mustache, he said, "You don't really 'spect us to believe that a man you didn't know just left you over one hundred thousand dollars, do ya?"

Actually, I didn't expect them to believe it, and it certainly looked as if neither of them were going to let me down. However, since it was the truth, what did they want me to do? Think up a more convincing lie? I shrugged. "That money being left to me has got to be some kind of mistake."

Reed ran a beefy hand through his white hair. As if clearing away any cobwebs up there. "All right. Enough," he said. Joe Friday sounded as if his patience was being severely tested. "We're not playing games here, Mrs. Ridgway. It's obvious that you and Mr. Cross had an intimate relationship, and—"

The man's hearing must be bad. Or maybe he should take English as a second language. I interrupted. "I not only did *not* have an intimate relationship with Ephraim Cross, I had no relationship at all." I leaned forward and carefully enunciated every word. *"I have never met the man."*

Reed made a noise in the back of his throat. It sounded like the one Ice Breath had made Saturday when I'd told her the same thing.

At that point, Reed must've decided to try a different tack. For the next few minutes, he didn't mention Ephraim Cross at all. Instead, he asked me the kind of questions you get asked when you're applying for a loan. How long I'd been at this address, place of employment, marital status, that kind of thing. Then he said, very fast, like maybe he was trying to catch me off guard, "So. What's all this about a raisin debt?"

I blinked. "Raisin debt?"

Reed cleared his throat, flipped his notebook to a page toward the front, and read, "—to my beloved friend, Schuyler Ridgway, who has given me passion, joy—"

It was all I could do not to wince while he was reading this part.

"—and a raisin debt—"

I glanced over at Constello. Reed was kidding, right? I shifted position on the couch. It looked as if I might be tempted to laugh in Reed's face whether he mentioned that "nothing but the facts" thing or not. "That's, um, French," I said. "*Raison d'être*. It means a reason for living."

"Aha." Reed exchanged glances with Constello.

I may have been a little oversensitive here, but it seemed to me as if that "aha" sounded pretty significant. That glance the two of them exchanged didn't look any too casual either. I wondered now if Reed hadn't just been playing dumb, in order to see if I myself knew what the French phrase meant. I cleared my own throat. "Look, it's not unusual that I know that. Everybody knows what raison d'être means. *Everybody*."

Reed gave me a flat stare for an answer. Apparently, he didn't agree.

Bad Cop #2 didn't look as if he agreed either. Constello pulled out a small color photo from his inside coat pocket, and handed it to me. "Know what this here is?"

I stared at the picture. It was a close-up of a small flower, its petals like several rows of yellow ruffles encircling a pale center. I recognized the flower right away, of course. When I was little, my grandmother's flower garden every spring had been bordered in these flowers. Grammy's flowers had been in a variety of colors—white, pink, red, and, of course, yellow, like this one.

The flower in Constello's photo looked a little worse for wear. It had shriveled some, and its ruffly petals were edged in brown. Like maybe it hadn't been in water for some time. Or, say, it had lain around for too long in the lap of a murdered man.

I suppressed a shudder and handed the photo back to

Constello. "It'a a buttercup." My grandmother had also called this flower a ranunculus, but I decided I wouldn't mention this to the Bad Cops. The way things were going, it probably wasn't a good idea to sound too knowledgeable about a flower involved in a homicide.

Evidently, however, just knowing one name of this flower was one too many.

Reed and Constello exchanged a glance that looked even more significant than the first. Their glance said I was two for two. I knew what raison d'être meant, and I knew a buttercup when I saw one. Apparently, I met all the qualifications for their job of Murderer At Large.

I hurried to explain. "My grandmother used to grow flowers like that. That's how I happen to—"

Reed clearly wasn't interested in how I came by my horticultural knowledge.

"You have a garden yourself?" Reed asked, interrupting. I think he tried to make his voice sound casual, but when you're doing a Joe Friday impression, sounding casual is pretty much out of the question.

"No, I don't," I said. "Unless you count three tomato plants." I was just trying to be absolutely truthful, but Reed gave me a look. Like maybe what *he* thought I was trying to be was a smart aleck.

Constello cleared his throat. "Reckon you wouldn't mind tellin' us your whereabouts on Wednesday night?"

I swallowed. And, for the first time since they walked in here, I actually felt a twinge of fear. Lord. These guys were serious. They actually thought *I* might've committed a murder. I couldn't bring myself to step on *spiders,* for God's sake, and they thought I could shoot a man.

This thing was getting out of hand.

It took me a minute to remember what I'd been doing that night, but when I did, I didn't feel any less afraid. I believe I could guess—even *before* I told Reed and Constello that I'd been home alone on Wednesday, watching an HBO movie—that the Bad Cops were not going to be impressed.

Sure enough, their eyes narrowed the second I spoke. "Look," I hurried to add, "I can *prove* what I was doing that night. I can tell you the entire movie plot. I can even tell you who starred, how the thing ended—"

Neither Reed nor Constello said anything for a second—they both just sat there with twin skeptical stares—so I launched into it. It had been an unbelievably stupid movie about this gorgeous woman lawyer and her less-than-trustworthy-but-terribly-handsome client. These two fall madly in love practically during the opening credits. Without so much as an extended conversation, they were suddenly so nuts about each other, they were risking life and limb to be together. Apparently, in TV world, good looks was one powerful motivator.

Bad Cop #2 evidently had heard enough. Constello held up his hand. "I don't reckon we need to hear a play-by-play, okay?" He cleared his throat, glanced over at my console TV sitting directly across from me against the opposite wall, and then said with studied nonchalance, "You got a VCR?"

He was looking straight at it, sitting on top of my TV, out in plain sight. For a second I stared at him. Was this some kind of test? Did he actually think I was going to lie about having a VCR when the thing was right here in the room with the three of us?

Well, if this was a test, I intended to pass. I nodded. "Yes, as a matter of fact. I do have a VCR."

Constello nodded too. "Well, then," he said.

I stared at him again. Well, then what? His point, however, was as obvious as the answer to his question. I could easily have recorded the movie during the time I was off murdering Ephraim Cross, then watched it *after* I got home. Murderers probably have been known to plan ahead.

I took a deep breath. "All right," I said. I no longer sounded like Good-Citizen-Anxious-to-Help. I sounded like Irritated-Citizen-Anxious-to-Get-These-Guys-Out-of-Her-House. "I cannot tell you why on earth Cross's will said what it did, or why he left me that money, but I can tell you this. I did *not* know the man. *At all.* I'm telling you the truth!"

"If it's the truth," Reed said, his voice infuriatingly

calm, "then you wouldn't mind us doing a little looking around, now would you?"

Having watched all those TV detective movies I mentioned earlier, I knew full well that this was the part where I was supposed to ask to see a certain piece of paper. I folded my arms across my chest. "Do you have a search warrant?"

You might've thought I'd asked if they had BO. Reed and Constello both looked offended. "Why, Mrs. Ridgway," Reed said, "could there be something around here that you don't want us to see?"

I glared at him. "No, of course not—"

"If'n you don't have anything to hide, then why would you mind us taking a look-see?" Constello rubbed his mustache speculatively.

I sat there for a long moment, trying to control my temper. I have never believed that it was a good idea to get into a shouting match with anybody who regularly carries a firearm. However, *this* was an outrage. I'd done nothing wrong, and yet, now—just because a total stranger had left me some money, for what reason I could not possibly imagine—I was being treated like a criminal. The *police* actually wanted to sift through my things.

How rude.

On the other hand, maybe Constello had a point. Maybe getting mad and demanding to see a search warrant did only make me look more guilty. If I wanted the Bad Cops to believe I'd been telling the truth—and that I really did have nothing to hide—why shouldn't I let them do a little snooping?

The reason I shouldn't was abundantly clear about an hour later when Reed and Constello finished poking around inside my house and headed outside to do the same to my car. By that time I was back in the living room, seated once again on my Ethan Allan sofa.

When they'd first started their search, I hadn't been able to resist following the Bad Cops around. After, however, watching them pull open all the dresser drawers in my bedroom upstairs and see with their own eyes that not only did I not keep my clothes folded neatly, but apparently, a grenade had gone off in my underwear drawer—I couldn't take it any longer. I decided it would be less humiliating—and it probably wouldn't look so much as if I were terrified they'd actually *find* something—if I just sat this one out downstairs.

When Constello and Reed went out my front door, I was just sitting there, idly flipping through the latest Spiegel catalog, trying to look casual. Like maybe the police dropped by to search my house a couple times a week.

I don't think I looked at all casual, however, when not ten minutes later Constello came swaggering back into my house. Reed followed him, holding a plastic bag that looked a lot like a Seal-A-Meal.

I recognized Reed's Seal-A-Meal immediately. It was an evidence bag. I'd seen quite a few of them on those HBO movies I'd watched.

I got to my feet and stared at the bag. Exactly what kind of evidence did Reed and Constello think they'd turned up? The thing in Reed's Seal-A-Meal looked to be a white piece of paper. "Well, well, *well,*" Reed said. His tone was triumphant.

I was game. "Well, well, well, what?"

It was Constello who answered me. "Look-a-here what we found in your glove compartment. Pushed to the back. *Hidden,* you might say. Just *look.*"

I looked. Through the clear plastic, you could plainly see a handwritten note on a sheet of linen-finish stationery. The stationery had a single line of embossed gray type at the top. Embossed gray type that said very plainly, "Ephraim Benjamin Cross."

My mouth went dry.

Chapter 5

I couldn't help myself. I stared at the note in Reed's hand pretty much the same way I expect I would stare at the Loch Ness monster. With a mixture of curiosity—and horror.

The note had been written in wide, bold strokes obviously made by a fountain pen. That made sense. Ephraim Cross probably wouldn't have been caught dead with a Bic.

No sooner had the thought occurred to me than I started feeling glad I hadn't voiced it aloud. The Bad Cops probably would've taken that little comment to be a Freudian slip. I took a deep breath and hurriedly finished reading the body of the note.

It had pretty much the same tone as Cross's will earlier.

"Schuyler, my darling, you are so *wonderful*! To understand the way you do. I wish I could give you *everything* I want to, but you even understand why I can't. One day, my *darling*, we'll be together! Until then, we'll be together in our hearts. All my love *forever,* Ephraim."

I read the thing through twice, the second time noting the underlines and the exclamation points. Lord. It looked like one of the articles in *Cosmopolitan.* Or maybe a note from some lovestruck school kid.

And yet, how could Ephraim Cross have been lovestruck over *me*? Even on that idiotic HBO movie, it had taken the opening credits and a sentence or two before the lawyer and her client were gaga about each other. Surely, you'd think such devotion did actually require *meeting* each other.

I swallowed, and made the mistake of lifting my eyes

to those of the Bad Cops. Reed and Constello were both staring at me. For a second I tried to remember where I'd seen eyes like that before. Let me see. Cold. Remorseless. Predatory.

Then it hit me. Those very same eyes had been on yet another HBO movie I'd seen recently.

Jaws.

Except, of course, in *Jaws* I believe that big white shark had radiated quite a bit more empathy than Reed and Constello here.

I took a deep breath. "Now, wait a minute. *This* isn't mine. I've never seen this note before in my life."

Reed and Constello exchanged another one of their significant looks.

I was getting tired of them doing that. "Look, you've got to believe me! This note had to have been *planted* in my car. Somebody is trying to make it look as if I really did know Ephraim Cross!"

Reed cleared his throat. "They're doing a good job," he said quietly. He moved his thumb so that it was pointing directly toward what, in high school English, we used to call the salutation. "Dear *Schuyler*—"

I had to admit, Reed's point was well taken. Having a letter begin this way *might* make a person think it was addressed to me.

And yet, how could it be? How on earth could Ephraim Cross be writing to me, if he didn't even know me?

I took another deep breath. "Maybe this note isn't even in Ephraim Cross's handwriting. Maybe somebody faked this thing, just to implicate me!"

Constello actually snickered. "Now, Mrs. Ridgway, that sounds real farfetched, now doesn't it?" He pronounced the word "doesn't" as if it were spelled "dudn't."

I took an exasperated breath. "Just because something sounds farfetched doesn't necessarily mean it isn't true! When Columbus decided the world was round, everybody in *Spain* thought it sounded farfetched!"

Maybe I shouldn't have brought up Columbus. I think it makes you sound a little desperate if you're reaching back a few centuries to come up with somebody to back up your argument. Constello obviously concurred. He gave me a contemptuous look. "Mrs. Ridgway," he said, "the world *is* round—"

He made this sound like news.

"—and I'd bet my paycheck that this here note I'm holding *was* written by Ephraim Cross." His Eastern Kentucky drawl now sounded testy.

I decided to move on. "Well, anybody could've hidden this letter in my car! *Anybody.* Particularly if you found it in my glove compartment!" I was trying to remain calm, but by now I was practically babbling in my rush to explain.

If the Bad Cops had found this note where Constello said they did—pushed into the back of my glove compartment—it was no wonder I hadn't seen it. I never looked in there. I'd decided it was something to be avoided, oddly enough, the day I took my car into one of those instant oil change places, and the guy on duty found a mouse nest in my air filter.

That had to be over a year ago. The attendant cleaned the nest out and threw it away, and at the time I even managed to laugh about it with him. Ever since then, though, I've made it a point *not* to look into any dark place in my car that might possibly appear homey to a mouse family. I don't look under my hood, or into my glove compartment, or even under the driver's seat—for fear I'll see assorted little rodent hitchhikers looking back at me.

"In fact," I finished, "the last time I can remember even *opening* my glove compartment was about three months ago when my front left tire went flat, and I'd needed to get out my owner's manual to figure out how to assemble the jack and put on the spare. So, see, somebody could easily have hidden that note in there, and I'd never have seen it!"

In the future, if the police ever question me again, I believe I'm going to have to remember one thing. Don't babble.

Reed and Constello were both looking at me as if they were now not only considering arresting me, but taking out a mental inquest warrant. "Let me get this straight," Reed said. "You want us to believe you never open your glove compartment because of *mice*?"

Constello's tone was, if anything, even more incredulous than Reed's. "You can't change a tire without reading the *manual*?"

I took still another deep breath, and tried to speak calmly. "What I'm trying to tell you is that there's somebody out there trying to make me *look* guilty." Just saying the words made me feel cold. My God. It was really true. Somebody wanted me arrested for *murder*. "And whoever's doing this is obviously the person you're really after!"

This particular somebody had, no doubt, gone to no little trouble to plant this little epistle in my glove compartment. And yet, when? How? The answers to those questions came to me immediately. They were: "Just about any time they wanted," and "Very easily." Respectively.

The reason I was so sure about this is that I keep forgetting to lock my car doors. You'd think, being afraid of mouse-hitchhikers, I'd be more conscientious about this sort of thing. But I always seem to be rushing to a showing or a closing or one thing or another, and locking my car doors gets to be way down on my list of priorities. Besides, I'm pretty sure that my air filter mouse didn't just mosey up, open the door, and get in.

Given how lax I am, putting that note in my glove compartment had probably been a cakewalk.

"That note could've been put in there when my Toyota was parked out in front of Arndoerfer Realty," I told Reed and Constello. "Or when it was parked out in front of any one of several houses I've shown this last week. Or it could even have been done when my car was parked in my own driveway!"

The thought of somebody out in my driveway hiding a note in my car while I was inside my house, only a few steps away, made me feel even colder. I'd been staring at the note in Reed's hand while I talked. Now I drew my suit jacket a little tighter around me, and looked up, straight into Reed's eyes.

I was right the first time. That *Jaws* shark had Reed beat bad in the empathy department

I held up my hand. "Hey, I know this *looks* bad—"

Reed interrupted. "You got that right."

I went on as if he hadn't said anything. "—but I'm telling you the truth, somebody is trying to frame me!"

The words were no sooner out of my mouth than I got the feeling that Reed and Constello weren't buying it.

Maybe it was the grin on Constello's face that was the tip-off. Or maybe it was the way Reed gave this little snort of disdain. "Mrs. Ridgway," he said, "what kind of fools do you take us for?"

I just looked at him. Reed had asked me about a "raisin debt," and now he was asking me *this*? I was pretty sure he didn't want to hear my answer. I was also pretty sure he could read in my eyes exactly what I was thinking, so I quickly glanced back down at Cross's note.

Until then we'll be together in our hearts, it said. Together in our hearts, my eye. The man was *married.* The way I saw it, Ephraim Cross was together with his wife on a pretty much permanent basis, and it didn't much matter *who* he was hanging around with in his heart. I blinked, staring at that note. What kind of woman would buy this load of garbage?

A total fool, I believe, would be my first guess.

It was painfully obvious, however, that both the Bad Cops were now looking at *me* as if I were the total fool in question. A total fool who had perhaps only just recently gotten tired of being one.

And had done something about it.

"You don't really think we're going to believe that there's some big plot against you, do you?" Reed went on. "I mean, it sounds kind of paranoid, doesn't it?"

What is it they say? Even paranoiacs have enemies.

"I don't care what it sounds like, it's the truth! I did *not* know Ephraim Cross—" I realized I'd said this before, but it seemed worth repeating. "—so he could *not* have written to me. Do you two think I'd have given you permission to search my house and car if I'd had *any* idea this letter was in my glove compartment?"

Constello shrugged. "Maybe you forgot it was in there."

I threw up my hands at that. "For crying out loud, there are a *lot* of people who benefitted from Cross's death more than I did!" Mrs. Cross and both her children immediately came to mind, as a matter of fact. "And, surely, a man as rich and powerful as Ephraim Cross had to have made a few enemies along the way. It seems to me that before you decide to home in on *me,* these other people should be checked out."

I didn't mean that the way it sounded. Reed and Constello both bristled. "Mrs. Ridgway, you can rest assured we're pursuing *all* possibilities," Reed said, jabbing his finger in my direction. "I don't think we need you to tell us how to do our job."

With that, apparently both Reed and Constello decided that their aforementioned job now entailed going through my house all over again. With renewed energy.

I believe I showed real restraint at this point. I actually settled myself back down on my Ethan Allen couch, even picking up the Spiegel catalog again to look as if all this wasn't bothering me a bit. It was, however, getting more and more difficult to pull this one off. Particularly with Reed and Constello noisily opening drawers once again all over my house, and stomping around in their heavy shoes on the second floor just above my head.

I considered more than once storming upstairs and telling them enough was enough, I'd decided I needed to see a search warrant, after all. And yet, every time it crossed my mind to do such a thing, I decided against it. I think I could be pretty sure that if I started ranting and raving, the Bad Cops would only get more convinced of my guilt. And they'd just stay that much longer. They might even end up arresting me for something like obstruction of justice. Or disturbing the peace. Or even having a sloppy underwear drawer. Whatever.

Assuming, of course, they didn't find enough evidence to arrest me for murder.

Had anything else incriminating been hidden around here? I never forget to lock up my house when I leave, so planting something in here would not be as easy as my car. I'd certainly noticed no evidence of a break-in, or anything like that, but how could I be sure?

After about the first hour, I dared breathe a little easier. It started looking fairly obvious that everything significant to be found in my house and car had already been put into the Bad Cops' Seal-A-Meal bag. And yet, they kept right on. Making their way very slowly this time through every single room. Fortunately, my house isn't that big—it's just three bedrooms and one bath upstairs, a kitchen, dining room and living room downstairs, and a small basement underneath that—or else the Bad Cops might've stayed around for the next year or so.

I probably would've had to declare these guys as dependents on my income tax.

The two of them really lingered in the kitchen. I wasn't sure what in the world they expected to find in there. A love letter under my toaster? A few candid photos of Ephraim Cross hidden in one of my canisters? No doubt, in the one marked "Sugar?"

If Reed and Constello had any idea how little time I myself spend in that particular room in the house, they probably wouldn't have spent so much time in there themselves. I believe the Bad Cops were making some assumptions here. Assumptions that could easily be called sexist. Apparently, Reed and Constello had concluded that, since I'm a woman, the kitchen must be an important part of my life.

Talk about a wrong number. The stove I currently have is the one that was here the day I moved in twenty years ago. I'm pretty sure that if I wanted to sell that stove today, I could describe it truthfully as "like new." In fact, I might even be able to drop the word "like."

I guess I take after my mother as far as cooking skills go. Mama never did exactly teach me how to cook. What she taught me was how to open and heat.

I admit all this freely. I continue to admit it even though several of the times when I've admitted in public what a rotten cook I am, I've gotten horrified looks from men *and* women standing nearby. The consensus of opinion seems to be that, as a woman, I should be too ashamed to admit such a shortcoming.

They've *got* to be kidding.

The way I look at it, if people are going to judge me solely on the basis of my cooking expertise, it could very well be that I don't value their opinions enough to care.

I would've admitted all this to Reed and Constello, too, had they asked. If, however, the boys in blue—or, in this case, *tan*—wanted to leap to conclusions and spend an inordinate amount of their time in there, who was I to tell them that they were way off base?

At one point, Reed wandered out of the kitchen into my dining room, opened the French doors out there, and went out onto my screened porch. That screened porch is one of the best things about my house. It permits me to sit out there and enjoy all the flowers in my neighbors' gardens without actually having to do the work of having a garden of my own.

Reed stood out on my screened porch for the longest time, staring out at my backyard. He did not appear, however, to be enjoying my neighbors' flowers. Not with that frown on his face. Finally, Reed wandered back in, closed the French doors, and without looking in my direction, headed right back out to the kitchen.

I knew then what Reed had been doing out there. He'd actually been checking to see if I'd been lying about having a flower garden. Apparently, he really thought there might be a possibility that I had a few buttercups hidden away in my backyard. Right next to my three tomato plants. All ready for use in my next murder.

I must not have an honest face.

Or else, I must look unbelievably stupid. Because what kind of murderer would leave buttercups growing in her backyard right after leaving one in the lap of her victim? You'd think even an idiot would head straight home after the heinous deed and dig every one of those babies up.

After a while I started wondering if maybe Reed and Constello were taking their sweet time just so that I'd break down and confess. Maybe they thought that by rattling all the pots and pans in my kitchen cabinets and leafing through every one of my cookbooks, they'd drive me over the edge. Maybe they fully expected me to collapse into sobs and scream, "All right, you guys, I've had enough—just take your grubby paws out of my silverware drawer and I'll tell you the truth!"

Before I got to that point, though, the Bad Cops and I were interrupted. Just as it was getting dark—in fact, just as I was starting to wonder if, in spite of my remaining as calm as I could, and not causing any scenes, the Bad Cops were never going to leave—two people walked in my front door. These two people are probably the only two people in the entire world that I'm pretty much always glad to see. On this particular evening, however, these two people would probably have headed my list of Folks I'd Just As Soon Not Drop Over When the Police Are Searching My House.

In through my front door walked my sons, Daniel and Nathan.

O joy. Another golden opportunity to set a good parental example.

Chapter 6

My sons have never gotten over the fact that my house has been their home for as far back as they can remember. So, even though the two of them moved into their own apartment a little over a year ago, they still never bother to knock. The boys always just open my front door, and walk right in.

"Yo, Mom," Daniel said as he came into the living room. This is what Daniel always says these days by way of greeting. I've decided that I should never have taken him to see any of those *Rocky* movies. They obviously hit him hard.

Nathan was not two steps behind Daniel. Nathan is the exact same height and weight as Daniel—six two and about one hundred ninety pounds—but the two of them would never be mistaken for twins. In fact, they're the nineties' version of the Odd Couple.

Daniel, the oldest at 21, always dresses in jeans and T-shirts, always chooses black as his predominant fashion color, and always wears a silver hoop earring in one ear. That is, at one time, that hoop in Daniel's ear was silver. These days it's more a gray-black. I try not to notice it, but frankly, every time I see Daniel, I fight an almost overpowering urge to dip the right side of his head in Tarn-X.

Had he lived back in the sixties, Daniel no doubt would've been called a hippie. A free spirit. A flower child. Unfortunately, in this day and age, what Daniel is called is a slob.

Among other things.

Daniel's jeans and T-shirts never look completely clean. They also never fail to look as if just before he put them on, Daniel took out his trusty machine gun and blew a few well-placed holes in them. Either that, or every time Daniel steps out his door, he's caught in cross fire.

Today's gun battle must've been particularly fierce. Both knees of Daniel's faded jeans were torn away, the shoulder of his black Grateful Dead T-shirt was ripped open, and the front was peppered with jagged holes. Daniel usually wears his black hair in a long shaggy mane below his shoulders, but today, no doubt in a concession to the hot weather, he'd pulled it back with a rubber band.

According to Daniel, he dresses the way he does to make a statement. In my opinion, the statement he appears to be going for is: "Yuck."

Nathan, only one year younger than Daniel, is so unlike his older brother, it's hard to believe they grew up in the same house. Nathan's sandy brown hair is a little shorter than a Marine's, he won't wear anything that doesn't have a designer label, and to put an earring in one of Nathan's ears would require anesthetizing him first. It would also be advisable *not* to be within a five-mile radius when Nathan woke up and found out what you'd done.

If Nathan has a fashion fault—other than paying far too much money for his clothes in relationship to his income—it would be that he dresses in shorts nearly all-year long. Nathan does have long, muscular legs, but you'd think he'd confine himself to showing them off only during summer months. Last year Nathan showed up at my mother's on Christmas Day in red tartan plaid shorts. His knees were as blue as my mother's hair, and yet he insisted he was comfortable.

Maybe that saddle block they gave me when Nathan was born affected him permanently—from the thighs down.

Today Nathan was once again wearing his plaid Christmas shorts, a yellow oxford shirt with a button-down collar and rolled-up sleeves, and leather tasseled slip-ons with no socks. Unlike Daniel, Nathan didn't even say "Yo" to me as he walked in. He just went right on talking to his brother, as if he didn't even see me sitting there on the couch. "You could've done *my* laundry, too. It wouldn't have killed you, Daniel. It was lying right there on top of the hamper, all you would've had to do was—"

Nathan and Daniel always seem to arrive in the midst of a fight. They've done this so often here lately that I've decided they're doing it on purpose. Obviously, they're counting on me to jump in and act as referee. Which, of course, like an idiot, I often do. A lot of the times when I'm refereeing, what had started out as a quarrel between Nathan and Daniel ends up as a quarrel involving all three of us. That's the kind of talent I have as an arbiter of problems.

Still, the boys keep doing this. I think they've made up their mind it's either me or Judge Wapner. I may not be as wise as the judge, but at least I won't televise their arguments.

"Oh, yeah?" Daniel was now saying to Nathan. "Well, maybe I don't think I should have to do laundry for somebody who left all his dishes in the sink the night before for *me* to clean up—"

Daniel and Nathan must've been concentrating all their attention on their argument because neither one of them seemed to notice the Bad Cops. This was pretty amazing since by the time the boys walked in, Reed and Constello had finally finished with my kitchen and were working their way through my dining room. My dining room is only separated from my living room by a large open archway, and both Bad Cops were standing in plain view, not more than eight feet away from where I was sitting, their hands rifling the top two drawers of my buffet.

"—and you *knew* I was bringing home a date, but did you clean up the kitchen? No, you—" Daniel broke off at this point. Evidently, he'd just caught sight of Reed and Constello. "Uh, Mom," he said, "there are two guys out in the dining room going through your stuff."

Daniel actually said this as if it were a tiny, inconsequential thing that he thought he probably ought to mention. Daniel has always been the more laid back of my two sons, but then I guess if you're the sort of person who feels at ease walking around with bullet holes in your clothes, it would take a lot to get you rattled.

"I know, Daniel. It's okay," I said.

Unfortunately, at the exact same time I was saying this, Nathan was also just catching sight of the Bad Cops. Nathan took this opportunity to demonstrate just how unlike his brother he really was. *"Oh my God!"* Nathan yelled, completely drowning out what I was saying to Daniel. "Mom, you're being robbed! Quick! Call the *police!*" He gestured wildly toward the cordless phone I keep on the end table next to my couch.

I just stared at Nathan. Sometimes I think the boys are just waiting for something to happen to confirm what they've suspected all along: I don't have good sense. Apparently, Nathan actually believed that I could have thieves break into my house, start rifling through my buffet drawers right in front of me, and it wouldn't occur to me to pick up the phone and call 911. Unless, of course, Nathan himself was there to suggest it.

This could be construed as insulting.

If *I* was feeling insulted, I had nothing on Reed. He took his hands out of my buffet drawer, whipped his badge out, and said, "Son, we *are* the police."

Nathan actually gasped.

Daniel, as laid back as ever, shrugged.

"I'm Murray Reed and this is my partner, Tony Constello." Reed was doing his Joe Friday impression again. I could've told him it was a waste on Daniel and Nathan. I don't think either of my sons have ever seen a single episode of *Dragnet.* Not even on the Nostalgia Channel. I believe, in fact, that unless Joe Friday has a video out, and it's being featured prominently on MTV, it's unlikely that Daniel and Nathan have ever heard of him.

"We're looking into a homicide, and we're asking your mother a few questions." All the time Reed was talking, Constello was standing next to him, giving Daniel a slow, up-and-down look. I swallowed uneasily. If Daniel didn't look like an unsavory character, nobody did. No doubt, Constello was now flipping through his mental list of Wanted posters.

Nathan, King of the Yuppies, oddly enough, didn't warrant so much as a glance.

Which was just as well. Nathan was mainly glancing at *me,* his mouth pinched, his blue eyes demanding an explanation.

I gave Nathan what I hoped was a reassuring smile. Nathan did not smile back, but I didn't really expect him to. Nathan always has had a lot of his father in him. I believe, if we put it to a vote, Nathan would definitely agree with Ed on the mop-shaking issue. The way Nathan feels about cops dropping by to search your house goes without saying. He stared at me the way he probably would have if he'd just found out I was Ma Barker.

Daniel, on the other hand, looked as if Ma Barker was his idea of the perfect mother. Daniel's brown eyes actually lit up at the word "homicide." "You're investigating a *murder*? And you're questioning *Mom*?" he said to Reed. "Cool."

Reed blinked at that one.

And then he and Constello started in, questioning Nathan and Daniel. I tried to object. "Is this really necessary?" I said. "My sons don't know anything about—"

It was Daniel, believe it or not, who jumped in at this point and pretty much let the air out of any argument I might've had. "Oh, that's okay, Mom," Daniel said, "it's cool. We don't mind a bit."

Apparently, Daniel was under the impression that being a part of a murder investigation came under the heading of "fun." Someday I need to have a long talk with that boy.

Nathan, however, looked as if he wanted to beat me to it. The look he gave Daniel was not the least bit "cool."

After that, Reed and Constello went right ahead and asked Daniel and Nathan the same sort of credit application questions they'd asked me. Name, address, place of employment. Thank goodness, though, it wasn't a real credit application. Having to sit there and listen to Nathan and Daniel blithely go over how much they owe and how little they make would definitely constitute cruel and unusual punishment.

In fact, if Reed and Constello only knew, this could

be a lot more effective technique than the Bad Cop, Good Cop routine. Just have Nathan and Daniel start talking about how they both opened up MasterCard accounts their first year in college—without my knowledge, I might add—and then have them move on to how they both immediately charged these cards up to the limit, and *then* have them mention how they weren't even employed at the time. That ought to soften me up some. For the clincher, Reed and Constello could have my sons go over slowly and in some detail just how they'd both managed to flunk out of college almost exactly a year ago this month.

Nathan and Daniel, amazingly enough, *were* like twins in this one instance. Last June they'd received identical letters from the University of Louisville informing them that their presence would not be required for the next term. These letters arrived shortly after grade reports mainly featuring the letters D and F.

Nathan, of course, had the record. He'd achieved flunking out after only one year of higher education. Daniel, the slaggard, had taken twice that long to earn his dishonorable discharge.

Oh yes, listening to all this would definitely break me down. After no time at all, I'd probably be reduced to a quivering heap, blurting out secrets that even *I* didn't know I knew. Particularly if either one of my sons happened to also mention that they'd done their flunking out at *my* expense.

That's right. Their father, in a rare moment of real insight, had flatly refused to pay any of Daniel's educational expenses, and then two years later, he'd even more flatly refused to pay any of Nathan's. At the time, of course, I'd been outraged. After all, it wasn't as if Ed were strapped for cash.

Back when we were married, Ed had limped along making not much better than minimum wage as a computer programmer. Shortly after our split, though, wouldn't you know it, Ed changed companies, began working his way up the corporate ladder, and three years ago he was made vice president in charge of computer operations at Klein Conveyor. In the world of conveyor belts, Ed was, according to the boys, one of the "head muckety-mucks."

A head muckety-muck who wouldn't contribute a dime toward his own sons' education. A head muckety-muck who at the time was dating Cindy, a blond beauty with a dazzling smile, who incidentally happened to be Daniel's age. Today—now that they've been broken up for almost eight months—Ed refers to Cindy less than fondly as "that high-maintenance chick." Meaning, I believe, that she required frequent gifts of jewelry and perfume to keep her smile dazzling.

This did not come as a surprise. In fact, when Ed kept on refusing to contribute anything to the boys' educational cause, I had no doubt it was because a major chunk of Ed's budget had already been labeled "Cindy." After the boys flunked out, though, I decided Ed's reluctance might've just been shrewd fiscal planning.

No doubt, Cindy—while she lasted—was a much better return on Ed's investment.

Thank God, neither Nathan nor Daniel mentioned any of this to Reed and Constello. I noticed moreover that neither one of my sons even looked in my direction while they were telling Reed where they were currently employed. Daniel had held four different jobs in the past year, but at that moment he was working at a Taco Bell. Nathan, on the other hand, actually told Reed with some pride in his voice, "I'm pursuing a career in dishwashing."

Reed blinked once more, but quickly moved on. Handing Nathan a glossy black-and-white photograph of Ephraim Cross, Reed asked, "Ever see this guy around here?" The photo must've been one taken for an annual report or a corporate brochure. In it Ephraim Cross was seated in a leather chair behind a desk bigger than my dining-room table. Cross had a telephone to his ear, and was looking directly at the camera. It was one of those poses that's supposed to look candid and unstaged, but never does.

Nathan stared at the photo. "No, sir." Even back in elementary school, Nathan had always been extremely polite in the presence of authority. "I certainly haven't seen him around here, sir."

Daniel, I don't believe, has ever said the word "sir" in his life. He was fiddling with his tarnished earring when Constello handed him the photo. Daniel took a quick look and said, "Uh, this is that Cross guy, right? The guy that was killed the other night? Man, I read about that in the paper." Daniel glanced over at me, and then back over at Reed and Constello. "Hey, wasn't this guy pretty much *loaded*? I mean, like, mega-rich? You don't really think my *mother* actually knew this guy, do you?"

At this point Daniel looked as if he were actually on the verge of laughing out loud at the very idea. I do believe I was being insulted again. Thanks a lot, Daniel.

Reed looked annoyed. Apparently, not only was Daniel one really unsavory-looking character, but Daniel also had the audacity to snicker at his prime murder suspect. "You didn't answer my question." Joe Friday was back. "Have you seen him around here?"

Daniel shrugged again. Apparently, he thought he'd made himself perfectly clear. "Uh, no," Daniel said.

Reed and Constello left soon after that. Either they'd decided that they'd found out all they were going to for the time being. Or else, they'd made up their mind that I probably wasn't going to break down and confess in front of family.

Judging from the expressions on Reed's and Constello's faces, it didn't seem to make much difference what Daniel and Nathan had just told them. Reed and Constello were obviously both still looking at me with more than a little suspicion.

Of course, they did have a letter with my name on it. And I guess they'd pretty much expected Daniel and Nathan to say what they did. No doubt, sons could be expected to lie for their own mother. Besides, even if Nathan and Daniel *were* telling the truth, I was supposed to be meeting Ephraim Cross on the sly, anyway, wasn't I? No wonder my sons hadn't seen him around.

"Don't be leaving town any time soon, ya hear?" Constello said on his way out the door.

The Bad Cops took the letter from Cross with them. Not exactly a surprise. They both were quick to tell me that they were just taking it in order to check to see if the handwriting really was that of Ephraim Cross, but they didn't fool me. I knew damn well they were taking it with them to make sure *I* didn't destroy it.

As soon as the Bad Cops went out my front door, Daniel and Nathan picked up where Reed and Constello had left off. "What's this all about?" "What's the cops doing asking *you* questions?" "You're not involved in anything we don't know about, are you, Mom?"

The last question was from Nathan. The trusting soul.

I explained the whole thing to them, but Daniel's and Nathan's reactions weren't exactly what I'd hoped for. "Uh, really, Mom?" That was as far as Daniel went in expressing what was clearly disbelief.

Nathan was a little more explicit. He ran his hand through his sandy hair and said, "Let me get his straight. You're saying that a rich total stranger left you over a hundred thousand dollars?"

I nodded.

Nathan exchanged glances with Daniel, and looked back at me. "Whatever you say, Mom." Nathan's tone lacked sincerity

I gave Nathan the look I used to give him when he wet his training pants. "Do you think I'm lying?"

Nathan must've remembered that look all these years later. "Oh, no," he said, holding up both hands defensively. "We believe you, Mom. We really do."

It was obvious that neither he nor Daniel did. At least, not completely.

I just stared back at them. It wasn't as if either one of them really considered for a second that I could actually be involved in Cross's death. I don't believe Nathan or Daniel would ever think me capable of doing anything illegal worse than speeding. However, both of them clearly thought it possible I might've actually been carrying on with Ephraim Cross.

Their own *mother,* they didn't believe. Was nothing sacred in America anymore?

Fortunately—or maybe, unfortunately, depending on

how you looked at it—Nathan and Daniel had other fish to fry. This fish was one they'd been frying with me a lot lately. In fact, this particular fish has got to be pretty crispy by now.

"So, Mom," Daniel said, "now that you're a rich woman and all, uh, I guess you wouldn't mind lending us fifty dollars until Friday, huh?" Daniel is always the one who asks. I don't know if it's because he's the oldest, so the boys have decided it's his responsibility. Or if Daniel just does it because he's so laid back, it doesn't require any real effort for him to beg for money.

Nathan always does his part by standing right in back of Daniel, giving me one of his best, endearing smiles.

Usually, I'm a sucker for one of Nathan's smiles. This probably has a lot to do with the way I happen to believe that both my sons are the handsomest young men on earth. My judgment, of course, might be a bit prejudiced, but even allowing for that, let's face it, they're still adorable.

Usually.

This moment, however, might've been a notable exception. I stared back at Nathan and did not return his smile. Nathan and Daniel, you see, are supposed to be self-supporting these days. As I mentioned before, the two of them decided a year ago—oddly enough, the very week they received their mutual dishonorable discharges from U of L—to move into a third-floor apartment in one of the old Victorian houses within walking distance of the university. It's my opinion that their move might've had something to do with how well acquainted they both were with my views on higher education.

I myself, in a moment of great stupidity, had dropped out my freshman year to marry their father, and had not returned to school until after Ed and I were divorced. Working full-time as a secretary, with two elementary-school-age boys at home—and only being able to attend classes part-time—I'd finally given up on a four-year degree, settling instead for a two-year Associate degree. I believe they call this particular degree an *Associate* degree because, if you have it, people will associate with you. It's certainly not good for anything else. Right after

I got my Associate degree, I enrolled in a real estate course and began the illustrious career I have today.

Both boys are very well aware how much I regret not finishing my baccalaureate. They're also very well aware how much I want *them* to do what I myself had been unable to do. No wonder they'd decided to move out when they did. After flunking out, they were probably afraid I might poison their food.

Which was a thought.

Nathan and Daniel have both assured me that they moved close to U of L because they have every intention of going back. According to them, they're going to re-enroll as soon as the university will let them back in. This next time, they insist, they're going to foot the bill themselves. And they're really going to buckle down.

I'd love to believe every word, but frankly, I'm not so sure. I hate to think it, but it does occur to me that another compelling reason for the boys to live close to a college campus is that this general area appears to be a magnet for young women the boys' age. And young women do seem to figure prominently in both their lives these days. Oddly enough.

In fact, I think I'll only believe that the boys have actually re-enrolled when I see a grade report at the end of a semester. With something on it higher up the alphabetical chain than a D or an F.

Talk, unlike an education, is cheap.

Not to mention, Nathan and Daniel were the same people who also told me the day they moved out, they were going to financially "float their own boat" from then on. And yet, this boat of theirs seems to be continually taking on water. How in the world were they going to afford tuition if they kept needing *me* to help bail?

Daniel was now trying to top his brother in the Most Endearing Smile Contest. I sighed heavily. "Guys, I don't understand why in the world you don't handle your finances better—"

It's what I always say. I could see both their eyes glaze over the second the words were out of my mouth.

I was about to start my usual speech about fiscal responsibility—the one they've probably got memorized by now—but Daniel played his trump card. "Mom," he said, "if you don't give us any money, we can't buy groceries. We're, uh, tapped out until we get paid."

Nathan piped in with, "Our refrigerator is empty, Mom."

I just looked at them. This was a persuasive argument, all right. What kind of mother would let her own kids go hungry?

On the other hand, I couldn't help remembering that the last time Nathan and Daniel had asked me for money, it had turned out that there was a Rod Stewart concert in town. Standing there, with both of them smiling at me pleadingly, I knew very well that I should go immediately and check the *Courier-Journal.* Just to make sure there weren't any rock concerts in town for which the tickets just happened to be $25 apiece.

And yet, I felt too drained to do it. When it came right down to it, I just didn't feel like arguing. I guess being accused of murder takes a lot out of a person.

As soon as I gave in to the boys, though, I regretted it. Not, of course, for the reasons I should have. Not, for example, because I was passing up a chance to teach my sons to be self-supporting and independent and all that good stuff. Oh no, I regretted it because almost the second I wrote them the check, Nathan and Daniel left. They gave me their usual hugs and kisses and multiple "Thank you's," and headed out the door. Headed for the grocery, they said, but for all I knew, it could've been to the nearest Ticketron outlet.

Once Nathan and Daniel were gone, there wasn't much else to do other than think about the mess I suddenly found myself in.

What the hell was going on? Who in the world could've put that note in my car? Had someone really been following me all over town, just waiting for the opportunity to plant a note in my glove compartment?

It was an unsettling thought.

Equally unsettling was this one: Was I going to be arrested for murdering somebody I didn't even know?

Chapter 7

The next morning was a Tuesday, which is one of the days of the week I usually dread. The other day is Friday, believe it or not. I know, I know. The rest of the world is practically holding its breath until Friday finally rolls around, and me, I see it come and groan. I hate Fridays for the same reason I hate Tuesdays. They're the two days of the week I have floor duty at Jarvis Arndoerfer Realty.

Floor duty shouldn't be all that bad. At most real estate firms, all you have to do is deal with walk-ins—either taking them yourself as new clients or if you're too busy, passing them on to another agent—and answer the phone.

Floor duty, in fact, should be something I look forward to since it's the way you generally come by new business. Most new clients either phone or show up at your office, having seen your firm's sign in front of a house for sale or having read one of your ads. And, while people who phone or come by seeking more information about one particular house almost never end up buying that house—I believe the actual figure is 3 out of 100—it's a great way to get leads. In a minute or two, you can find out who they are, and what they're looking for, and when they're planning to move, and you can take a giant step toward convincing them that you're just the person to help them out.

This is how floor duty is *supposed* to work. At Jarvis Arndoerfer Realty, there's a slight twist. Mainly because Jarvis is such a cheapskate, he refuses to hire himself a secretary. Instead, he insists that all the agents who work for him fill in as his secretary on their floor duty days.

So instead of just answering the phone and dealing with potential clients, you're answering the phone and dealing with Jarvis's wife, and his mother, and often one of his five grown children. You're also taking Jarvis's messages, and typing his letters, and doing his filing and whatever else Jarvis can think up. It's my fear that one day Jarvis's idea of floor duty will include just that—doing the floors.

It's not, of course, always as bad as it sounds. If it were, I probably would've moved on to another agency long ago. On some days Jarvis's wife, Arlene, is in the office, and *she* plays secretary. Not, mind you, anywhere near often enough, but occasionally she *is* there.

On the other hand, there have also been those Tuesdays and Fridays when I've had so much to do as Jarvis's secretary that I've actually let callers hang up without getting their name and phone number. Which is the same as flushing a perfectly good lead down the toilet.

In spite of all this, amazingly enough, when I woke up on the Tuesday after the Bad Cops' visit, I was surprised to find I was almost looking forward to going into the office. For one thing, it would take my mind off wondering about what in the world I could do to erase my name from the Bad Cops' list of suspects. I was positive that there *had* to be something I could do, but I wasn't at all sure what that particular something could be.

I would've liked to have found out more about Ephraim Cross, maybe even question his relatives as to why he might be corresponding with a woman he didn't know. I believe, however, I could pretty much guarantee that none of the Cross family would be willing to talk to me.

So what could I do? Other than worry about how I was going to look in prison stripes. Or if they even wear stripes anymore, prison fashions being something I've not exactly kept up with. It's a thing, I suppose, I've always expected to learn on a "need-to-know" basis.

I got out of bed, pulled a robe over my nightshirt, and went downstairs to the kitchen to make my usual breakfast—a large glass of Coke, heavy on the ice. I may have given up potato chips and ice cream to lose weight, but I drew the line at giving up brown carbonated beverages. Besides, without the bracing shock of an ice-cold Coke to pop open my eyes every morning, I'm sure I'd walk around half asleep all day long.

I guess I might've been able to give up Coke, too, if I'd ever learned to like coffee. I can't stand the stuff, though. I've hated coffee ever since high school when I stayed up all night cramming for U.S. History finals and drinking coffee by the gallon. Now I can't even smell coffee without it bringing back that unnaturally wide-awake, nauseated feeling and the agony of trying to memorize dates of Civil War battles at three o'clock in the morning.

I realize, of course, that it's probably the caffeine in Coke—not the ice—that pops open my eyes every morning. And, yes, I have read all those magazine articles about how bad caffeine is supposed to be for you. However, since I don't smoke, and since I've already given up the aforementioned potato chips and ice cream, I think I've probably got a wide margin of error here that allows me to throw caution to the wind, consume vast quantities of the Real Thing, and still live to be a very wrinkled old lady.

Not to mention, with the police making house calls these days, I needed a good drink.

I polished off two full glasses of icy Coke while I got dressed, and then I headed into work.

Jarvis Arndoerfer Realty is just five miles away, but allowing for the tangle of traffic on Bardstown Road in the mornings, I usually give myself ten minutes to get there. In the last month, I've even added another ten minutes. This is because they're doing something to Harvard Drive right in front of where it intersects with Bardstown Road. From what I can tell, going by in the car, it looks as if they're fixing the sewers or rerouting the water lines or maybe widening the street a couple inches. The city of Louisville is always doing something like this. I've lived here all my life, and Louisville has never been finished. They're always widening a street, or adding another lane to the expressway, or doing something else than necessitates putting large holes in the street.

I think this is a rule in Louisville. No matter what public project is being done, it has to require putting large holes in the street. I think if they were stringing Christmas lights, it would require holes. Big, deep ones that could gobble up your car if you're not careful when you drive around them. I deftly dodged a few car-gobbling holes, ignored a couple members of the street crew who—judging from their hand signals—wanted to become close friends of mine, and turned right onto Bardstown Road.

The traffic on this road might not be so bad, but as I've mentioned before, most of my neighbors are elderly. I've always pictured my own retirement as definitely including sleeping late in the morning, but for some reason, a great many of the older people who live near me get out in their cars between eight-thirty and nine. Advanced age has evidently made them cautious, because once out on the road, apparently they've all agreed that the safest driving speed is 25 miles an hour. They also have apparently decided that you should start braking for a red light at least three car lengths before you get to it. There are four red lights between me and Arndoerfer Realty. Between silver-haired drivers stopping for distant red lights and city buses abruptly pulling out right in front of you, it's a wonder the traffic on Bardstown Road moves at all.

Turning from Bardstown Road onto Taylorsville Road was its usual death-defying feat, but I actually felt my spirits lifting as soon as Arndoerfer Realty came into view. It really was going to feel good to be busy.

Arndoerfer Realty occupies a two-story building located on the left-hand side of Taylorsville Road right next to Radigan's Meat Market. The Arndoerfer Realty building was at one time a private residence, but Jarvis has knocked out a few walls, bulldozed some trees, and made a parking lot out of what was once, for the Highlands, a very spacious lawn. This is what Jarvis calls progress.

The bottom half of the building is brick, and the top

is shingles, but you don't notice this right away. This is because the entire thing has been painted bright yellow. Even the roof has been done in mustard-yellow shingles. I think Jarvis read somewhere that yellow is the most visible color, and he decided to make his real estate office the most visible thing on Taylorsville Road. If that was his aim, Jarvis has certainly succeeded. If it was also his aim to create an eyesore, Jarvis has succeeded there, too.

Arndoerfer Realty shares its parking lot with the meat market next door, so if there's a sale on veal cutlets or if, say, sirloin is on special, you have to park in the back. Today, however, all the meat must be at regular price. There was actually a parking space right next to the front door. I don't know if it was finding this space, or anticipating doing something that would get my mind off murder, but I was actually smiling as I walked into the office.

Because Jarvis knocked out the aforementioned walls, the front door opens immediately into one huge open room with four metal desks—one in each corner. I think Jarvis did this on purpose so that he can make sure none of his agents ever slack off. It only takes one glance around the room, and you can see everybody that's there.

Jarvis's own office is, of course, upstairs.

Arndoerfer Realty is not a very large firm—it has only five agents, and that's counting Jarvis and his wife. One quick glance told me that everybody except Arlene Arndoerfer, Jarvis's wife, was present and accounted for. This little fact usually would've made my stomach tighten, but today I was almost pleased. So I was going to be very busy. Good.

Barbi Lundergan and Charlotte Ackersen, two other real estate agents, were both at their desks, and over at the coffee machine in the back corner was Jarvis himself. My glance around the room also told me something else. Everyone in the room had stopped in the middle of what they were doing, and were openly staring at me. It was almost as if I'd walked into a surprise party, only nobody yelled surprise.

I swallowed uneasily. What was wrong here?

Jarvis was the first to break the silence. "Well, Schuyler, good morning!" In his early fifties with a good-size gut hanging over his belt, Jarvis stands about 5'5" in his stocking feet—and that's only when he's wearing *very* thick socks. For as long as I've known him—and I've worked here for the last five years—poor Jarvis has suffered from SMD, Short Man's Disease. One of the symptoms of SMD is that the sufferer apparently feels compelled to dominate every conversation, and that if there are more than two people in the room with him, he insists on being the center of attention. Another symptom of SMD is knowing everything there is to know about everything and being only too glad to tell you about it.

Jarvis, as usual, was in the throes of his illness. His voice was so loud it seemed to ricochet off the walls. "My, my, my, Schuyler," he boomed, "how *very* nice you look today!"

I was wearing a floral print Liz Claiborne dress that I'd found last August marked less than half price in the Galleria downtown. One reason this dress was on sale, I'm sure, was because it was a size 12 Petite. There can't be that many size 12 Petites walking around, size 12 and Petite being, I believe, mutually exclusive. I myself am not a Petite either—far from it—in spite of Jane Fonda's efforts to the contrary. However, Liz Claiborne dresses often run so oversized that I can wear Petite in quite a few of them. I'd been so delighted to find this Liz on sale that I've worn it about a million times to the office.

This was the first time Jarvis had commented on it. A major red flag.

Jarvis followed up his comment with a simpering smile. Yet another red flag. Jarvis doesn't waste his simpering smiles on just any occasion.

"Why, thank you, Jarvis," I said warily.

Jarvis had apparently decided a long time ago that if he was going to be short, he was not going to go unnoticed. Today he was wearing rust red slacks, a grass green blazer, and a tie that looked as if somebody had spilled an entire set of watercolors all over it and left it there to dry. Some of the colors had run together, but none had lost their luminosity. With thick lips, a bulbous nose, and that tie, Jarvis needn't have worried. You noticed him, all right. It was entirely possible you'd notice him five miles away.

In addition to being short in stature, Jarvis is also a little short in the hair department. Most of what Jarvis has left makes a shadow just above his ears and around the back of his head. To give Jarvis credit, though, at least Jarvis doesn't grow it very long on one side, and comb it over the way some balding guys do. What Jarvis does do, however, is constantly swipe at his forehead as if he's brushing great quantities of hair out of his eyes.

Jarvis apparently thinks that if he goes through the motions of having lots of hair, people might be fooled into thinking that he really does have more than a few strands up there.

He was swiping at nonexistent hair now as he said, "My, my, yes, that *is* a very pretty outfit."

"Thanks," I said again, as once more I glanced around the room. Barbi and Charlotte were still looking my way. What on earth was up? Was Jarvis going to tell me that from now on I would be expected to not only play secretary on Tuesdays and Fridays, but that I should also start washing his car?

Jarvis's simpering smile grew. Incidentally, not a pretty sight. "By the way," he said, "Daniel called. I told him you weren't in yet."

I stared at Jarvis. This, of course, explained everything. My blabbermouth son, no doubt, had phoned, found that I wasn't in, and then, just to make sure the phone call wasn't a complete waste, proceeded to tell the entire office about my sudden good fortune. Emphasis on the last word—*fortune*.

I went over, put my purse under the front desk, and took a deep breath. Maybe I could help the Bad Cops come up with another crime to charge me with. Killing Daniel, for example.

Daniel's babbling, however, wasn't exactly a surprise. This was the same son who, almost fifteen years ago, at the age of seven, had announced loudly and clearly at the traditional Thanksgiving dinner at my parents, "Mommy and Daddy don't sleep in the same bedroom anymore."

What an adorable kid.

That Thanksgiving I'd seriously considered strangling Daniel, but eventually I'd decided Daniel's big mouth wasn't so bad. At least, no one in my family had been surprised when I filed for divorce a few months later. Still, if Daniel were going to go around spreading rumors, I'd wished at the time that he'd also thought to mention—in an equally loud voice—exactly how many girlfriends Ed had calling the house during the eight years we were married. Then maybe my mother wouldn't have spent so much time trying to talk me into going back to Ed.

And now, adorable Daniel had done it again. One thing about it, Daniel seemed to have covered this last bit of news a lot better than he'd reported on mine and Ed's marital problems. Everyone in the office—from Jarvis Arndoerfer right on down to Barbi Lundergan—seemed to know every detail. They all even knew the exact amount that Ephraim Cross left me.

I found that out when Barbi came hurrying over to my desk, right after I'd returned Jarvis's pointed smile and taken my seat at the front desk. "One Hundred and Seven Thousand, Five Hundred and sixty Dollars!"

I don't think I've heard a sum of money spoken with such breathy reverence since the last time I watched *The Price Is Right.*

"Oh-h-h, Schuyler," Barbi went on, "aren't you excited?"

"Excited is not the word for it," I said.

Barbi blinked and nodded as if she knew precisely what I meant. It is no doubt less than kind for me to say this, but unfortunately, it's true: Barbi Lundergan is that rare thing—a dumb brunette. I found this out the day she asked me, in all seriousness, how many quarters were in a football game. Barbi drives a bright red Corvette with a personalized license plate that says, TRU LUV,. and, believe me, there's every chance that Barbi thinks that the words on her plate are spelled correctly.

Up until recently, however, Barbi and I were pretty good friends. If Barbi was not exactly what you'd call a brain trust, I can't say I particularly cared. It wasn't as if we were going to sit down any time soon and do a few calculus problems together. Barbi was still fun to be with, and we had a lot in common. She, too, was divorced; she, too, was just about my age; and she, too, had two children—a boy and a girl, nineteen and twenty. Barbi also had a particularly endearing way of referring to my ex-husband as "Mr. Ed." I wasn't sure if she was doing this on purpose, or if it just happened to come out that way. I did, however, enjoy hearing it.

With her own ex-husband, Marvin, Barbi didn't bother being particularly inventive about what she called him. "Asshole" was the name, I believe, she preferred to use most often.

Barbi and I used to spend quite a few evenings together after work, having dinner together and sharing horror stories about our kids and our ex's. Neither of us was dating anybody in particular, so each of us, I think, enjoyed having somebody to do things with.

All this, however, abruptly ended two months ago on the day Barbi turned thirty-nine. That particular birthday must've been a rough one for her. I tried getting her to go out with me and celebrate, but Barbi just kept looking at me all day long with those big blue eyes of hers and saying in a mournful voice, "There's nothing to celebrate, Schuyler. *Nothing.*"

The "nothing" she was referring to, I soon realized, was the absence of a man in her life. Because ever since her birthday, Barbi has spent every minute on The Great Man Hunt. I'm not kidding. Barbi is apparently bound and determined to snag another husband before she turns forty.

Toward that end, in the weeks since her birthday, Barbi has undergone a less than subtle metamorphosis. At first, she still wore the tailored suits I'd been accustomed to seeing her in, but her blouses got progressively a little more low cut, a little more clingy, a little louder in color. Her jewelry got a little bigger, her perfume a little more potent, her makeup a little more thickly applied.

These changes must not have attracted quite the attention Barbi had anticipated, however, because her next move was to abandon the suits altogether in favor of body-hugging dresses and hems above the knee. This, too, apparently didn't do the trick, so Barbi moved right along to giving up her low-heeled sensible shoes in favor of high-heeled, patent leather sandals that looked, at best, painful.

Two weeks ago, Barbi evidently decided even bigger changes were in order. She went from brunette to platinum blonde overnight, and actually acted surprised the next day when everybody in the office noticed.

None of Barbi's recent changes, however, are anywhere near as bad as the one she made the very next day after her birthday. That was the day Barbi apparently decided that every other female on the planet is competition in The Great Man Hunt. It is now not a good idea to be anywhere near Barbi if there's an eligible male within a five-mile radius. She's okay if it's just the two of you, but let a single guy show up, and Barbi will turn on you with, I believe, a little more ferocity than a hungry pit bull.

Thank God, today the only man around was Jarvis. And he was already married. "You lucky, lucky, lucky duck," Barbi was saying, her voice a trill of envy. Today's outfit was a skin-tight, fuchsia knit with gold studs all over the bodice that looked as if maybe Barbi had ordered it straight out of the latest Frederick's catalog. The dress had a neckline that revealed a good inch of cleavage and a skirt decorated with what looked to be short gold chains ending in coins all around the hem. Sort of a money fringe.

I couldn't help staring at that fringe. Barbi has made it no secret that one of the requirements for the man she's seeking is wealth. As she so charmingly puts it, "He's got to have *oodles* of money." Judging from the fringe, I'd say Barbi has decided that the way to attract a man with oodles is with oodles itself. Barbi's earrings were also gold coins dangling from chains, and she had several chains with dangling gold coins wrapped around her neck and on each wrist.

Barbi jangled when she moved.

She also reeked. That, I believe, is the only way to describe it. Barbi had apparently dipped herself in Joy perfume. Much the way you might dip your dog in flea and tick repellant. With pretty much the same results, I expect. I don't think any self-respecting flea—or tick, either, for that matter—would come within a foot of Barbi. I myself tended to agree with the fleas and ticks. Standing near Barbi made my eyes water. I blinked and said, "Well, I don't know if I'd say I was *lucky,* exactly."

Barbi blinked, too, cocking her platinum head to one side. Maybe it was because I was already thinking about dog dips, but it seemed to me that Barbi cocked her head in exactly the same way a dog does when you've given it a command it doesn't understand. "Well, of course, you're lucky!" she said. "Of *course* you are! You're a lucky, lucky, lucky *duck!*" As she said this, Barbi waggled a fuchsia fingertip in my direction. "And to think, you didn't even give me the slightest *hint* what was going on." Now there was a faint, but unmistakable rebuke in Barbi's voice.

I don't know. I guess being accused of murder and all makes me a little testy. I stiffened. "What do you mean, Barbi?" I said. "What do you think was going on?"

Barbi actually giggled. "Oh, *you know.* You and Ephraim Cross. I didn't have any idea that you and he were—well, *you know.*" Every time Barbi said "you know," she wrinkled her nose. I wasn't sure if she was doing that because she found the whole idea distasteful, or if her own perfume was beginning to get to her. Barbi now leaned toward me and lowered her voice. "His dying is terribly convenient, too, isn't it?" Barbi actually smiled when she said this, as if she and I were enjoying a private joke.

I leaned away from her. Now, not only was her perfume giving me a headache, but what she was saying was getting fairly irritating, too. Next, Barbi would be turning me in to the police. Reed and Constello, I do believe, would be only too happy to hear from her.

"Barbi," I said flatly, "I didn't even know Ephraim Cross."

Her reaction was a bit disappointing. This time Barbi not only giggled, she *laughed.* Holding a fuchsia-tipped hand in front of her fuchsia mouth. "Oh, of course, you knew him, you silly thing," Barbi said. "Of *course* you did!" She leaned toward me again, and lowered her voice even more. "You don't have to lie to *me,* Schuyler. I think it's just great!"

I cleared my throat. "Barbi, I'm telling you, I've never met Ephraim Cross in my life. Really. Think about it—" Here I realized, even as I said it, that what I was asking might require real effort on Barbi's part. "—did you ever actually *see* me and Ephraim Cross together?"

Evidently, what I was asking required even more effort than I thought. Barbi screwed up her heavily mascaraed eyes, pursed her fuchsia mouth, and cocked her head to one side again as she considered my question. After about a minute, she shook her platinum curls. "Well, no, I never actually *saw* you together." She wrinkled her nose again. "But, Schuyler, surely somebody as important as Ephraim Cross would know how to be discreet, wouldn't he?"

This seemed to be the consensus of the office.

Even Charlotte Ackerson, a woman with whom I thought I'd become fairly good friends ever since she'd started working at Arndoerfer Realty some five months earlier, reddened when I glanced her way. Charlotte immediately looked down at her desk as if maintaining eye contact with me was too embarrassing for both of us.

I couldn't believe it. I was actually being indicted by people who *knew* me. These people actually believed that I'd been carrying on shamelessly with a married man. It seemed pointless to stand up and announce to the office at large that, contrary to popular belief, I didn't even know the late Ephraim Cross.

Although the thought did cross my mind.

My mood had taken a nose dive. Lord, if *these* people would think me guilty, what would everybody else think?

I found out the answer to that question about three that afternoon. By that time everybody but me had been in and out of the office several times, showing houses, taking clients to lunch, and in general, doing the sort of things a real estate career entails. I, on the other hand, had been extremely busy doing the sort of things a secretarial career entails. I'd gotten one lead off the telephone, but other than that I'd spent my time doing a pretty fair impression of Della Street.

By three, everybody had returned to the office. Barbi had even brought me back some lunch—a big Mac and, you guessed it, a large Coke—and she and Charlotte were at their desks, catching up on paperwork, Jarvis having disappeared upstairs to his office.

So, as luck would have it, everyone was there when Matthias Cross walked in the front door.

He'd shed his pinstripe gray funeral suit in favor of worn blue jeans, scuffed boots, and a blue chambray shirt with rolled-up sleeves, but I didn't have any trouble recognizing him. The beard was the same, of course, as was the hostile look on his face.

If anything, Matthias Cross managed to look even more angry than he had in Addison Glassner's office. His green eyes were all but shooting fire as he walked straight up to me and said, "I've just been going through my dad's effects, and guess what I found in his office? Right on top, in one of his desk drawers. Guess what I found?"

He didn't give me a chance to guess. Right away he pulled a small color Polaroid out of his right front shirt pocket and slammed it down on the desk in front of me.

I stared at the snapshot and actually gasped.

It was a picture of me in a bikini.

Chapter 8

There are a lot of bikinis in this world far skimpier than the one I had on in the Polaroid Matthias Cross slammed down on my desk. It wasn't even a string bikini. It wasn't even one of those thong-type things that were popular a while back—the kind that just has this string in the back that goes between your hips. "Anal floss," I believe, is what my sons call these particular suits.

The suit I had on in this Polaroid was far from anal floss. It was, in fact, modest by today's standards. A sedate navy blue, the bikini bottom very nearly reached my navel, and the bikini top completely covered my chest.

To look at Matthias Cross's outraged face, however, you might've thought that all I was wearing in the Polaroid was three Band-Aids. Not the big wound size, either. The little spot ones.

If Matthias was outraged, he had nothing on me. "Hey!" I said. "Give me that! That's *mine*! What the hell are you doing with that?" As I said all this, I made a quick grab for the Polaroid.

Matthias was even quicker. He snatched up the picture and actually had the gall to wave it in my face. "*Now*, do you still say that you didn't even know my father?"

As Matthias spoke, I suddenly became aware of the unnatural silence around us. Taking a quick glance around the office, I could see that both Barbi and Charlotte were now looking my way. And that even though Barbi was on the phone, she wasn't saying a word. In fact, Barbi was even holding the receiver away from her

ear a little, so it wouldn't interfere with her eavesdropping on Matthias's and my conversation.

I'd been considering making another wild grab for the
picture, but I reconsidered. Instead, I took a deep
breath, turned back to Matthias and lowered my voice.
"Yes, I do still say that I did *not* know your dad." My
voice was practically a hiss.

"Then how did this get in his desk? Tell me *that*."
Matthias's voice was definitely not a hiss. It was more
on the order of a roar. Barbi, I noticed, moved the
phone even farther from her ear as she and Charlotte
continued to look my way.

"How do *I* know how it got in his desk?" I hissed. I
reached under my desk, grabbed my purse, and took out
my wallet. "All I know is that picture belongs to me,
and—"

I broke off here as I stared at the empty clear plastic
sleeve that was now between an old baby photo of Daniel and my Social Security card. I had to swallow once
to make sure my voice didn't crack when I spoke. "*This*
is where I used to have that picture," I finally got out.
"Somebody obviously stole it!"

I cleared my throat. Whoever had put the note in my
glove compartment had clearly been busy.

Matthias didn't look as if he were buying a word of
it. He gave me a level look and cleared *his* throat. "What
the hell are you talking about?"

Apparently, in situations requiring tact and diplomacy,
Matthias—unlike yours truly—could not be counted on
to be a calming influence.

I just stared back at him for a long moment. Lord. I
hated to explain. I had, of course, recognized the Polaroid the second Matthias put it on my desk. It was a
Polaroid that Nathan had taken of me nearly two years
ago on one of our infrequent trips to Florida. In this
particular Polaroid, I am ten pounds lighter, and—if I
do say so myself—I don't look half bad. As Nathan
snapped the shot, Daniel had been standing directly behind him making faces, so in the picture I'm laughing
my head off, looking directly at the camera. It's about
the only picture I've ever had taken in my whole life in

which I don't look self-conscious. I look, in fact, relaxed and happy. And, not incidentally, *thin*.

Like I said, *ten* pounds lighter. This, of course, was the reason I recognized this Polaroid so quickly. It was my willpower photo. The one I keep in my wallet so that every time I feel the urge to reach for a Caramello bar, I can take this picture out and look at it. It was a "there but for the grace of chocolate-chip cookies, go you" sort of picture.

I did not feel at all inclined, however, to discuss willpower techniques with a man who at that very moment was looking at me as if I were Lucretia Borgia.

I did it, though. I took another deep breath, and forcing myself to speak calmly, I said, "Look, I can't tell you how my picture ended up in your dad's desk, but I *can* explain."

The whole time I was talking, I didn't look at Matthias once. Instead, I stared at the photo in his hand as I found myself admitting to practically a total stranger that, yes, indeedy, I am now quite a bit heavier than I was in that particular picture and, in spite of that irrefutable fact, I continue to have a profound weakness for things made of chocolate and caramel.

As I spoke, I could feel my neck getting warm. All my life whenever I've gotten nervous or upset, my neck always gets these huge red blotches. It's the reason I spent quite a few months looking for a turtleneck wedding dress before, of course, I realized it was hopeless. I'd ended up settling for a dress with the highest lace neckline I could find. Now I was sure, without even looking, that large portions of my neck were close to the same shade as my lipstick.

Not only was it embarrassing to have to admit to a stranger that, yes, I did appear to be on the road to total blimpiness, but it also occurred to me that if Matthias happened to show this particular Polaroid to the Bad Cops, the prospect of my becoming well acquainted with prison fashions could become a certainty.

Of course, Matthias had said that he'd *just* found the photo, so apparently, he'd come straight here after the find. If that was so, maybe he hadn't yet shown the photo to the police. So there was still hope. If I could do the best sales job I'd ever done in my life, and convince a totally hostile man that I was telling the truth.

That ought to be easy.

When I finally finished explaining about my willpower photo, Matthias didn't say a word. He just stood there, staring at me. I wasn't sure if he was looking at me that intently because he'd noticed the blotches on my neck and was trying to decide if he should run out for some antihistamine, or if I was actually starting to make a dent.

Matthias cleared his throat again. "You really expect me to believe that you carry around a picture of *yourself* in your purse?"

He made it sound as if it were a framed 11" × 14" glossy. It was a *Polaroid,* for God's sake. I'd even cut it down a little to get it to fit in the plastic sleeve. "It's the truth," I said.

Matthias ran his hand over his beard while he considered what I'd just said. It seemed as if it took him about an hour, but I guess it wasn't even a minute. "You know," he finally said, "that is such a ridiculous story, it actually makes me wonder if you could've made it up that quick."

I stared at him. I probably should've eased up a little at this point, but as somebody who makes her living closing deals. I guess I couldn't resist trying to hammer home the sale. "Well, of *course,* it's ridiculous!" I said eagerly. I couldn't believe what I was saying. In another minute, I'd be admitting I was too *stupid* to have come up with a story like that, so it *had* to be true. "Here," I hurried on, "let me call my son, and he'll tell you the exact same thing I just told you. You'll see, he'll tell you that he's the one who took that photo, here, let me get him on the phone—" My smile at that moment was probably a shade brighter than my neck.

Matthias was already starting to look doubtful again even as I punched line two and started dialing. This is one of the first things you learn in sales. Don't push too hard, or your prospect will start getting antsy. And once your prospect starts feeling as if he's having something crammed down his throat, he's going to stop swallowing.

It was Daniel who answered the phone. He told me Nathan had just left to pursue his career in dishwashing, but that he himself would be more than delighted to talk to Matthias. "The *son* of the guy who was murdered?" were Daniel's exact words. "Uh, sure, Mom, put him on!"

No doubt, Daniel wanted more information that he could spread around my office.

I handed over the phone and stood there, listening. I could only hear Matthias's end of the conversation, which mainly consisted of "Yes," and "Yes," and "Okay," but apparently, Daniel did indeed verify everything I'd just told Matthias.

At least, that's what Matthias said when he handed the receiver back to me. He was still looking skeptical, though. "Just because your son took the photo doesn't mean you didn't later give it to my father." Shrugging his broad shoulders, Matthias added in a nonchalant tone, as if the thought had just occurred to him, "I guess your own son *would* lie for you, wouldn't he?"

I just stared at him, feeling tired. What was I going to have to do to convince everybody I was telling the truth?

I didn't have a chance to defend myself further, though, because at that moment Barbi Lundergan wandered over, coin fringe jangling away. I can't say I was surprised to see her. In fact, I had no doubt that Barbi would've trotted over sooner except that she couldn't get off the phone.

Barbi's thickly mascaraed eyes were riveted on Matthias. "Excuse me, aren't you Matthias Cross?" she said. Her voice was suddenly so breathy, if I hadn't known better, I would've sworn she was having an asthma attack.

Barbi must've already known the answer to her question because she went right on. "I just wanted to come over and offer condolences on your recent loss. We all thought the world of Mr. Cross here. He was a wonderful man."

I stared at Barbi. I hadn't even known that she knew

Ephraim Cross. Had she decided he was wonderful from what she'd read in the paper?

Not to mention, wasn't this the same woman who shortly ago had referred to Cross's death as "terribly *convenient?*"

Evidently, Barbi's distress over Cross's demise had increased by leaps and bounds since I'd last talked to her.

"It was just a tragedy," she was now saying. She was also leaning so close to Matthias, he couldn't help but reap the full benefit of her perfume. It was sort of like watching someone being sucked into a perfume tornado. I couldn't be sure, but I thought I saw in Matthias's eyes a fleeting glimpse of the same sort of stunned expression I remembered seeing in the eyes of Ray Bolger in the *Wizard of Oz* just as the cyclone hit.

"Your father's loss is a loss to us all," Barbi was saying. Her asthma had gotten worse.

Matthias said something back to Barbi, but I didn't catch it. I'd just realized that the receiver in my hand was squawking, "Mom! Mom! *MOM!*"

"Daniel?" I said, putting the phone to my ear again.

I immediately regretted this, because Daniel was in mid-yell. *"MA-A-A-AHHHM!"*

"Daniel," I said, "I'm back." I thought about adding, "—and in a couple of years, my hearing will probably be back, too," but I didn't. I really do try not to make my kids feel guilty. It's one of the things I've been determined to do differently from my own mother. Mama was of the old school of parenting. "Spare the guilt, spoil the child," I believe, was her motto.

"I thought you'd hung up on me." On the other hand, Daniel seems to have no compunction about making *me* feel guilty. His tone was clearly aggrieved. "And I, uh, needed to ask you one thing before I go. My Nikes are falling apart, and now that you're coming into some money, I wondered if you could, uh, spare ninety dollars for some running shoes? I saw them on sale at the Galleria, and they're a real bargain—what do you say?"

Barbi had now managed to move even closer to Matthias. In another minute she'd have him pinned against my desk. I watched her, idly wondering if she did indeed pin him, whether or not I'd be able to wrench my photo out of his hand.

"You know," Barbi was saying, "if there's anything—anything at all that I can do—just ask, okay?" At this point, Barbi gave Matthias a long, suggestive look through her eyelashes. It was a wonder she could see at all through that much mascara. In fact, it was a wonder she could even open her eyes.

"Daniel," I said, "this isn't exactly the best time to talk about running shoes—"

The closing-the-sale instinct must be a genetic thing, and Daniel had gotten an ample helping of it directly from me. He wasn't about to give up. "But you'll think about it?" he said. His voice was hopeful.

"You're very kind," Matthias was now saying to Barbi.

"No-o-o, I'm not," Barbi replied, her asthma really bad now. The woman no doubt needed a paramedic.

"Daniel, I'll think about it and get back to you," I said.

Funniest thing. The second I hung up the phone, Barbi left. She did, however, give Matthias one final come-hither look before she went.

I watched her go. You had to admire the woman's technique. Of course, I had too many problems of my own to give Barbi much more than a passing thought. Matthias Cross, when he wasn't looking at me as if mentally picturing me in the electric chair, probably was an attractive man, but it wasn't my concern if Barbi Lundergan wanted to throw a net over him and drag him off to her condo. What *did* concern me, however, was clearing up this entire mess. And getting my willpower photo back. And finding out who'd taken it out of my purse.

My *purse.*

Lord. I don't know how other women feel, but as far as I'm concerned, purses are private. Sacred. You could have your house broken into, or your car, and that's pretty bad. But when somebody starts rummaging around in your purse, that's a *violation.* The thought of somebody fingering all the school and baby pictures of Daniel and Nathan that I keep in my wallet, or looking at the embarrassingly low balance in my checking account, or, God forbid, staring at that frightening picture of me on my driver's license—the one that has me smiling so big my upper gums show—well, the very thought made me so mad, I could hardly see straight.

I swallowed uneasily, remembering exactly when I'd seen my willpower photo last. It had been last Wednesday night. *The night Ephraim Cross was killed.* That night, on the way home from work, I'd had a wild craving for Baskin-Robbins Rocky Road ice cream—and I'd stared at the photo for some time to fight the urge.

So somebody had to have taken the photo out of my wallet since then. In fact, the picture could've been gone ever since then for all I knew because I hadn't even glanced at the picture section of my wallet until today.

All of this was going through my mind as Matthias was evidently somewhat distracted, watching Barbi return where she came from, back to her desk in the far corner diagonally opposite from mine. Rolling her hips, of course, in that tight fuchsia dress. With all those coins on the hem jangling away.

When Matthias finally turned back to me, I thought his eyes looked a bit unfocused for a second, as if maybe he'd been momentarily hypnotized by the lights dancing off gold coins. His eyes cleared up immediately, though, and he said, "Okay, let's just say you really are telling the truth and the photo *was* stolen out of your wallet, do you have any idea who could've done it?"

I just looked at him. Was it possible Matthias was actually starting to believe me? Or was he just humoring me? The man was standing there, arms folded across his broad chest, giving me a convincingly earnest look, but he could very well be just playing along, hoping I'd say something incriminating.

I tried to pick my words carefully. "Well, other than when I was at home, the only time I can remember leaving my purse unattended was right here at work."

My purse is a brown and black Dooney & Bourke handbag that I gave myself for Christmas two years ago. I'd read in one of those "How-to-look-rich-even-though you're-not" books that one of the secrets was to carry an expensive designer handbag. Apparently, the thinking here is that women who have obviously spent an outrageous amount of money on their purse probably carry around an even more outrageous amount of money inside it.

I wasn't sure about this logic, but in my line of work, it pays to look affluent. Mostly because if prospects think you haven't collected very many commissions lately, they tend to think you're too inexperienced to list their house with you.

So, in a blatant effort to look like I make a great deal more money than I actually do, I blew two hundred and seventy dollars on something called a "dome satchel." I've wished ever since I hadn't done such a frivolous thing. It's so contrary to my basic ultra-thrifty nature to spend this much money on something that doesn't even have a motor that it immediately made me paranoid. Right after I started carrying the Dooney & Bourke, I started envisioning purse snatchers lurking around, making unseen grabs at my dome satchel as I walked by. If I was that paranoid with the thing slung over my shoulder, you can imagine how often I actually put my purse down. Even when I'm showing a house, I always keep my purse with me.

In fact, to the best of my recollection, the only times I don't have my purse with me is here at the office and at home. Being purse-picked at home seemed unlikely since I'd had no visitors in the last two weeks other than the Bad Cops and my sons yesterday. Surely if a burglar *had* dropped by, he'd have left some mementos of his visit. A broken window. A busted door. Something.

I had to face it. It was most likely that my purse had been rifled while I was *here.* This office, since I knew and trusted everybody here, was the one place I always felt perfectly at ease leaving my purse unattended. I always just blithely left it under my desk, while I went off to the copier, or to the ladies' room, or into the kitchen to get myself a Coke.

I swallowed as the implication of all this hit me. As much as I hated to think it, I had to admit that it was highly unlikely that a total stranger could ever waltz into this office and start going through my purse without somebody noticing. Not to mention, how would a total stranger have known to even *look* for my willpower photo?

The inescapable conclusion appeared to be, then, that my purse had been rifled by somebody I knew. Somebody *right here* in this office. The thought was not exactly the most comforting thing that's ever crossed my mind.

My God, was it possible? Could somebody I actually work with have stolen the photo out of my wallet?

As all this occurred to me, I resisted an almost overpowering urge to give both Barbi and Charlotte a piercing stare. Instead, however, I gave Matthias a *Reader's Digest* Condensed Version of everything I was thinking. "And since I've only been here in the office for any length of time today and on Friday of last week, then— if the picture was stolen after Wednesday evening when I saw it last—it had to have been on Friday," I finished.

This was not exactly a lot of help because on Friday everybody working at Jarvis Arndoerfer Realty had been in the office at one time or another. Barbi, Charlotte, *and* Jarvis were all here that day. Even Jarvis's wife, Arlene, had been in last Friday. As I recalled, Arlene had come in around noon to meet her husband for lunch. While I was occupied with a client or whatever, any one of these people could have gotten to my purse.

And yet, why would anybody here want to make it look as if *I* were having an affair with Ephraim Cross?

I went right on, explaining everything to Matthias, but inwardly, I was thinking: Why indeed—unless, of course, one of these people had actually killed Ephraim Cross and was now trying to divert suspicion from themselves?

Just thinking such a thing made a shiver go down my back.

After I finished telling him all this, Matthias had a question that was equally unsettling. Lowering his voice at last, he said, "So. Who in this office knew about the picture?"

I stared back at him. His question could be taken two ways. Matthias could be asking in order to help me determine who might've known about the photo's existence in order to figure out exactly who could've taken it.

In which case, he was being kind and helpful.

Or Matthias could be asking just to see if there was somebody else in the office who could verify my story. To see if I was lying about having a willpower photo in the first place.

In which case, he was being sneaky and underhanded.

I took a deep breath. And I thought my *purse* was making me paranoid.

Whatever Matthias's reason for asking, it took me a second to consider the answer. The best I could come up with was something that I dimly recalled happening a couple weeks ago. "I was getting ready to leave, and I was in a hurry to get to an appointment, and I picked up my purse by just one strap, and it upended," I told Matthias. "It dumped all over the floor. My wallet fell out, a couple lipsticks, my compact, mascara—" Here Matthias started to look impatient, so I called a halt to my list of purse contents. "When my wallet hit the floor, several of the pictures came out of their sleeves and scattered all over. I think my willpower photo was one of them." I stopped here, trying to picture who in the office had been standing near me when my purse fell. Someone *had* been here—someone had, in fact, even helped me pick up my stuff—but who? Try as I might, I couldn't get a face. Finally, I had to admit to Matthias, "But I can't remember who was standing around then."

Matthias gave me a look that said that was pretty much what he expected me to say. Cold-blooded killer that I was.

I gave *him* a look that said, well, what do you expect? Dropping your purse on the floor is not the sort of earth-shaking world event that burns itself into your memory. It's not exactly up there with tearing down the Berlin Wall.

"Well, I guess the only thing we can do, then, is show this Polaroid to everybody here," Matthias said, emphasizing his words by waving my picture in the air, "and find out if anybody has ever seen it before."

I don't know what I'd been expecting him to say, but this wasn't it. My mouth actually dropped open. "What? You're not serious, are you?" Matthias actually intended to go around the place where I *worked,* and show them a picture of me in a *bikini*? For crying out loud. This could be even more humiliating than having the Bad Cops go through my underwear drawer. While Matthias was at it, maybe he'd like to show everybody in the office that gum picture on my driver's license. "Oh no," I said. "You are *not* going to—" I broke off here because I was using all my concentration to make a grab for my picture.

In the game of Polaroid-Keep-Away, Matthias had a distinct advantage, being almost ten inches taller than me. It looked as if it were no effort for him at all to keep the photo out of my reach, switch it to the other hand, and deftly move away from me.

I have never been all that great a loser. "Now, just a minute," I said. I was so angry, my voice was shaking. "That is *my* picture. You've got no right—"

Matthias, at this point, amply demonstrated just how much weight he gave to *my* rights. He turned on his heel and headed across the room toward Barbi's desk. Without even looking back.

Chapter 9

When I'm mad, I sometimes do the dumbest things. Can you believe I actually followed Matthias across the room, saying, "Hey. I mean it. Give me that picture! *Now*!" As if I actually expected Matthias to suddenly stop, turn around, and hand it over. No doubt, saying something like, *Sure, Schuyler, all you had to do was ask. I didn't know you really wanted it.*

Uh-huh. *Right.*

Instead, Matthias totally ignored me.

When Barbi saw Matthias headed her way, her eyes lit up like two neon signs. Barbi apparently took Matthias's approach as a definite indication that he found it impossible to stay away from her for long.

Unfortunately, when Barbi noticed *me* following along right in back of Matthias, her neon eyes looked as if they'd been connected to a dimmer switch.

And when Matthias showed her the Polaroid of me, Barbi's eyes looked positively short-circuited.

One thing I have to say for him, Matthias certainly doesn't waste time on small talk. "Ever seen this before?" Matthias asked.

At that point, there didn't seem to be a whole lot I could do except stand there while Barbi peered intently at my photo. I'd been right, of course. This *was* more embarrassing than having your house searched.

Barbi blinked a couple of times before she answered. "Have I seen *what* before? The beach or the bikini?" she said, tapping her front teeth with a fuschia fingertip.

I believe I've mentioned before that Barbi is not exactly Phi Beta Kappa material.

Matthias blinked. "No," he said slowly, his tone now

amazingly patient, "I mean the Polaroid itself. Have you ever seen this *Polaroid* before?"

"Oh," Barbi said. She actually stared at the Polaroid for another long moment before she answered. "Matthias, I have never seen this picture before in my life." Barbi's asthma was acting up again.

Glancing my way, however, her condition underwent an instant cure. Barbi's voice was not the slightest bit breathy as she said, "If I *had* seen that picture earlier, I would've been sure to tell you right away, Schuyler, honey, that too much sun causes skin cancer. You really ought to get yourself checked out by a dermatologist. *All* over."

I took a deep breath. What a sweet thing to say. Apparently, my bikini photo had brought out every one of Barbi's fuschia-lacquered claws.

I wasn't sure what Barbi's line of thinking was here. Did she actually believe that Matthias was now going around the office taking applications for the position of "Next Girlfriend?" Could Barbi be under the impression that I'd given Matthias this photo as part of my résumé? Did she really think, since the dad was out of the picture, that I was now setting my sights on the son?

Barbi, however, wasn't through. Before I could put in a word, she went smoothly on, "You really should be more careful, Schuyler." She gave me a saccharine smile. "Skin cancer is a lot more likely for somebody *your* age."

Barbi is only two years younger than me, but from the way Barbi emphasized the words, "*your* age," you could get the idea that I was out on a day pass from a nursing home.

Oh yes, Barbi was suffering from Pit-Bull Syndrome, all right. It was with considerable effort that I managed to keep my eyes from narrowing to slits. "Thanks so much for the advice, Barbi," I said through my teeth.

Barbi turned back to Matthias. "Schuyler here is such a dear. You needn't worry, Schuyler is telling *everybody* she didn't even know your dad."

I did a quick intake of breath.

Maybe that old cliché was right. With a friend like

this, I didn't need enemies. "Barbi—" I had every intention of telling her exactly how much I appreciated her
endorsement, but Matthias interrupted me.

His green eyes were fixed on Barbi's face. She didn't
look at all unhappy to have his undivided attention.
"Miss Lundergan," Matthias said, "are you saying that
you saw my father and—?"

Barbi interrupted. "Actually, it's *Mrs.* Lundergan. But
I'm no longer married." Barbi punctuated this statement
by batting those heavily mascaraed lashes once again,
her tone indicating that this information was significant.

Significant or not, Barbi's information seemed to be
lost on Matthias. He gave a quick nod of his head and
began again. "I just wanted to know if you'd ever—"

Barbi interrupted again. "Call me Barbi."

I took another deep breath. If Barbi didn't tell Matthias soon what she'd told *me* earlier, I would be forced
to pull her platinum hair out by every one of its dark
roots.

"*Barbi,* then," Matthias said evenly. The man could
give Job lessons on patience. "What I wanted to know
was if you'd ever seen my father and Schuyler
together?"

Barbi batted her lashes four more times before she
answered. I counted. "Well, no, Matthias," Barbi said,
"I can't say I've ever actually *seen* them together." Her
asthma had returned with a vengeance.

"Never?" Matthias persisted.

"Nevah," Barbi said. Now her asthma had taken on a
Southern accent. "Like I said, you don't have to worry.
Your dad was real discreet."

I glanced over at Matthias. Surely he realized that this
was just *Barbi's* assessment of the facts. That the important thing here was that she had never actually *seen*
me with his father.

Barbi, however, seemed determined not to give Matthias a chance to think of anything other than *her.* She
stood slowly and leaned toward him. Her cleavage grew
before our eyes from a small crack into a veritable cav-
ern. It was a little like watching an earthquake. "You

know, Matthias, I'm not like Schuyler. I prefer my men
a *lot* younger."

This was probably all Barbi had to say, and Matthias
would've gotten the point. There are, no doubt, Mack
trucks that have been more subtle. Barbi, however, apparently wanted to make absolutely sure that Matthias
understood *precisely* what she was getting at. Her eyes
traveled slowly over his faded jeans, took in the broad
shoulders beneath his blue chambray shirt, and finally
ended on his face. "In fact," Barbi went on, "I prefer
men just about *your* age."

What a revelation. Thanks so much, Barbi, for sharing
this late-breaking bulletin with us.

Matthias, however, didn't seem to pay all that much
attention to Barbi's news. He didn't even seem to notice
the obvious results of Barbi's earthquake. "If you never
actually *saw* them together," he said, "then what makes
you so sure that Schuyler and my dad were—"

Barbi evidently had the smarts to see where this question was headed. She answered before Matthias finished.
"Well," she said, twirling a platinum curl around her
finger, "*of course* they were seeing each other, silly. Why
else would your dad have left her all that money?"

That summed it up nicely, I thought.

Matthias was now looking at Barbi as if maybe it had
just occurred to him that Barbi might not be elected to
Mensa this year. "Thanks for your help," he said and
turned to go.

Barbi's face fell. "Oh," she said. "Well. I guess this is
goodbye." As I said, Matthias had already turned to
leave, so Barbi was saying this to his back. This didn't
seem to deter her, though. She hurried right on, "I have
an appointment in ten minutes to show a house out in
Beckley Woods, so I guess I have to be going, too—"

This was an understatement. Beckley Woods is one
of several subdivisions located off Shelbyville Road in
Louisville's East End. It is, in fact, located so far east
in Louisville's East End that this area isn't even called
Louisville. It's called Middletown, a place midway between Louisville and Shelbyville, Kentucky. Hence the
name, I guess. Even if Barbi broke every speed limit

between here and there, there was no way she was going to make it to Beckley Woods in ten minutes. Evidently, Barbi had decided that if it came down to a choice between flirting with Matthias Cross and a little thing like making an appointment on time, Barbi chose flirting.

When Barbi started making conversation with his back, Matthias obligingly turned around. It was a good thing because Barbi was now extending her business card. "Here," she said. Her asthma had gotten much worse. "In case you need me for anything." I was fairly certain I could assume here that Barbi was not talking about listing his house. "My home phone is on the card, too," she added.

I think I was wrong before. Mack trucks are a *lot* more subtle than Barbi. Having pressed her card into Matthias's hand, she was now waggling her fingers in what she clearly thought was a seductive wave. "See you soon, I hope," she said. The wave looked a little on the silly side to me, but since I wasn't the one Barbi was waving at, my opinion probably didn't count.

Matthias, I noticed, did not wave back. He did smile, however. I couldn't tell if it was because Barbi was finally getting to him, or if Matthias was just smiling to keep from laughing in her face.

When we moved away from Barbi's desk, I started acting stupid again. "Look, I want that photo, okay? It's mine. Give it to me. *Now.*" This was pretty much the gist of what I had to say to Matthias as he walked purposely away from Barbi's desk, his eyes traveling around the room.

As I followed him, I made a couple more grabs at the photo in his hand. For all the impact I made, though, I could've been a gnat. Matthias didn't even glance my way as he held the photo out of my reach, and said, "Where's the other woman who was in here?"

"Oh no," I said. "You're *not* going to show my picture to her!"

Matthias didn't even answer me. He'd spotted Charlotte and was headed toward her.

From nine in the morning to five at night, Jarvis leaves the front door to Arndoerfer Realty standing wide open.

That means there's only a storm door protecting the front office from the elements. A drafty, ill-fitting storm door, I might add. This is not a problem on mild days, but on very cold days or on very hot days closing the front door might actually keep the office from becoming either a refrigerator or an oven, respectively.

If you close the front door on refrigerator/oven days, however, Jarvis immediately opens it again. I believe Jarvis does this because he doesn't want to take the chance on a closed front door possibly discouraging potential prospects. For those prospects who might find the idea of actually having to reach out and turn a doorknob far too taxing, thoughtful Jarvis has solved the problem.

With the front door standing wide open as usual, it was easy to see Charlotte Ackersen through the glass of the storm door. Slender and petite, she was standing just outside, peering down Taylorsville Road, obviously waiting for somebody.

Dressed today in white opaque hose, low-heeled black pumps, a pink jumper and a lace-trimmed white blouse, with her shoulder-length blond hair held back from her face by a wide, pink headband, Charlotte was wearing the kind of outfit I picture a grown-up Alice in Wonderland wearing to work.

I knew immediately, of course, who Charlotte was waiting for out there, since she had mentioned to me earlier that he was coming by. Of course, even if Charlotte hadn't mentioned it to me, it wouldn't have been hard to guess who it was.

Her husband, Leonard.

At least, I guess you'd still call Leonard her husband. Charlotte and Leonard have been separated for almost five months now. According to Charlotte, she and Leonard would've already been divorced by now except that about two weeks before they separated, the Ackersens had moved to Louisville from a farm just across the bridge over in Indiana. This move delayed the Ackersens finalizing their divorce, because Charlotte couldn't serve divorce papers on Leonard until she'd established residency in Kentucky. Which takes six months.

Charlotte insists that the second—no, the *milli*second—that she's established residency, she's heading straight downtown to file the papers. Frankly, I have my doubts. You know how love is supposed to mean never having to say you're sorry? Divorce, I believe, means never having to lay eyes on the sorry son of a gun again unless he's coming around for visitation with the kids. At least, that's what divorce means to *me*. What it means to Charlotte must be something else again. Because, from where I stand, it looks as if she sees more of Leonard now that they're separated than I'd seen of Ed when we were married.

Not to mention, this morning when Charlotte told me that Leonard was going to be arriving this afternoon to take her to get her driver's license renewed, she'd sounded perfectly happy about it. The place where you get your driver's license is just five miles down Taylorsville Road, and yet Leonard was showing up to personally escort Charlotte there. "Leonard's trying to be helpful," Charlotte had explained.

Charlotte has this high-pitched, Minnie Mouse voice that I'd thought at first she had to be faking. In the five months I've known her, though, Charlotte's voice has never varied. So I guess, it's got to be genuine. If for no other reason than surely no adult would fake a voice like that one.

"Leonard just wants to make sure everything goes all right," Charlotte had added.

I hadn't said anything at the time, but I couldn't help thinking, *what could go wrong?* Charlotte's current driver's license hadn't yet expired. She wasn't going to have to take the road test or anything. She was just going to stand in line a few minutes, answer some questions, and get an eye exam. That was it. Did Leonard think one of the driver's ed cops might pull a gun?

Some of what I was thinking must've shown in my face because Charlotte had added, her tone a little defensive, "Leonard is just looking out for me, Schuyler."

I had been struck speechless. Evidently, it hadn't occurred to Charlotte that for a lot of women, renewing your driver's license is not a group project. It did, however, occur to *me* to wonder why Charlotte bothered to renew the thing at all. Because Leonard was always around, driving her somewhere or another. He even drove her to and from some of the open houses she was supposed to attend.

In addition to chauffeur duties, Leonard also sent Charlotte flowers a couple times a week, phoned her several times a day, and mailed her little gifts.

It didn't take a genius to figure out that Leonard was doing his dead-level best to win Charlotte back.

Leonard, of course, should've thought of doing all these things a bit earlier. When they were still together, from what Charlotte had told me, Leonard had been dead set against her working outside the home. In fact, he'd gone so far as to forbid her to ever take a job.

"And with both kids in school, there just wasn't enough to do at home to keep me busy," Charlotte had told me. "Besides, I'd never held a job before. I married Leonard right out of high school, so it was high time I got out into the world."

I'd stared back at her and thought, *I'll say.*

After Charlotte got herself a lawyer and started talking divorce, insisting that Leonard pack up all his stuff and move out, Leonard, oddly enough, had a change of heart. He suddenly felt compelled to pay for the real estate course Charlotte had enrolled in. He also outfitted her home office with a new rolltop desk, a word processor, an answering machine, an electronic calculator, a fax machine, and—as best as I could tell from just listening—pretty much anything else that he could think of that Charlotte might possibly need in her new chosen profession.

Leonard was obviously trying to prove to Charlotte that he was now a New and Improved Leonard. Kind. Caring. Supporting. A Phil Donahue Leonard.

I'd heard all about the New and Improved Leonard, believe it or not, from Leonard himself. Leonard had actually called *me* up at work more than once to find out if Charlotte was weakening toward him. Leonard was a successful building contractor with a thriving business, and yet, every time he'd phoned, he'd sounded as if he were back in high school, trying to get the home-coming queen to go out with him. Leonard had actually begged me a couple of times to put in a good word for him.

In my opinion, my good word was hardly necessary. It was clearly only a matter of time until Charlotte went back to him, but I'd never tell Leonard that. For one thing, if Leonard had any idea that it was pretty much a done deal, he might stop buying Charlotte all the stuff he was getting her. I'd sure hate to spoil her fun.

No one had asked me, of course, but it sure looked like a good idea to me if the two of them got back together. Especially since Charlotte and Leonard have two children—a son, Donnie, age eight, and a daughter, Marie, age six.

That's right. Donnie and Marie. Charlotte and Leonard had actually named their kids after the Osmonds. The way I saw it, it was entirely possible that they were uniquely suited to each other.

And even if they weren't, take it from me, being a single parent is definitely something you should do only if you absolutely have to. If I could have convinced Ed that he really did not need to subscribe to the Girlfriend-of-the-Month Club, I certainly would have.

When Matthias and I walked out the front door of Arndoerfer Realty, Charlotte shot a quick glance our way, and then immediately resumed looking down Tay-lorsville Road as if she hadn't seen us. This was fairly typical behavior for Charlotte. Although the woman was really very pretty with big gray eyes, high cheekbones, and the kind of ultra-straight blond hair that back in the sixties people actually *ironed* their hair to get, you could tell Charlotte's goal in life was to be the human equiva-lent of wallpaper. Pretty and decorative, but not some-thing you'd notice when you walked into a room.

I had a sneaking suspicion that leaving her husband might've been the first assertive thing Charlotte had ever done in her life.

As a matter of fact, when Charlotte first came to work, I'd thought her retiring nature might hinder her success as a real estate agent. Since something like 40 percent of each year's crop of new agents drop out their first year, I'd had my doubts about Charlotte. And yet, she seemed to be doing just fine. In fact, Charlotte was so shy, so totally unpushy, that some clients actually *preferred* to work with her. So that they'd be totally free to make up their minds, unhampered by aggressive sales pitches.

I genuinely liked Charlotte—she really was a nice person—but I admit, sometimes when she did her shrinking violet impression, I had a strong urge to grab her by both shoulders and give her a good shaking.

Of course, right now I would've also liked to give Matthias a good shaking, too. If it were possible. His broad shoulders did look pretty unshakable. "Look, Matthias," I said, "I've got rights, you know. You can't just go around, showing—"

That was all I got out before Matthias interrupted me. "Hi," he said to Charlotte, "I'm Matthias Cross, and I'd like to know if you've ever seen this picture before."

So much for my rights.

Charlotte took a lot less time than Barbi to answer. "Oh, no," she said, immediately averting her eyes, "I don't remember *ever* seeing that picture."

Charlotte had only taken the briefest of glances. "Are you sure?" Matthias asked.

"Oh my yes," Charlotte said, her hand now at her throat. "Goodness me." Minnie Mouse sounded shocked. The implication in Charlotte's tone seemed to be that nice women didn't even look at photos of bathing suits like this, let alone wear one.

I stood there, wondering if maybe I shouldn't start sewing scarlet A's on all my clothes. Things were not looking good. So far the only person who'd corroborated my story about this Polaroid was Daniel. My own son. And, if that wasn't enough to discredit him as a witness, I was pretty sure that if Matthias ever talked to Daniel in person, rather than just on the phone, the sight of Daniel's bullet-ridden wardrobe might cast more than a little doubt on his credibility.

If I thought Charlotte was shocked by my bikini photo, she outdid herself when Matthias asked her his next question. "Have you ever seen Schuyler and my father together?"

"Why, no," Charlotte said, reddening all the way to her hairline, "I—I've never seen them together." Her eyes at that point were focused on her shoes. "Goodness, no, I don't believe that I've—"

Charlotte broke off with a transparent look of relief as a late model burgundy Toyota Camry pulled into the parking lot. Her husband, Leonard, was out of the car and walking over to us, smiling amiably, in a matter of seconds.

A tall, thin, muscular man, Leonard would've been a lot more attractive if he didn't have so much nervous energy. He was always waving his arms in the air or bouncing on the balls of his feet or fiddling with something he was wearing. It was no wonder that Leonard stayed so thin. A perpetual motion machine, he had to be burning off every ounce of excess fat.

Sure enough, as he walked toward us, Leonard was pulling at the sleeves of his navy blazer and straightening his red print tie and running his hand through his thinning blond hair. In a blur of motion.

Charlotte cleared her throat and immediately started the introductions. "Um, Leonard, you already know Schuyler here, and this—this is, um, Mr. Matthias Cross. Arndoerfer Realty did some business with Mr. Cross's father just before his, um, passing, and Mr. Cross here and Schuyler have, um, just been asking me some questions."

I stared at her. Charlotte sounded as if she were reporting to a parent.

Charlotte's report must've been adequate, because Leonard didn't seem to want to hang around to hear anything more. Or maybe with all that nervous energy, he just couldn't stand still for long. In the space of about a minute, Leonard had nodded at me, given Matthias a handshake, offered his condolences at Matthias's loss, taken Charlotte's elbow, and steered her toward the waiting Camry.

The second the Ackersens were out of earshot, I started in. "Okay, Matthias, you've asked *your* questions. Now I want to ask you one. Are you going to give me back my Polaroid?"

It was a question Matthias apparently didn't even have to think about. "No," he said.

I was not surprised at his answer. I swallowed my anger, and took a deep breath before I asked my next question. "Are you going to give it to the police?"

Matthias didn't hesitate this time, either. "Well, I can't say I completely buy your story about this picture," he said, rubbing his beard thoughtfully. "*Nobody* but your son has backed you up, you know."

I just stared at him. *I knew,* for God's sake. "Then you've made up your mind? You've decided to judge me solely on the basis of finding this picture in your dad's desk? *Anybody* could've put it there!"

Matthias returned my stare. "I *have* made up my mind yes. But only about one thing. I've decided I'm not going to give this picture to the police—"

My heart did this joyful, little leap, and then Matthias finished, "Not yet, anyway, not until I've decided whether you're telling the truth or not."

I blinked. So, this wasn't a *permanent* stay of execution. Matthias was just giving me the chance to convince him I was telling the truth before he threw me to the wolves. What a guy. I did, however, feel a little relieved, anyway. Not a *lot* relieved. But a little.

I would've liked to have enjoyed feeling a little relieved for a while longer, but almost immediately another thought occurred to me.

So far everything that the Bad Cops and Matthias had linking me to Ephraim Cross's death was pretty circumstantial. Was Matthias just agreeing not to give my Polaroid to the police so that he could follow me around for a while and find out something else that would definitely incriminate me?

I didn't have time to mull this one over, because in back of us the door to Jarvis Arndoerfer Realty opened and Jarvis himself walked out.

Chapter 10

If there were ever a contest between Jarvis Arndoerfer's voice and thunder, Jarvis's voice would easily win out. "Hello, there!" he boomed, grabbing Matthias's hand in what looked to be a bone-cracking grip. "I am *so* glad to meet you!"

I didn't know about Matthias Cross, but *I* believed Jarvis. Jarvis looked as if he were about to weep from the sheer joy of it.

"Glad to meet you," Matthias echoed, but his tone was uncertain. His uncertainty might've had something to do with the way Jarvis continued to aggressively work Matthias's hand. Jarvis could've been milking a cow.

"I was *so* sorry to hear about your poor father." Jarvis went on. "It's a tragedy, just a *tragedy*." After saying this, the tears sparkling in Jarvis's eyes looked a lot more appropriate.

Releasing Matthias's hand, Jarvis immediately started brushing great quantities of nonexistent hair out of his eyes. "Allow me to introduce myself. I'm Jarvis Arndoerfer," he said. "*Owner* of Jarvis Arndoerfer Realty." I believe Matthias might've figured this one out for himself, but Jarvis seemed all too willing to help Matthias out. Jarvis's tone implied that Matthias should be impressed.

I took a quick, sidelong glance at Matthias. He didn't look impressed. He looked relieved that Jarvis had finally released his hand before it required medical attention.

"I'm Ma—"

That was just about all Matthias got out of his own

introduction before Jarvis interrupted. "Good heavens, you don't have to introduce yourself to *me*, Matthias!"

Just like that, Jarvis and Matthias were on a first-name basis. Jarvis, no doubt about it, *is* slick. I do believe it would take him no more than sixty seconds to get on a first-name basis with the pope.

"No introductions whatsoever are necessary," Jarvis went smoothly on, waving his hand in the air. "I daresay, *everyone* knows who you are." Jarvis smiled once again and added, "Everyone who's anyone, that is." Apparently, Jarvis was including himself in this last group. With all the other anyones in Louisville. "I just can't believe you've been here all this time," he said, "and nobody even told me you were here!"

The last part of Jarvis's statement was clearly directed at me. If I'd had any doubt about that, Jarvis followed up what he said by a dark glance my way. *You're supposed to be secretary today, and you didn't even tell me MATTHIAS CROSS was here?* his eyes seemed to say.

I returned Jarvis's look. If Jarvis could read *my* eyes, they were saying loud and clear, So don't ever let me play secretary again. *Break* my heart.

My eyes can be very sarcastic.

Since I seemed unrepentant, Jarvis gave up glaring at me and gave his undivided attention to Matthias. "I *must* apologize—I was upstairs, talking on the phone, and I had no idea you were here. If I'd only known, Matthias, of *course* I'd have gotten off immediately and rushed right down! My staff"—here Jarvis shot another unforgiving look my way—"has been instructed to inform me *immediately* when VIPs come in, but in this case, I'm afraid I'd never even have known you were here if I hadn't happened to walk by and see you! I am *so* sorry. I hope you haven't been waiting for me long—"

Jarvis was babbling. He was also obviously making an assumption here. He does this a lot. Jarvis definitely feels that if you're wealthy or well-connected, there's only one person you'd ever drop by Jarvis Arndoerfer Realty to see. The Man himself.

I know it was mean of me, but I couldn't resist saying, "There's nothing to be sorry about, Jarvis. Matthias came by to see *me.*" It didn't seem at all necessary to add that the main reason Matthias dropped by to see me was apparently to accuse me of lying, to show me what he thought was incontestable proof that I'd been engaging in lascivious acts with his father, and, oh yes, incidentally, to imply that I was guilty of murder.

There didn't seem to be any reason to burden Jarvis with all these ugly details.

Especially when poor Jarvis looked so burdened already. His round face had paled. "Oh." That Matthias had not come by to see *him* was evidently such an unexpected turn of events that for a second Jarvis seemed unsure what to say next. Which might've been a first for him. Jarvis fiddled for a second with his watercolor tie, looked momentarily disconcerted, and then, in my opinion, recovered nicely. Pushing more invisible hair out of his eyes, Jarvis said heartily, "Well, I don't have a doubt in the world that Schuyler here is giving you *all* the help you need—"

There is a code of ethics among realtors that strictly forbids one realtor from bad-mouthing the competence of another. Particularly when they're listening.

"Schuyler here is an experienced professional," Jarvis went on, "and we're certainly proud to have her associated with *Jarvis Arndoerfer Realty.*" Jarvis said the name of his firm with the same unnatural enthusiasm with which Sam Donaldson says the words *Prime Time LIVE* on TV every week. "I know you're in good hands, Matthias. Schuyler is one of the best. She's thorough, diligent, hardworking—"

Code of ethics aside, Jarvis seemed to be overdoing it a bit. I stared at him. Jarvis was making me sound like Wonder Realtor. Standing there, listening to Jarvis go on and on about how great I was, right in front of me, made me feel a little strange—and yet, when somebody is praising you, you don't exactly want to tell him to shut up.

This was not at all like Jarvis. Jarvis never wants to build up the competition, even if it's one of his own realtors. In fact, I do believe the last time I'd heard

Jarvis say something nice about another realtor, he was delivering the guy's eulogy.

And he'd been somewhat restrained, even then.

"Schuyler is always very punctual, she's always extremely professional, and—" This was getting weird. Why on earth was Jarvis going on like this? At first, listening to him, I thought maybe it might've had something to do with the way—as an independent contractor working out of his office—I have to give Jarvis 40 percent of every dollar I make. I thought maybe Jarvis had quickly decided that, if he couldn't hog the entire commission himself, it would be enough just to land Matthias Cross as an Arndoerfer Realty client.

So, I decided, that must be why Jarvis was obviously trying to hard-sell Matthias on *me*.

However, as Jarvis continued to extoll my virtues—he was now going on about my "attention to detail," believe it or not—I began to wonder. Jarvis was actually acting as if it hadn't even *occurred* to him that Matthias could've come by to see me for any other reason than a strictly professional one. This, even though Jarvis had found out this morning, along with everybody else in the office, that Matthias's father had just left me a good deal of money.

I shifted my weight from one foot to another, and continued to stare at Jarvis. Could it be that Jarvis considered an illicit relationship between one of his real estate agents and one of his more prominent, married clients to be too indelicate a matter to even acknowledge? This was a distinct possibility. And yet, knowing Jarvis, I suspected something else. Particularly after Jarvis said, without batting an eye, "Our Schuyler never needs supervision, either. Matter of fact, she's *very* independent. She actually *prefers* to work alone."

Now this was a crock. Jarvis was making it sound as if realtors usually work in packs. And that I, unusual Wonder Realtor that I was, was one of the very few who were inclined to see clients and show houses all by their lonesome.

Offhand, I couldn't think of any realtors who worked in pairs. Most of the realtors I knew were too worried that somebody was going to steal their leads to ever work with anybody else.

I glanced over at Matthias to see if he was buying any of this.

"Yes, our Schuyler," Jarvis was now saying, "is what they call a self-starter. My goodness, I never know where she is or *what* she's doing—"

Oh yes. This explained it. No wonder Jarvis was doing this. Like that tape said just before it disintegrated at the beginning of the old *Mission Impossible* TV show, Jarvis was "disavowing all knowledge of my actions." Jarvis clearly was afraid that Matthias might not be in his best mood. So, brave soul that Jarvis was, he was covering all his bases. If Matthias was here on business, then Jarvis was convincing him what a competent realtor I was. And if perchance Matthias was here to put some heavy blame on the person—and the firm—who'd made it possible for his father to meet me and subsequently begin to break one of the ten commandments, not to mention, eventually get himself murdered, Jarvis was making his position on that very clear. He was making it sound as if I were such a terrific realtor, that of course, he'd made me part of his staff. Who could pass up Wonder Realtor? And that, in light of my unbelievably amazing professional expertise, who also could've suspected what a sleazy temptress I was in my spare time?

"—everyone Schuyler has ever worked with has *nothing* but praise for the way she's handled their listings," Jarvis was now saying.

By this time the only virtue of mine that Jarvis had not yet mentioned seemed to be how well I alphabetized. Even Jarvis seemed to realize that he was now sitting on empty. His voice trailed off like a faucet run dry. There was an awkward pause while Jarvis obviously racked his brain for yet another wonderful thing to say about me. Finally giving up, Jarvis took a deep breath, and abruptly changed the subject. "You know, Matthias, everyone here was *devastated* to hear of your dear father's passing. Simply *DEVASTATED*. It was such a shock, *such* a shock."

I blinked. Jarvis could easily quality for a black belt in fawning.

'How kind of you to—" Matthias started to say, but Jarvis apparently wasn't through fawning yet.

"I *so* enjoyed working with your dear father. Ephraim was a great man, a *GREAT* man. I daresay we're all going to feel his loss for years. *YEARS*, I dare say. Whoever cut that dear man's precious life short, well, I can only hope that they prosecute this—this *monster* to the full extent of the law!"

I blinked at that one. Was it really possible that it had not occurred to Jarvis that Matthias might have the idea that the thorough, diligent, hardworking Wonder Realtor that Jarvis had just gone on and on about could be the monster in question? Or could this be another reason why Jarvis had insisted that I worked independently?

Matthias, by this time, evidently had given up trying to get a word in because all he did was just nod solemnly.

Jarvis nodded, too. For a second Matthias and Jarvis looked as if their heads were keeping time to music only the two of them could hear. Jarvis evidently thought he'd covered Ephraim Cross's demise every bit as much as was necessary because now he abruptly cleared his throat and moved on to the topic he always seems to be eventually headed for. Business. "Now, Matthias, if there's anything, anything at all, that I can do for the son of the late, great Ephraim Cross, I stand ready to serve."

There was also a good chance Jarvis could be called upon to do any bootlicking that Matthias might need done, but I didn't think I should mention it. Glancing over at Matthias, I had the feeling he probably already knew it, anyway.

Evidently, Matthias had spotted his opening at last. "Well," he said very fast, "you could take a look at this photo and tell me if you've ever seen it before."

My stomach dropped to my knees. Oh, for Pete's sake. I'd been so mesmerized by Jarvis's list of my remarkable talents that it hadn't occurred to me that Matthias intended to show Jarvis my Polaroid, too. "Matthias, is this really necessary?" I was pretty sure that if it had been Jarvis that day who'd helped me after I dumped my purse, I would've remembered. "I really don't think it was Jarvis—" I said, but, as usual, Matthias had apparently undergone a massive hearing loss. He continued to hand the photo to Jarvis without even looking my way.

I made a quick grab for the thing, but only succeeded in grabbing Jarvis's sleeve.

With the Polaroid already in his hand, Jarvis gave me a strange look, moved the photo closer to his eyes, and peered at it.

Once again, all I could do was just stand there. With my neck blotching up.

Jarvis, on the other hand, looked as if he were enjoying himself. His round eyes widened, and then he actually whistled. "Nice," he said, "very nice."

Jarvis must not get out much. From the sudden leer that crossed his plump face, you might've thought he was looking at a *Playboy* centerfold.

I decided this was a good time for *me* to jump in. And perhaps move things along. "Jarvis, what Matthias wanted to know was: Have you ever seen this photo before?"

Jarvis's eyes were still glued to my Polaroid. The expression on his face had undergone a less than subtle change. When his eyes lifted to mine, you could see what he was thinking almost as clearly as if it were running in a ticker tape across his pupils.

No wonder clients want to work with you instead of me.

Jarvis actually looked hurt. I do believe if Jarvis ever became convinced that distributing a Polaroid of *himself* in a bikini would help him land more clients, he would rush right out and have one printed on his business card.

The thought of Jarvis in a bikini was not, however, an image I personally wanted to dwell on.

"Jarvis?" I said again.

"No, I can't say I've ever seen this picture before." He looked over at me and then took a step closer to Matthias. Lowering his voice as if I couldn't hear him even though I was standing not two feet away, Jarvis actually said, in a companionable aside, "It kind of makes you understand why your dad left her all that money, doesn't it?"

I did a quick intake of breath. Apparently, seeing my picture had made Jarvis decide this topic wasn't taboo, after all.

Matthias blinked. "You saw my father and Schuyler together then?" You could tell Matthias tried to ask this casually, but there was an unmistakably tense undercurrent in his tone.

Jarvis's eyes widened. "Oh no. Never. Don't you worry, Matthias, your dad was always the gentleman. The *perfect* gentleman."

This was a bit much. Apparently, Jarvis's idea of a perfect gentleman was a man who could sneak around on his wife in such a competent way that no one ever suspected. No doubt, Jarvis's own wife, Arlene, would love to hear this.

I cleared my throat. "Jarvis, the reason you never saw us together was that I didn't even *know* Ephraim Cross! His leaving me that money is a mistake!"

Jarvis gave me a smile now that looked very close to patronizing. "Of course, Schuyler, whatever you say." He shot a sly look at Matthias, Jarvis's eyes now clearly saying, Isn't she cute when she's lying?

It was that sly look that did it. Up until that moment I had, of course, realized that Jarvis Arndoerfer would sell his own grandmother if it meant he'd collect 7 percent commission on the deal. Now, however, for the first time I wondered if Jarvis could possibly be even worse than the simple money-grubbing social climber he'd always appeared to be. Could Jarvis actually be capable of doing something really terrible? Like, for example, *murder*? I'd thought it couldn't have been him, but now I wondered: Had it been Jarvis who'd taken the Polaroid out of my wallet?

Jarvis, after all, *had* personally handled the sale of Ephraim Cross's rental property. Could something have been wrong with that sale? Could that have led Jarvis to do something even worse, to cover his tracks? My God, could this short, squat, balding man in a watercolor tie actually be capable of shooting somebody?

It seemed unbelievable, and yet—

I glanced over at Matthias, wondering what he thought of Jarvis. Matthias, however, was at that moment putting my Polaroid into his left front shirt pocket. His eyes, surprisingly enough, were on me.

Matthias's expression, unlike Jarvis's, was totally unreadable.

In the split second it took me to glance over at Matthias, Jarvis produced a business card. How Jarvis does this is beyond me. I think there's every possibility that Jarvis keeps his business cards connected to some kind of magician's contraption under his sleeve, so that whenever he needs a card, one shoots into his hand.

Jarvis pressed the card into Matthias's hand. "Here, take this. I know Schuyler is helping you, and yet—"

The realtors' code of ethics also dictates that one realtor is not supposed to deliberately try to steal another realtor's client. Jarvis is well aware of this, so, of course, at this point, he started doing some truly talented verbal tap dancing.

"—as I said, Matthias, you are in the *most* capable of hands. Schuyler is one of the best. However, since your dear father and *I* had such a good business relationship, I would feel remiss if I didn't also offer you my assistance—"

Usually, listening to Jarvis blatantly try to steal one of my clients right out from under my nose would've made me seriously consider going for his throat, but this time I stayed completely in control. It helped, of course, to know that Matthias wasn't really a client. "That's right," I said to Jarvis, as if the thought had just occurred to me. "You did recently handle the sale of some commercial property for Ephraim Cross, didn't you?"

Jarvis glanced my way and immediately nodded. As he did so, though, I could've sworn I saw something flicker in his eyes.

I tapped my chin. "Who did you say was the attorney who handled the closing?" I asked.

Matthias was looking a little puzzled at my sudden interest, as was Jarvis, but I noticed that Matthias watched Jarvis intently as he answered.

"I didn't say, but it was Addison Glassner." Turning to Matthias, Jarvis added, "Addison is a *wonderful* attorney. A credit to his profession. A *joy* to work with. *Really.*"

Why Jarvis was now gushing over Glassner like he'd gushed over me was beyond me. Of course, maybe Jarvis just wanted Matthias to know that he now considered anybody even remotely connected with the Cross family to be firmly entrenched in the *wonderful* category. Next, he'd be raving about their mailman.

Having finished worshiping Glassner from afar, Jarvis was suddenly eager to leave. "Well, I have some appointments," he said, glancing at his watch. "It was *so* nice to meet you at last." Once again, Jarvis attacked Matthias's hand. "*Please* convey my heartfelt condolences to your lovely mother. And remember what I said about being of help to you. Just give me a call. Any time. *Any time* at all."

With that, Jarvis all but ran to his black Mercedes, parked directly across from where we were standing.

Jarvis's haste made you wonder if his sudden departure could have something to do with his wanting to avoid further questions that made his eyes flicker.

Chapter 11

Standing beside me, just in front of the open door to the Arndoerfer Realty office, Matthias was rubbing his beard, watching Jarvis speculatively.

Jarvis got into his black Mercedes, started it, and pulled away without looking over in our direction once.

I was getting used to being blunt by now. "So, tell me, who *else* are you going to show my picture to? Old Man Radigan next door at the meat market?"

Matthias gave me a look that I guess he thought would be withering. "How *else* was I supposed to find out if anybody had seen the photo," he said, "if I didn't show it to them?"

I refused to wither. "Did it ever occur to you that whoever took my photo is going to lie about it? You don't really think somebody is just going to take a quick peek and admit, *oh, yeah, I saw this a couple of weeks before I stole it*?"

Matthias gave me another withering look.

I didn't wither this time, either. I took a deep breath. While I was bringing up things that Matthias might not react well to, I thought I might as well mention something else that had just occurred to me. "Look, I don't know how friendly you are with Addison Glassner, so maybe I shouldn't mention this. But isn't it possible that Glassner could be in cahoots with Jarvis? I mean, it could easily have been Jarvis who took that Polaroid out of my purse. *And* it could easily have been Glassner who altered your dad's will, leaving all that money to me."

Matthias, amazingly enough, did not double over with laughter. Instead, he just gave me another long look.

Since Matthias wasn't laughing, I pressed on. "Don't

you think it would be a good idea to talk to Glassner?"
When Matthias didn't immediately answer, I added,
"And don't you think you ought to have somebody
along who knows something about real estate? Who'd
be able to spot right away if something was wrong with
the sale of your dad's building?"

I really hadn't planned on adding that last part. My
mouth seemed to sort of take off on its own. It does
that sometimes. However, my being a part of a meeting
with Glassner did seem like one of my mouths' better
ideas.

Besides, there was no harm in asking. The worst Matthias could do was say no.

As a matter of fact, I half expected Matthias to look
at me as if I were crazy, but he didn't. Instead, he just
turned on his heel and headed back into the office. Once
inside, he picked up the phone on the front desk, dialed,
and asked for Addison Glassner.

I was amazed. Good heavens, it looked as if Matthias
was actually taking what I had to say seriously. When,
to be honest, I wasn't even sure *I* took it seriously myself. Now that I thought about it, the idea of Jarvis being
in some kind of plot with Addison Glassner did sound
farfetched. What could they possibly have hoped to gain
by giving *me* a lot of money? Was I grasping at straws
here, trying to divert suspicion in any direction other
than my own?

I had followed Matthias into the office, and now I
shamelessly eavesdropped. Evidently, Glassner was not
in, and Matthias was now making an appointment with
him for nine the next morning.

It was, amazingly enough, an appointment for *both*
of us.

As a professional salesperson skilled in persuasive
technique, I don't think it's a good idea to look surprised
on those occasions you talk somebody into doing things
your way. I don't think it's a good idea, but I must've
looked surprised anyway, because when Matthias hung
up, he said, by way of explanation, "Like you said,
you're the one who knows real estate. *I* teach printmaking at the Kentucky School of Art. I wouldn't know if

something was wrong with a sale if it were right in front of me."

I blinked. An *art teacher*? This bearded blacksmith of a man was an art teacher? I'd just naturally assumed that he held some outrageously overpaid job in his daddy's company. Moreover, I was sure Jarvis—and Barbi, too, for that matter—had assumed the same thing.

"I'm going to need you there to look over the papers on the sale of my dad's apartment," Matthias was saying, "to see if you can spot anything that seems odd."

Now it was my turn to stare at him. Was Matthias actually starting to trust me? Did he finally believe what I'd been telling him—that I didn't even know his dad, let alone kill him?

Eager to show just how helpful I could be once you stop suspecting me of murder, I said, "You know, maybe I can find out about that sale even before tomorrow's meeting."

Jarvis keeps all his expired listings in tall, gray metal file cabinets lined up against the back wall of a small room that had once been this house's pantry. I headed in that direction.

In the ex-pantry, I went immediately to the file cabinets, opened the drawer marked C, and started flipping through folders. All the expired property listings were filed under the owner's name, so it took me only a couple minutes to locate the file labeled "Cross, Ephraim."

A lot of good it did me.

The folder was practically empty. In fact, the only thing that was still there, as evidence that the transaction had ever taken place, was a black-and-white glossy of the apartment building—the one that had appeared in *Homes,* the local real estate listings magazine. That was all.

For a long moment I just stood there, staring at the folder.

And feeling oddly cold.

I had not told him to follow me, but Matthias had, anyway. He was now standing at my elbow, looking down at the manila folder in my hand. "Anything wrong?"

I shrugged, not sure how to answer. "The papers on the sale of your father's apartment building aren't here." I frowned, staring down at the empty folder. "Sometimes, a file is cleaned out after a sale, but Jarvis *always* keeps a copy of the settlement statement."

The settlement statement generally consists of two legal-size sheets summarizing the real estate transaction. It lists how much money came from the buyer, how much went to the seller, and it documents things like attorney's fees, taxes due, and the way the broker's commission is divided up. Jarvis always highlights in yellow marker the broker's commission earned on each sale that goes through his office. That makes these file cabinets, in essence, the Arndoerfer Realty trophy cases. And now one of Jarvis's trophies were gone? This particular transaction would've have been one of Jarvis's prize trophies, too, since the illustrious Ephraim Cross had been the client.

How could this have happened? Jarvis's wife, Arlene, Charlotte, Barbi, and I all played Jarvis's secretary, so all of us did his filing. Could the settlement statement for the Cross closing have simply been misfiled?

Or had it been filed correctly, and then someone had purposely taken it?

I could feel Matthias eyes on my face, so I tried for a casual tone. "Of course, it could be that the statement's just been accidentally misplaced."

I knew, however, even as I said the words, that the chances of the papers being lost by accident were pretty unlikely.

About as unlikely, in fact, as somebody *accidentally* putting that note in my glove compartment. Or that same somebody *accidentally* stealing my willpower photo out of my wallet, and then *accidentally* planting it in Ephraim Cross's desk.

Matthias's green eyes were intense. "Do you really think it's just an oversight?"

I shook my head. "No," I said.

Matthias didn't even blink. "Well, I don't, either," he said. He took a deep breath. "So. Who has access to this filing cabinet?"

I just looked at him. "Everybody who works here," I said. "Jarvis, his wife Arlene, Charlotte, and Barbi."

Just saying their names made me cold again. Lord. These people were people I knew. People I worked with. They might be guilty of misfiling, maybe, but I couldn't believe any of them could really be guilty of murder.

I had, of course, left somebody off my list. Matthias, thoughtful soul that he was, added it for me. "And you," he said quietly.

I stared back at him. This being accused of something I hadn't done was really starting to get on my nerves. "Do you actually think I'd have shown you this folder if I'd been the one who'd taken the papers out of it?" My voice was testy. "Do you really think I'm that stupid?"

"No," he said, "I think you could be that smart."

I think I could safely assume here that the man was not paying me a compliment. "Look," I said, "if you don't have any more trust in me than that, why in the world are you taking me to Addison Glassner's with you?"

For an answer, Matthias had the colossal gall to actually smile. It was one of those wide, boyish smiles I think are supposed to be disarming.

I just stared back at him. I didn't feel disarmed.

Matthias shrugged. "I didn't say I don't trust you," he said. "If you'll recall, all I've ever said is that I haven't made up my mind about you yet."

Then, as if to prove his point, he stood there and stared at me. Searchingly. For a long, long moment.

I was taken off guard. Otherwise, I certainly wouldn't have stood there, staring into his eyes, suddenly aware that Matthias Cross and I were very much alone in a very small room. And I most certainly wouldn't have stood there, growing more and more aware that Matthias Cross did happen to have the greenest eyes I'd ever seen, that his dark beard really did look as if it might be extremely soft to the touch and very nice to run your fingers through, and that for a man in his forties, he did appear to have the broad-shouldered, muscular body of a man at least ten years younger. I also became aware, not incidentally, that the man was wearing Aramis after-shave—a scent that has been known to make me a little dizzy.

When worn by the right person, of course.

I blinked and took a deep breath. Matthias Cross was not, however, the right person. Even though, at that moment, something did seem to be happening in those green eyes of his. If I hadn't known better, I could've sworn the look in his eyes had suddenly softened into a look of frank interest.

I did know better, though. Let us not forget that this was the same man who had just finished showing my bikini photo all over the office, totally ignoring my objections. *And* this was the same man who not an hour ago had all but accused me of murdering his father. Call me pessimistic, but I don't think these things portend a promising relationship. While it was true that it had been months since I'd met a really interesting man—the last one being the CPA with the S fetish that I mentioned earlier—I didn't think I was getting so desperate that I needed to start considering as a possibility the one man in the world who might most want to see me on Death Row.

Besides, it was transparently obvious that Matthias, in the absence of Reed and Constello, was playing Good Cop in a big way, trying to worm his way next to me with those mesmerizing green eyes of his.

What did he take me for—an idiot?

I would've taken a quick step away from Matthias, but there wasn't space in that small room. Instead, I stayed right where I was, abruptly turning around to face the file cabinet, so that Matthias couldn't see that my hands had actually started to shake a little.

I shoved the folder back where I'd gotten it, and then, of course, I did what I always do when I get nervous.

I acted like an idiot.

"Well," I said brightly, turning back to Matthias, "just look what time it is. Where has the day gone?" *After* I said that, I actually thought to glance at my watch. It was a little after four. "I'd better get back to work."

With that extremely smooth exit line, I stepped awkwardly around Matthias and hurried back into the front office so fast you might've thought something—or some-one—was chasing me.

Which, now that I think of it, might've been true.

On my way I didn't bother to glance into the antique mirror on the wall just outside of the file room. I didn't need a mirror to tell me that my neck was blotching up again. No doubt, at this moment, leopards and I had a lot in common.

Out in the front office, there actually wasn't much for me to do. The phones were not exactly ringing off the hook. I tried to make a good show of it, though, walking purposely over to the computer and printing out the day's update of the Hot Sheet.

The Hot Sheet is a long page of new real estate list-ings, expired listings, listings that have changed in some way, and the like. Because of the Hot Sheet, some of the new listings in the Multiple Listings book—which only comes out once a week on Thursdays—are already sold by the time the book is printed.

I hoped if I acted busy, bustling around the office, calling for information on various listings, checking back with clients who'd expressed an interest at the open houses over the weekend, that Matthias would take the hint and leave. Matthias, however, was either dense or deliberately ignoring the obvious. For the next hour, up until closing time, he lounged around the front office, watching me. Even the times when I was on the phone, Matthias continued to sit in the chair beside my desk, making no pretense of not listening.

When I wasn't on the phone, he followed me around, asking questions. As if he were suddenly very interested in how you go about getting the computer to do a com-parison study in order to determine the fair market price of a given home. Or that the Hot Sheet is updated at four every afternoon. Or that the test to get your real estate license in Kentucky takes four and a half gruel-ing hours.

I considered, of course, just showing Matthias to the door, telling him rather curtly that I'd meet him tomor-row at Glassner's office. Every time I was tempted to do that, though, I couldn't help remembering all those Columbo movies on TV. Didn't the guilty guy *always* try to get Columbo to just go away? If Matthias was determined to play Columbo, far be it from me to look any more guilty than I already did.

Not to mention, if Matthias really hadn't yet made up his mind about me, as he insisted, I certainly wasn't going to push him in the wrong direction by looking as if his being around totally unnerved me.

At five, while Matthias watched me in either amusement or amazement, I wasn't sure which, I went through all my closing-up motions, making sure the fax and the computer were still in receive mode, turning on the answering machine, and finally locking the front door behind us. All the time, of course, chattering away about the real estate business, and about how we leave the computer and the fax on all night, in order to be on call twenty-four hours a day for our clients.

By the time Matthias and I stepped into the parking lot, even *I* was getting sick of my own voice. Fortunately, Matthias jumped in at this point. "Well, now that you're off work," he said, "how about you and I—"

Believe it or not, it had actually sounded as if he might be asking me out, but I didn't get to hear the rest. Matthias was interrupted by what I thought at first had to be a car backfiring on Taylorsville Road.

I changed my mind when the small, arched window in the front door of Arndoerfer Realty in back of us shattered in a small explosion of glass.

And when Matthias dropped like a rock to the ground, pulling me down with him.

Chapter 12

They say you'll never hear the gunshot that kills you. This was not a particularly comforting thought as I lay flat on my stomach in the parking lot outside Arndoerfer Realty, a couple feet from the front door. The shots appeared to have come from the direction of the dense shrubbery at the edge of the parking lot directly in front of us. I continued to lie there, not moving a muscle, rather anxiously waiting, please, oh, please, oh, please, to *hear* the next shot.

The bottom part of Matthias's legs seemed to be lying diagonally across my ankles, but I wasn't a bit inclined to lift my head to find out for sure. In fact, I wasn't the least bit inclined to move even so much as my little finger. I don't know all that much about guns, but I *was* pretty sure that your average, garden-variety pistol was capable of shooting more than just two bullets. So, since I'd heard only two shots, my vote was to stay right where I was, flattened against the pavement until, oh, say, the next frost. By that time maybe the trees and flowering shrubs lining the parking lot would've lost their leaves, and I'd have a much better idea if there was anybody still hiding behind them.

I might easily have still been there, with people no doubt wiping their feet on me before they entered the Arndoerfer building, if Matthias hadn't lifted his shaggy head and said, "Are you okay?"

"Yes, are you?" I whispered this, just in case anybody hiding behind one of the trees or in the shrubbery might decide I was being left in too good a condition and want to rectify his error.

"Well, I'm as good as I can be for somebody who's

just been shot at," Matthias said, raising up all the way
and looking around us. He sounded angry. I can't say I
blamed him. Being shot at does not exactly do wonders
for the old disposition. After I got through being scared
silly, no doubt I myself would be more than a little irritated. "I think they've gone," Matthias went on. "I believe I heard whoever it was running away right after
we hit the pavement."

It was the words, "I think," and "I believe," in those
sentences that bothered me. I'd heard nothing that
sounded even remotely like somebody running away. Of
course, it would've been difficult for me to pick up the
sounds of a *train* going by over the racket my heart was
making. It sounded as if somewhere in the middle of my
chest, a thunderstorm was raging. It wasn't at all hard
to believe that Matthias might've heard something I'd
missed. However, what I really wanted was documentation before I got to my feet the way Matthias was doing.

It dawned on me, however, as I watched Matthias
brushing off his jeans and eyeing the shrubs directly
across from us that continuing to lie there at his feet
was awkward. Not to mention, once Matthias leaned
over and took my hand, clearly expecting to help me to
my feet, there wasn't any way I could continue to lie
there. Unless, of course, I wanted Matthias to drag my
limp body behind him as he headed back inside to call
the police.

I took a deep breath, squeezed my eyes shut, and let
Matthias help me up. I don't know why I shut my eyes.
It didn't make any sense at all. It wasn't as if the rule
for homicide was: If the victim doesn't actually *see* the
bullet heading toward him, the bullet can't hurt him. If
that were the case, I probably would've kept my eyes
shut until Christmas. Matthias would've had to lead me
inside like a guide dog.

It seemed to me that Matthias held onto my hand a
little longer than absolutely necessary, helping me up,
but I could've been imagining things. Things seem a little
more magnified when your eyes are shut.

After I got to my feet and I didn't hear a shot—or,
more importantly, didn't *feel* one—I forced myself to

open my eyes and survey the damage. My panty hose now had a huge run down the right leg, both my palms had been scraped raw when I'd tried to break my fall, and my bargain Liz Claiborne floral dress now had some dirt smeared among its flowers.

I also surveyed the look on Matthias's face. Getting up with your eyes shut evidently makes people look at you funny. "Are you okay?" he said again. He'd moved a little closer as if maybe he were expecting me to faint.

Matthias didn't look the least bit woozy himself so even though I *was* feeling a bit light-headed, I wasn't about to have him think that I was the sort of helpless female who swooned on a regular basis. "Oh, sure, I'm okay," I said, waving my hand in the air like maybe this was the tenth time this week I'd had bullets whizzing by within inches of my head. "No problem." I knew, of course, that I was not at the moment capable of giving Matthias a smile that didn't shake badly, so I settled for just nodding in his direction. "I am just *fine,*" I said with a little extra emphasis on that last word.

Unfortunately, I couldn't say the same for Jarvis's front door. In addition to the shattered arched window, there was another hole about six inches above the door-knob. Just looking at the thing made my heart thunder a little louder. I averted my eyes, stepped gingerly over the broken glass, inserted my key, and moved inside as fast as I could, Matthias at my heels.

While Matthias phoned the police out in the front office, I did what I usually do when I'm very upset. I walked straight into the tiny kitchen in the back, opened the refrigerator, took out one of the plastic two-liter bottles of Coke I always keep in there, and poured myself a tall one. Very heavy on the ice. When Matthias walked into the kitchen minutes later, I'd just downed a little over half the glass in one large gulp.

Which meant, of course, that, having just ingested a large quantity of carbonation, I wanted to burp very badly. My mother, however, taught me while I was still in elementary school that Southern ladies *never* do such things. I'd known, of course, even back then that she was lying. It stood to reason that Southern ladies had to burp occasionally, or else the poor things would build up so much internal air over the course of their lives that one day all the Southern ladies you knew would explode. I'd never heard of this actually happening so I'd known Mama was telling me another one. I'd mentally filed it with "Southern ladies always take dainty steps." And with "Southern ladies always let the boys win." And, later on, when I was in high school, with "Southern ladies *never* French kiss."

Still, with all that antiburp training from an early age, I couldn't bring myself to do it right in front of Matthias. Instead, while Matthias talked, I tried to let it out a little at a time. Sort of like letting air out of a tire.

Matthias, true to form, didn't waste any time beating about the bush. "So what's your guess?" he said. "Who do you think was shooting at us?"

I just looked at him, wide-eyed, loudly clearing my throat to camouflage my tire-deflating. There was no way I could say anything without taking a chance on the entire tire going at once so I just shrugged and shook my head. Which, I hoped, was universal language for "Hell if I know."

I must've been right about this universal language. Matthias nodded as if he understood. "Whoever it was has to be either one unbelievably lousy shot, or he was just trying to scare us," he told me. Having bullets singe his hair must've rattled Matthias more than his casual tone belied because Matthias began to do a fair-to-middling imitation of Leonard Ackersen. He couldn't seem to stand still. Instead, Matthias paced the small kitchen like a caged animal.

I stared at him. What did he mean, *trying* to scare us? I couldn't vouch for Matthias, but the shooter, as far as *I* was concerned, had certainly succeeded in the Scare-the-Daylights-out-of-Schuyler department. My heart was still having a thunderstorm. I reached for the Coke bottle again and refilled my glass.

Remembering my manners somewhat belatedly, I waved the bottle toward Matthias. Which, I hoped, was universal language for "Do you want a Coke, too?"

I must've been right this time, too. Matthias shook his

head and went on pacing. "It must've been somebody who knows we're asking questions," he said. "Somebody who thinks we could find out something they don't want us to know—"

I just stared at him. Lord. My life was starting to sound like a B-movie.

I was still letting air out of my tire, bit by bit, so I couldn't say anything. If, however, I were forced to pick a somebody out of a hat, I'd have picked Addison Glassner. Hadn't Matthias just called Glassner earlier, more or less tipping him off that Matthias and I were together, and that we were snooping around? In the hour or so since Matthias's phone call, Glassner would've had plenty of time to get here from his downtown office and try to scare us off with a few well-placed shots.

Of course, it could also have been Jarvis. We'd talked to him, too, hadn't we? No doubt about it, it *was* odd that all the papers on the sale of the Cross apartment building were missing from the office file. Were Matthias and I on the verge of discovering something about that sale that either Glassner or Jarvis would kill to keep from being found out?

Having also discovered quite recently, however, exactly how wonderful it felt to be accused of something you didn't do, I wasn't about to do the same thing to somebody else. Not without concrete evidence. So, even though I was getting close to completely deflating my tire, I had no intention of mentioning either man's name to Matthias.

As it turned out, I didn't have to. "Glassner and your boss are obvious possibilities," Matthias said as he continued to pace the kitchen. "Of course, we're not even sure the gunman was shooting at *both* of us. With there being only two shots, how could you tell? Maybe the gunman had been aiming only at me, and he'd missed both times." Matthias darted a look in my direction then, and I didn't have to guess what he was thinking

Or I *alone* could've been the target.

If that were so, the way I'd been making friends and influencing people the last few days, I'd say the possibilities were endless. It could even include the *mother* of

the man pacing in front of me. Judging solely from the
warm reception Harriet Schackelford Cross had given
me on her way out of Glassher's office after her late
husband's will had been read, I wouldn't have put it past
the grieving widow to hire a hit man. This possibility, I
decided, probably wasn't worth mentioning to Matthias
any more than mentioning Glassner or Jarvis had been.
Matthias would, no doubt, be delighted to hear that I
considered his mom a prime suspect.

Once my tire was completely deflated and I could talk
without fear of explosion, I headed back out to the front
desk, glass of Coke in hand, and phoned Jarvis. I intended this phone call to accomplish two things: tell Jarvis that if he was counting on opening an intact front
door to his office tomorrow morning, he'd better think
again. And, yes, to check out his alibi. Jarvis lived in
Oldham County, some thirty-five minutes away. If Jarvis
were home, there was no way he could've been hiding
in the shrubbery outside with a gun.

Jarvis's phone rang and rang.

When Jarvis's answering machine finally picked up, I
kept my message every bit as brief as Jarvis's recorded
voice instructed. "Hi," I said, "this is Schuyler. Somebody shot the window out of the office door. Thought
I'd let you know."

If, of course, he wasn't already aware of it.

The police must've been in the neighborhood. Or else,
a phone call from a member of the Cross family gets
amazing results in this town. Less than five minutes after
Matthias phoned, an unmarked blue sedan, siren going
full blast, pulled into the Arndoerfer parking lot.

The second Matthias heard the siren, he headed across
the room to open the front door. I followed him, feeling
a wave of relief. Somehow, just having the police here
made me feel a little safer.

Until, of course, I saw that the police were Reed
and Constello.

Walking through the front door of Arndoerfer Realty,
the two of them looked even more like salt-and-pepper
shakers. Reed was wearing a light gray suit only a few

shades darker than his white hair, and swarthy Constello was wearing a navy suit so dark it looked black.

I guess it goes without saying that I wasn't all that glad to see them. I was even less glad after I found out that Reed and Constello had their own unique theory about the identity of the shooter. Reed and Constello didn't share that theory with us, however, until quite some time had passed. First, they called in a couple uniformed policemen who showed up about twenty minutes later to poke around in the shrubs outside.

Louisville is on daylight saving time in June so things stay fairly light until right around nine. I'd say the policemen outside probably needed every minute of this time, however, to do their poking. A sizable section of the shrubs around the Arndoerfer Realty parking lot backs up to Cherokee Park. The shrubs give way almost immediately to dense woods so the shooter would've had a lot of cover for his escape. He would also have had his choice of directions in which to go.

The policemen had their job cut out for them.

While the policemen outside poked, Reed and Constello talked with Matthias alone out in the kitchen for an unbelievably long time. It was obvious right from the start that the Bad Cops were interviewing me and Matthias separately just to make sure our stories matched. What a surprise. Maybe I was leaping to conclusions here, but it was enough to make you think they didn't trust me.

What was really a surprise, it also made you think they didn't quite trust *Matthias*. Maybe his being here with me, even in the capacity of co-victim, had tarnished his image.

The Bad Cops took so long interviewing Matthias that I started doing my own imitation of Leonard Ackersen. Pacing out in the front office. As I mentioned, I'd brought my glass of Coke with me out there, but it was empty all too soon. With all the ice I'd put in the glass, the thing probably only held about three tablespoons of Coke. At least, that's what it seemed like when I was drinking it. Once the glass was empty, it occurred to me that there was no way I could get myself a refill. I was pretty sure that if I suddenly showed up in the kitchen, the Bad Cops would never believe that the only reason I was there was that I needed another fix. Bad.

Without my Coke pacifier, there was really nothing to do but pace. And worry. Mainly, my worries seemed to center on one thing. Would Matthias decide to show the Bad Cops that photo of me? In spite of what he'd told me? The picture was right there in his left front shirt pocket. Easy to get to. Would Matthias decide that, since the police were already here, he might as well save himself some trouble later on by showing them the thing now? The thought made me thirstier.

By the time Matthias came out and told me the Bad Cops were now ready to talk to me, I was all but spitting cotton. In the kitchen, however, neither Reed nor Constello mentioned the Polaroid. Thank God. Instead, they began asking the same questions they'd, no doubt, just asked Matthias. "How many shots did you hear?" "When did this happen?" "Did you get a look at the shooter?" Etcetera, etcetera, etcetera. All my answers had to have been an echo of what Matthias had just told them. In fact, the only question that gave me any trouble was one asked by Constello. "By the way," he said in that eastern Kentucky twang of his, "what was Mr. Cross doin' here in the first place?"

I swallowed. The correct answer was, of course, "He'd dropped by to accuse me of murder," but I didn't think strict accuracy in this instance was really necessary. The problem was, since this would be the first instance in which I would not be telling them the exact truth, I wasn't sure what to say. I settled for telling them a half truth. "This firm handled the sale of an apartment building for his father. And he wanted to know the particulars." As I said this, I stared Constello straight in the eye, unflinching, the way you did when you were a kid, when you're telling a particularly big whopper.

I probably should've skipped the unflinching stare. My mother could always see right through that one. The Bad Cops evidently could, too. They exchanged one of their looks, and I knew at once that what I'd just said didn't match what Matthias had told them. "Is that right?"

Reed said, running his fingers through his white hair. "Mr. Cross told us he came by because he was thinking of buying a house in this area."

I blinked. "Oh, yes, *that,* too," I said. "He did mention he was getting ready to buy a house. He looked through our Multiple Listings book for quite a while."

It was obvious that the Bad Cops were not buying it. Reed's eyes narrowed as he said, "And did he find a house he liked?"

"Why, no," I said. "As a matter of fact, he didn't."

"Funniest thing," Reed said dryly.

"Funniest thing," I repeated.

They dropped it there, though. I halfway expected them to start shining a lamp into my face until I blurted out the truth, but they didn't. Probably because the only light in the kitchen other than the long, fluorescent one overhead was the small bulb in the refrigerator. That thing wasn't going to make anybody confess.

Unless, of course, you stuffed the person you were questioning *in* the refrigerator, directly under the bulb.

That might do it.

It was only after Reed and Constello finally finished their questioning—and had returned to the front room with me—that Reed at last shared his theory on the shooter. Reed was sitting on the edge of the front desk by then, facing Matthias who'd evidently tired of pacing and had dropped wearily into the gray metal chair right next to the desk.

"You say you called your son Daniel earlier?" As I already mentioned, Reed was facing Matthias. Reed was definitely *not* looking in my direction when he asked this. His eyes, in fact, were on his notebook. I believed, however, that I could just go ahead and assume that he was talking to me since I was reasonably sure I was the only one in the room with a son by that name.

"That's right," I said. I think I already had a dim idea what was coming, because my stomach tightened up.

Reed cleared his throat. "Well then, isn't it true that you could have told your son over the phone to get right over here and take a couple shots at Mr. Cross? Wouldn't that have been a smart thing to do? Not only to convince Mr. Cross here that you were innocent of any wrongdoing, but also to throw a little scare into him?"

For a second, I couldn't speak. Reed was actually saying this as if it were a real possibility. Did this man actually think that I would ever encourage either one of my sons to handle a loaded gun? Not to mention, did he really think that, having done such an idiotic thing, I would ever consider it "a smart thing to do" to tell Daniel or Nathan to point the aforementioned gun in the general vicinity of where *I* myself was standing? Lord. At least, if I really had done this, I could probably get off by pleading insanity.

"You have *got* to be kidding," I finally managed to say. "Why on earth would I want to scare Matthias?"

Reed shrugged, as if that was the easiest question he'd heard all day. "You might want to scare him off if he's nosing around asking questions. Questions you don't want asked."

I just looked at him. This man really did think I was Ma Barker.

It probably hadn't helped my case any to have told him my half truth earlier. Because, obviously, Reed had already made up his mind why Matthias had come by Arndoerfer Realty today.

Reed may have been convinced that his theory was correct, but Matthias didn't seem to be. "I was standing right there while she was talking to her son," he told Reed. "I didn't hear anything the least bit suspicious—" Matthias's eyes said unkind things about Reed's intelligence.

I gave Matthias a quick glance. My goodness. If you didn't know better, you'd actually think Matthias was *defending* me. Would wonders never cease?

Reed, however, did not appear to think this was as nice a thing as I did. He was now looking at Matthias with something close to contempt. "Didn't you say that part of the time that Mrs. Ridgway was on the phone, you were talking to this—this—" Here he consulted his notes. "—this Barbi Lundergan person?"

Reed's point apparently was that while Matthias was

distracted by Barbi, I could've been hiring a team of hit men, and he couldn't have noticed. Remembering Barbi's skin-tight fuchsia dress, I had to admit that it *was* a possibility.

"Well, yes," Matthias said, "I was talking to Barbi."

Reed shrugged. "Well, then, there you are."

There I was, all right. Once more at the head of the list of Most Likely to Have Committed a Murder in the Last Week.

Thanks so much, Reed, for the vote of confidence.

To give him credit, Matthias still didn't look convinced. Of course, he *had* talked to Daniel personally over the phone. Maybe that's all it took to realize what a preposterous notion Reed's theory really was.

Of course, on the other hand, Matthias could've just been *acting* as if he didn't put any stock by what Reed was saying so I'd still be willing to accompany him to Addison Glassner's office the next day.

Where, no doubt, I would be a lot of help hammering the last few nails in my coffin.

Chapter 13

When Matthias picked me up at my house the next morning for our nine o'clock appointment at Glassner's office, I felt as if I hadn't gotten a wink of sleep. Let's face it, it's a little hard to doze when you know that there might be somebody roaming around loose who'd be delighted to pump a few bullets into you.

And when you also know that there are *definitely* a couple of Bad Cops roaming around loose who'd be delighted to escort you to a cozy jail cell. Reed and Constello had not left Arndoerfer Realty last night before telling me once again not to leave town. "I've got my eye on you," Reed had said as he and Constello went out the front door.

I'd felt as if I were in a B-movie all over again.

I believe I could assume that Reed had not been referring to the way he intended to guard me against another possible attack. I believe I could also assume that if the Bad Cops were convinced that *I* had personally staged this shooting exhibition for Matthias's benefit, neither of them would be looking very hard for the real shooter.

All of which were definite sleep-inducers.

Another big help was getting a phone call from Jarvis just as I was finally climbing upstairs to bed. Evidently, Jarvis had just listened to the message I'd left on his answering machine. "What do you mean, somebody *shot out* the window in the door?" he yelled. "Why would somebody do that?"

The implication in Jarvis's tone seemed to be that *I* must've done something to provoke the attack. What did he think I could've done? Had I sold a home too far under the market value? Did the store-bought chocolate chip cookies I'd brought to my last open house send somebody into a homicidal rage? I took a deep, weary breath. "Jarvis, I don't know why they did it," I said. "I just know they did it, that's all. Just as Matthias and I were leaving the building, somebody—"

Jarvis interrupted. "Oh my God! You were with *Matthias Cross* when this happened?" Evidently, judging from his reaction, Jarvis didn't mind so much *my* being in harm's way, but having bullets head in Matthias's direction was cause for real alarm. "Oh my God, oh my God, oh my *God!*"

I interrupted Jarvis's oh-my-Gods. "Jarvis, neither one of us was hurt."

Jarvis didn't seem to hear me. "Oh, now, this is great. Just *great.* Matthias Cross will never come around the office again if *this* is the way he gets treated. I don't know how we'll ever make this up to him—"

It had been a very long day. My legs were actually starting to wobble a little. "Jarvis," I said, "why don't you send him a nice bulletproof vest, okay?"

And I hung up.

After that little conversation, I tended to think that even though Jarvis had not been home when I'd phoned earlier, Jarvis probably was not the shooter, after all. Jarvis was probably physically incapable of ever pointing a weapon at a potential client. Particularly a client with the kind of connections Matthias Cross had.

Unfortunately, once I eliminated Jarvis from my list of Most Likely to Wantonly Endanger, that only left Addison Glassner.

Which was yet another reason I hadn't slept any too well.

Matthias's car turned out to be an ancient MGB in a color, I believe, they call racing green. This was something of a misnomer for this particular car because judging from the way the engine sounded when Matthias turned on the ignition, I was sure racing had been beyond this car's capability for a long, long time.

I couldn't help being surprised when I first saw the thing. It certainly wasn't the kind of car I'd expect the son of a millionaire to drive. I was surprised even more when I got in on the passenger side and found out that most of the dashboard was gone, exposing a tangle of wires and God-knows-what-else where the glove compartment had been.

Naturally, the first thing I thought of, as I fastened the frayed seat belt around my waist, was the mouse that had been found in my own car. The second thing I thought of was that Matthias's car looked a *lot* more likely to shelter a few generations of rodents than my car ever did. In fact, compared to my reasonably well-kept Tercel, this bucket of bolts looked like the Mouse Hilton.

Matthias evidently took my widened eyes and total silence for awe. "Isn't she a beauty?" he said, backing out of my driveway.

It took me a second to realize that he was actually referring to the mouse hotel we were riding in. "I fell in love with her the second I saw her. It was at last year's car show at the fairgrounds. Can you believe it? I got her for only fifteen hundred dollars."

I could believe it.

"I'm restoring her," Matthias went on as we headed down Harvard Drive toward Bardstown Road. "I only have time to work on her on the weekends so it's taking me a while."

I was trying to follow what he was saying, but it was pretty difficult since a good deal of my attention was now focused on the dark crevices directly in front of me.

Was I imagining it, or were those sparkly little eyes in there?

I'd just decided that what I'd mistaken for eyes were just knots of shiny wires when I realized that Matthias had stopped talking and was now obviously waiting for a response. I glanced over at him. "You're restoring it, you say?" I said. "Well, it sure is"—I fumbled around in my mind for an appropriate adjective—"different," I finished.

Matthias immediately smiled. As if I'd said something funny. "It's different, all right," he said. "It's going to be nice someday, though."

Just glancing around us, I'd say that the someday to

which Matthias was referring ought to occur sometime toward the end of the 22nd century. I didn't actually say it, though. I just returned Matthias's smile.

The man did have the greenest eyes.

Today he was wearing jeans and boots again, with an acid-washed, short-sleeved, blue knit shirt. Matthias may have been going to see the family attorney, but evidently he didn't see it as an occasion requiring business attire. He hadn't even tucked in the knit shirt.

I, on the other hand, was wearing what the sales lady who sold it to me had called a "power suit"—a black, severely tailored linen with an ivory silk blouse, black Pappagallo heels that I'd found at a discount outlet, and carrying, yes, my overpriced Dooney & Bourke handbag.

It occurred to me that if a casual observer wanted to pick out the heir to millions, I probably would've been the more likely guess.

A casual observer might also have wondered why exactly was somebody with Matthias's money restoring a beat-up import? You'd think if he really wanted to bother having the thing restored, he'd just drop it off at the nearest expensive body shop and pick it up a week later, completely rejuvenated.

Actually, what you'd think was that he'd just go out and pick himself up a brand-new luxury sportscar that didn't need any long-term restoring.

And that had air-conditioning.

Even though it wasn't supposed to get nearly as hot today as it had been on Monday, Louisville was still going for the title of "Sauna City of the Century." Breathing the air outside was like sucking a too-thick milk shake through a too-small straw.

In the absence of air-conditioning, Matthias was thoughtfully driving with all his windows down. After the first mile—during which I could already feel the curl leaving my hair—I gave Matthias a quick glance. Was the man some kind of eccentric? Did he have something against brand-new automobiles loaded with all the latest options?

I might've thought about all this a little longer and perhaps even questioned Matthias about it, but I had more pressing things on my mind once we turned left onto Bardstown Road. In fact, what I had on my mind was so compelling, it even made me forget for a while to look for mouse hitchhikers.

It occurred to me, you see, that the last time I'd appeared in public with Matthias Cross, someone had decided to send a couple of bullets our way. Both bullets *had* missed, but in my opinion, it was the thought that counted.

The second we were in the middle of all the traffic on Bardstown Road, I found myself scooting down into the passenger seat of Matthias's MGB as far as I could.

Unfortunately, in an MGB, there isn't far to scoot.

Even more unfortunately, during rush hour this part of Bardstown Road is three lanes heading into downtown with only one lane headed out. Which meant, since Matthias chose to drive in the middle lane, that we had a constant stream of cars on both sides of us.

I tried to sit there calmly, but with the windows wide open the way they were, I couldn't do it. My eyes kept going from side to side. Almost like a reflex action. Just checking, of course—just making sure that no one was pulling up beside us with a loaded weapon.

There were, no doubt, coiled springs less tense than I was.

"Are you okay?"

Matthias seemed to be asking me this all the time. Admittedly, it could have something to do with the way I was now sitting, all scrunched down in his car, my eyes darting from side to side, like somebody watching a frenzied tennis match. I wasn't about to confess outright what a coward I was, though. I waved my hand as airily as I could from a near prone position. "Oh, sure," I said, "I'm fine. Just fine."

Matthias just looked at me, his eyes concerned. So I quickly added, my tone now a trifle defiant, "I'm just a little tired, that's all. I didn't get enough sleep last night."

That ought to explain why I was lying almost flat in his passenger seat. If Matthias wanted to know why I suddenly had a bad case of tennis eyes, he'd have to ask.

He didn't.

Maybe because he already had a good idea why. "You don't have to worry," Matthias said, glancing into the rearview mirror. "I don't think we're being followed or anything."

My response to that, of course, would've been "How would you know?" It's been my experience that art teachers are not all that well versed in the latest surveillance techniques. I decided, though, that maybe lack of sleep had made me a little grouchy. So all I said was, "That's good."

Between checking for hitchhiking mice *inside* the car and gun-toting assassins *outside* the car, the trip downtown fairly flew by.

We parked in the Citizens Plaza parking lot, and took the elevator to the twenty-third floor. There I found that Frosty Flossy had thawed considerably since I'd seen her last. Needless to say, there was a strong possibility that her meltdown had something to do with *Matthias* being the one who walked up to her, asking to see Addison Glassner.

"Oh, right this way," she breathed. "*Right* this way!"

Rolling her hips, Flossy all but danced down the hall ahead of us. Today she was wearing a white dress with big black polka dots, and it was like following the bouncing dots as we trooped down the hall toward the mahogany door of Glassner's office. Unlike Monday, Flossy glanced our way several times to make sure nobody got lost. Smiling at Matthias every step of the way, of course, and tossing her brown hair, and batting her brown eyes.

Me, Flossy ignored. Recalling, however, the reception I'd gotten from her the last time, I decided that this was a definite improvement.

Addison Glassner had changed his decor a little since Monday. Gone were the neat rows of wooden chairs. In their place were two large overstuffed chairs upholstered in green leather. The massive oak desk, though, was still there, as was the matching credenza, and the rest of the Basic Law Office kit.

"Come in, come in," Glassner said heartily the second we walked in the door. Seated behind his huge desk,

Glassner was wearing a silvery gray suit that set off his silver hair to perfection. He must've known it, too, because as we walked in the door, he ran his hand through his hair in a gesture that couldn't help but draw your eyes there. What also drew your eyes was the diamond stickpin once again sparkling away in his lapel, and, yes, Glassner's amazingly white teeth once again sparkling away in his mouth.

"It's good to see you again," he said, reaching over his desk to shake Matthias's hand. I did notice that as Glassner said this, his eyes remained riveted on Matthias's face. I might, in fact, have been the Invisible Woman. "Is there anything we can get you?" Glassner went on. "Coffee? A Danish?"

Flossy was still hovering around the door, clearly loathe to let Matthias out of her sight. "A donut, perhaps?" she added hopefully.

I'd already drunk two and a half glasses of Coke at home in a determined effort to wake up, but I would've loved another one. However, since Glassner and Flossy had yet to even acknowledge I was in the room, I decided I probably shouldn't push it. No telling what Flossy might put in a Coke she served *me*.

Matthias immediately said, "Nothing for me, thanks," and a crestfallen Flossy took her leave.

Once Matthias and I had settled ourselves into the green leather chairs opposite his desk, it took Glassner all of sixty seconds to go from overly friendly to overly hostile. This, I believe, can be directly attributed to what can only be described as Matthias's real talent for tact and diplomacy.

Since it had been Matthias who'd called to set up the meeting—and since I continued to be invisible—I'd decided to play it very low key and let Matthias start everything off.

This strategy probably needed some rethinking.

"The reason we came by," Matthias blurted, "is to go over some of my father's papers. His will, for starters. I'd like to take a look at the original, *not* a copy, the orig—"

Glassner's square jaw suddenly looked as if it had

been carved out of granite. "Now just a minute," he said, interrupting. "You're not implying that there might be something wrong with your father's will, are you?" Glassner drew himself up as tall as he could, considering that he was sitting down. "I'll have you know that I have been your father's attorney for the last thirty-five years, and there has never been the slightest hint of impropriety. Not the slightest! I don't know *who* you've been talking to—" Here, oddly enough, Glassner looked at *me* for the first time since I walked into his office. I decided it probably would not be the best time to give him a big smile. "—but I can assure you," Glassner hurried on, "that Ephraim Cross's will *is* genuine, and that it meets *all* the statutory requirements."

Goodness, this man sounded outraged.

I jumped in at this point and tried to put out the blaze. "Mr. Glassner, I'm afraid you've misunderstood. There are no accusations being—"

Glassner, however, was not to be extinguished. He glared at me, glared at Matthias, and interrupted again. "You two have my personal invitation to speak to all three witnesses to the document. They all work here, you know. In fact, one of them was the lovely lady who just directed you to this office."

Flossy Fenwick? *She'd* witnessed the will?

"They all *personally* watched Ephraim sign the document." Here Glassner gave me another look. If anything, this one was even more hostile than the last. "It's ironic that you'd walk in here hinting that *I,* of all people, might've actually had something to do with falsifying your father's will," Glassner went on, "when *I* tried to talk Ephraim *out* of making it."

That got Matthias's attention, all right. He leaned forward, rubbing his beard. "You did?"

Glassner lifted his chin indignantly. "Of course I did. I told Ephraim more than once that since he said he'd only known this—this person—" Again, the look my way. Again, not friendly. "—for a scant *three* weeks, that was hardly enough time to get to know anybody well enough to leave them over a hundred thousand dollars."

Glassner had a point. Three weeks *wasn't* much. Three

weeks was, in fact, so brief that I could pretty much remember the last twenty-one days in their entirety.

Ephraim Cross had not been featured in any of them in even the slightest way.

I hadn't passed him on the street. Or talked to him on the phone. Or even laid eyes on him. The transaction involving the sale of his apartment building had been *six* weeks ago. That was when I'd last seen him in the Arndoerfer Realty office.

So, why on earth had Ephraim Cross told Glassner that he and I had been carrying on for three weeks? Had the man just picked that number out of his hat?

Glassner was making clicking noises with his tongue. "No matter what I said, Ephraim wouldn't listen. He actually told me that, at the age of sixty-four, he'd fallen head over heels in love for the first time in his life." Glassner shook his silver head, pursing his lips in distaste. "Can you believe it? The man had been married for over forty years, and yet he said he'd never been in love before."

I sat there, my eyes glued to Glassner, purposely not looking in Matthias's direction. Glassner had just told us that Matthias's father had never loved his mother. That couldn't be a particularly terrific thing to hear.

In fact, I thought Matthias's voice did sound oddly strained when he said, "My father actually said that?"

Glassner was still shaking his head. "I tell you, Ephraim was just talking nonsense, that's all, nonsense."

Once again, I didn't move. I wasn't at all sure if Glassner meant that it was nonsense that Cross had never been in love before, or if it was nonsense that Cross had fallen in love with *me*. I decided, however, not to pursue it.

No use *asking* to be insulted.

Glassner was hurrying on. "Ephraim told me that he was changing his will because he wanted to make sure that his one true love was left something to remember him by—if anything should happen. In fact, Ephraim's exact words were, 'I just want to leave my little buttercup enough money to cover all the birthday presents I won't be there to buy for her.'"

I blinked and stared at Glassner. *Buttercup?* Ephraim Cross had referred to me as his "little buttercup?" Oh God, this didn't sound good. This had to be the significance, then, of the flower found with Ephraim Cross's body.

I shifted around uneasily in that green leather chair. "Have you, by any chance, told this to the police?" I tried to sound as if this were a casual question, but I don't think I fooled anybody.

Glassner gave me a nasty smile. "I most certainly have," he said.

My stomach wrenched. No wonder the police were so suspicious of me! With that flower being found in Cross's lap, it was almost as if his death had been *autographed* by his murderer. As the "buttercup" in question, even *I* had to admit things looked awfully suspicious.

The police were apparently not the only ones who were suspicious of me. The significance of what Ephraim Cross had said was apparently not lost on anybody. Glassner was now looking at me as if I were pond scum.

I returned his look with a flat stare. I believe I could assume then, that having been turned down for dinner, Glassner's opinion of me had taken a definite downturn. He appeared now to actually believe I was capable of murder.

Surely, he hadn't felt this way on Monday, or was it possible that Glassner *preferred* his dinner companions to have recently committed a homicide?

Matthias, however, was the one whose suspicious look really bothered me. He tried to look away before I saw it, but it was unmistakable. In Matthias's eyes, as clear as if he'd voiced it aloud, was a vast quantity of lingering doubt.

I took a deep breath. "Look, how many times do I have to say this? *I didn't know Ephraim Cross.* Why he left that money to me is beyond me."

Glassner made a scoffing sound in his throat. "Ephraim told me the day the will was signed, that once Tiffany was in college, he intended to divorce Harriet and marry *you*."

My stomach hurt again. *This* was news. Not being in

the habit of marrying men I didn't know, I'd say Ephraim had been overly optimistic.

I'd also say that this gave a very good motive to Harriet Schackelford Cross. If Ephraim had been serious about divorcing her, she might have understandably wanted to stop him.

On a permanent basis.

Glassner apparently also realized at about the same time that things didn't look completely rosy for Harriet, because he hurried to add, "Before you leap to some ugly conclusions"—here, Glassner gave me the pondscum look again—"let me assure you, to the best of my knowledge, Harriet Cross had no idea whatsoever that Ephraim was having an affair. And she certainly had no idea of Ephraim's long-range matrimonial plans."

I just continued to stare at him. What a cold and unemotional way to put that. Ephraim Cross was talking about dumping his wife of many years, and running off with some chick he'd allegedly just met, and Glassner referred to it as "long-range matrimonial plans." Leave it to a lawyer to make something like that sound like nothing more than a business transaction.

Glassner, however, had moved on. His eyes traveling back to Matthias, he said, "I want you to know that I resent very much any suggestion that I might have ever been involved in something illegal." Glassner was clearly working himself into a rage again. His voice was shaking. "If you're considering for even a moment trying to throw mud on me or on this firm with wild, unfounded accusations about your father's will being fraudulent, you can rest assured that I will fight back with my own accusations." At this point Glassner gave Matthias a pointed look. A look that said, *You know what I'm talking about.*

I now stared at both of them. Matthias may have known what Glassner was talking about, but *I* certainly didn't. Matthias, however, didn't give me a chance to dwell on it long. "Addison," he said, "you're getting all worked up over nothing. Like Schuyler said, neither she nor I are here to make accusations. We're just here to get information. That's all. Besides my father's will, we'd also like to see the papers on the sale of my father's apartment building. You did handle the closing, didn't you?"

Glassner nodded, his eyes narrowing.

Matthias didn't blink. "Well, then, I'm sure you wouldn't mind our taking a look at the papers," he said. "Since you have nothing to hide."

For a long moment, Matthias and Glassner seemed to be in a staring contest. Matthias, however, evidently won. Glassner abruptly cleared his throat, swiveled around to the credenza in back of him, and after a minute or so, tossed two manila folders in our direction.

"Why you want to see these things is beyond me," he grumbled. "Everything is completely aboveboard. If your father were alive, he'd never permit your treating me like this—"

Beside me, I could hear Matthias abruptly catch his breath. "Addison," he said, his tone crisp, "my father *is* no longer alive. And *that's* precisely why I have to do this."

While Matthias went over his dad's will, and while Glassner pressed his lips together in a very thin line, I looked through the real estate papers.

At first it all seemed to be in order just as Glassner said. Nothing unusual.

Until I turned to the second page of the settlement statement. Then something practically leaped off the page.

No wonder Jarvis had not kept a copy of these papers in his trophy case. This was certainly no trophy. In fact, according to the settlement statement, it looked as if Jarvis had handled the listing *for free*.

I looked up from the papers, directly into Glassner's eyes. "It says here that the listing broker waived his commission. Do you know why?"

Glassner shrugged and fingered his diamond stickpin. "I gather there was some irregularity. I don't believe I was ever told what the problem was, but Mr. Arndoerfer *insisted* on waiving his fee."

I just stared at him. The selling price of Ephraim Cross's apartment building had been $300,000, the commission 7 percent. So, according to Glassner, Jarvis had "insisted" on waiving *twenty-one thousand* dollars?

That was a hell of a lot of waiving.

I took another deep breath. The Jarvis I knew was no more capable of letting go of that much money than he was of shooting a gun at a potential client. So, either Glassner was lying through every single one of his amazingly white teeth, or I didn't know the man I worked for at all.

"Well, everything seems to be in order—" Matthias said shortly after that, handing Glassner his folder. That seemed to be the signal that the meeting was over.

Glassner shook hands stonily with Matthias, ignoring me, and Matthias and I were out of there.

After Glassner had practically dared us to question the three witnesses to the will, it seemed pointless to go through with it. It didn't seem likely that Glassner would want us to question his witnesses unless he was certain they were going to back him up. Besides, all the witnesses worked for Glassner. How likely would it be that anybody would blow the whistle on his own boss?

On our way out, however, Matthias and I did talk to Flossy Fenwick. It wasn't as if we had much choice. She planted her polka dots right in front of Matthias, and said brightly, "Matthias, I wanted to tell you personally that I am so-o-o sorry about your father."

She didn't look sorry. She looked as if she were about to spring, wrapping herself around Matthias so tight he'd need a crowbar to pry her loose.

Matthias gave her a quick nod and said, "You witnessed his will?"

Flossy nodded almost eagerly. The entire time she was verifying what Glassner had just told us—that she'd watched Ephraim sign his will personally—she was batting her eyelashes. If they ever make eyelash-batting an Olympic event, Flossy Fenwick and Barbi Lundergan will, no doubt, tie for the gold.

After she'd finished creating a breeze in Matthias's direction, Flossy turned to me. "Mr. Cross was in such a wonderful mood that day," she said. Her tone was sweet, but the look in her eyes was nasty. "He said he was doing all this just to make *you* happy."

I think Flossy got the reaction she wanted. I stared. Matthias frowned.

"What do you mean?" Matthias asked.

Flossy's wide smile revealed lipstick on her bottom teeth. "Why, Mr. Cross told everybody in the room that day that he'd already told Schuyler here that he was changing his will."

If I'd thought Matthias had looked suspicious of me earlier in Glassner's office, it was nothing compared to the look on Matthias's face now.

I took still another deep breath. "I. Did. Not. Know. Ephraim. Cross." I said each word as if it were a separate sentence.

Matthias, however, looked as if he doubted every one of my sentences.

Flossy, on the other hand, looked terribly pleased with herself.

"Matthias," I said, "I don't know how I can make it any clearer. I have never met your father."

Even I was getting a little tired of hearing me repeat myself.

Matthias's eyes met mine. "I believe you," he said softly.

I don't think, however, I have ever heard words spoken with less conviction.

Chapter 14

After what Glassner had just told us, the next step was pretty clear. Find out from Jarvis exactly what the problem was that had led him to bid a fond farewell to twenty-one thousand dollars.

What had Glassner called it? An "irregularity?" It sounded as if Jarvis had had some kind of intestinal illness. Of course, if he'd actually had to give up that much money, Jarvis probably *had* been sick. Intestinally and otherwise.

Before Matthias and I left Bentley, Stern, and Glassner, I phoned Arndoerfer Realty to see if Jarvis was in.

I got the feeling that if Matthias had not been standing right there when I asked to use the phone, Flossy would not have given me permission. Moreover, I think old Flossy would've actually *enjoyed* refusing me. With Matthias there, though, Flossy sounded as if it were the best idea she'd heard all day. "Oh, of course," she said, her eyes fixed on Matthias. "Help yourself. By all means!"

While I phoned, Flossy moved closer to Matthias and worked up a breeze again with her eyelashes.

It was evidently Charlotte Ackersen's day to play Jarvis's secretary. Charlotte picked up on the second ring, told me in her best Minnie Mouse voice that Jarvis had attended a closing early this morning, dropped by the office briefly, and then headed home. "He left only ten minutes ago so he's not home yet," Charlotte said. She took an audible breath and said, "Um, Schuyler? I might as well tell you. I think the reason Jarvis decided to go home so early is, um, he's still terribly upset." Charlotte said this in the same hushed, urgent tone I think I myself used back in high school to warn a friend that I'd heard the principal was mad at him.

"Oh? Is Jarvis upset?" I'm not sure why I said this. It definitely did not take a genius to figure out what Jarvis could possibly still be upset about.

Charlotte took another deep breath. "He sure is. About the, um, front door. I guess you saw today's paper."

Matter of fact, I hadn't even glanced at the *Courier* this morning. "Was it in the paper?"

Charlotte took a moment before she answered. It must require real effort for her to tell somebody bad news. "It was only a little bitty article," she finally said, "and it was, um, on the next to the last page of the front section, so probably not *that* many people saw it, but from the way, um, Jarvis carried on—"

Charlotte's voice trailed off, but I could finish for her. Jarvis had, no doubt, acted as if his damaged front door had gotten the same kind of media coverage as the *Hindenberg*. "Jarvis says," Charlotte added, "that this sort of thing isn't good for business. He thinks people will, um, start being afraid to come by the office."

Maybe I wasn't so far wrong about Jarvis after all. Because this was definitely the Jarvis I knew. The first thing he'd think of, if one of his real estate agents were shot at, would not be if the agent was okay, but how the incident was going to impact the flow of traffic through his front door.

What a humanitarian.

On the other hand, Charlotte, bless her heart, did seem to have a different set of priorities. "From what I read, it sounded pretty scary," she said. "Are you okay, Schuyler?"

"I'm fine, Charlotte," I said. "Thanks for asking."

"Do you have any, um, idea who could've—"

As much as I appreciated Charlotte's concern, I didn't particularly want to get into a discussion of who all might like to see me perforated by bullets. Especially with Flossy standing within earshot. It might give her an idea she hadn't thought of yet. "Charlotte, I'll tell you all about it when I get back into the office, okay?" That said, I got off the phone, Matthias said his goodbyes—nobody seemed to care if *I* said goodbye or not—and on the way out to the parking lot, I suggested we head for Jarvis's home.

As I mentioned before, Jarvis lives all the way out in Oldham County. In a mostly rural area, at least thirty-five minutes away.

If anything, the trip out to Jarvis's was even more fun than the trip into downtown Louisville had been. Mainly because now, not only did I have mouse hitchhikers and the possibility of an anonymous gunman pulling up alongside us to worry about, I also had something else to consider. Whether or not, after our little talk with Addison Glassner, the man sitting beside me was now totally convinced I'd murdered his father, after all.

It was not the sort of thing that makes for a relaxed drive into the country.

Matthias *was* being awfully quiet as we headed out of downtown, turned onto I–65 North, and finally turned again onto I–71. I kept glancing over at him, unable to decide if Matthias was mentally fitting me for handcuffs, or if he was just going over in his mind everything we'd learned from Glassner.

There *was* one thing that I myself had learned from Glassner that I was a bit curious about. Ordinarily, out of simple courtesy, I probably wouldn't have asked, but by the time we'd traveled about five miles down I–71 in the direction of Oldham County, it occurred to me that it probably wasn't possible to make Matthias think any less of me. If he already thought I was a murderer, for God's sake, it didn't seem to matter much if he also thought I was rude. And nosy.

"I've been wondering," I began, "what did Addison Glassner mean when he said he'd make his *own* accusations if you accused *him* of anything?"

I guess it being the first question I'd asked after so many minutes of silence made the thing seem more significant than I meant it to. Matthias shot me a quick look. But then, he just shrugged. "I'm sure somebody will tell you sooner or later," he said. "Dad and I were not on the best of terms."

From what he had to say next, that appeared to be an understatement. It sounded as if Matthias had gotten along with his dad a lot like Poland had gotten along with Hitler. According to Matthias, he and his father had been arguing on a regular basis ever since Matthias was in his teens. Their arguments had apparently started the day young Matthias made up his mind not to go into the family business, but instead to major in art in college.

"My father was furious," Matthias told me. "He said that a career in art was a silly pipe dream, and that if I continued being this stupid, he was going to disinherit me. In the meantime, Dad did the next best thing. He refused to pay anything toward my college expenses. Unless, of course, I agreed to change my major to something *he* approved of."

Matthias rubbed his beard and shrugged again. "So I paid my own way through school. It took me five years instead of four, and I worked at six different jobs over those five years, but I finally finished."

Even now, there was still a trace of defiance in his voice when he said the words.

I gave him a long look. You have to admire a rich man's son who chose to put himself through college. Particularly if you happen to have sons like Nathan and Daniel. Adorable, yet irresponsible, tykes that they are. Lord love 'em.

"I got my BFA," Matthias was now saying, "and then I went to IU for my master's. I've been teaching printmaking at the School of Art for almost thirteen years now, and today, at the ripe old age of forty, I can still say that I've never taken one dime from my father."

After Matthias said that, it was a real effort not to look surprised. Because, as Matthias spoke, two things hit me. The first one was: Matthias Cross, then, was not the rich man a lot of people seemed to think he was.

That certainly explained why he was driving the Mouse Hilton.

The other thing that hit me was not quite as big a shock, but it *was* something of one, nevertheless. With all that gray in his beard, I'd have guessed Matthias to be older than me. Now, it turned out, he was an *entire* year younger.

So what was all this he was saying about being a ripe, *old* age? I think I could get depressed here.

A dozen questions flashed through my mind after that, but the one that surfaced first, believe it or not, was, "What exactly is printmaking?"

I'm not sure why I asked that. I guess maybe, of all the questions that occurred to me, it seemed the least controversial.

Even Matthias seemed to have expected me to ask something with a little more meat to it. He gave me another quick, sideways glance before he answered. "Printmaking is just what it says. Making prints. I do lithographs, etchings, and a combination of techniques called intaglio. In addition to the workshop I use at KSA, I've got my own printing press at home. I've had quite a lot of my work accepted into national shows. Last year I had a show of my work at a New York gallery."

Now there was a hint of pride in his voice.

"Didn't that change your dad's mind a little?" I asked. "Your having that kind of success?"

Matthias shook his shaggy head. "Are you kidding? It only made him that much angrier. Dad took it as a slap in the face. My publicly showing work that he'd never wanted me to do in the first place." There was a long silence while Matthias stared at the highway stretching ahead of us. Even in profile, his face looked infinitely sad. "To tell you the truth, I was surprised my father mentioned me in his will at all. Dad and I have hardly spoken for years." Matthias's voice was now ragged with regret. He cleared his throat before he went on. "Anyway, I guess all this is what Addison was getting at." Matthias took a deep breath. "What Addison doesn't know, though, is just how guilty I feel about my dad. I guess I'll never forgive myself for not mending fences with him before it was too late."

I just looked at him. I wasn't sure what I could possibly say that would be any comfort. Matthias's father was dead. It really *was* too late.

Fortunately, I didn't have to say anything, because Matthias hurried on. "That's why I'm so determined to bring my father's killer to justice."

I swallowed uneasily. Did he think he was talking about *me*?

"Fact is, I feel like I owe it to my dad to get to the bottom of all this. It's the only thing left that I can still do for him."

I nodded, as if I understood. And yet, I still felt uneasy. The entire time he was talking, Matthias had certainly acted as if he were being totally frank, and yet, for some reason, I had the odd feeling that there was a lot more to this story than Matthias had just told me.

Maybe it was the way his eyes never quite met mine.

By this time, however, we were getting close to Exit 17—the exit we needed to take—so I didn't have a chance to ask Matthias any more questions. We made the turn-off on I–71, and after that, our conversation mainly consisted of my giving Matthias directions to Jarvis's house.

Jarvis lives in a town called Buckner, emphasis, I believe, on the first syllable of that word. Once just a small rural town, Buckner today is an up-and-coming community in prestigious Oldham County. The land out here is outrageously expensive, and new construction even more so.

Jarvis's home, built just three years ago, definitely cost *big* buckners.

A huge, three-story contemporary, Jarvis's home looks from the outside as if somebody stuck four odd-size cedar boxes together after cutting the top of each box off at a diagonal. The bottom half of three of these boxes is covered in creekstone, the fourth broken up by a wide, three-car garage door.

Jarvis's home, no doubt about it, is stunning.

In my opinion, it might be even more so if it weren't for one thing—the color Jarvis and his wife selected to paint the trim, the front door, and the garage door. Turquoise. This must be the Arndoerfers' favorite color, because—from having visited here before—I know that this color repeats itself all over their house. The wood trim in the dining room, one entire wall in their family room, the Formica countertops in the kitchen. If you ever had any hope of escaping this garish color, abandon all hope, ye who enter Jarvis's door.

It's sort of like Dante's Gates to Hell, in that respect.

Jarvis's home sits on 7.62 wooded acres—I know the exact figure because he's told everybody at the office so many times—and when the trees are filled out, you wouldn't know he had neighbors. It's a little bit of a surprise to find that a man who evidently enjoys making his living more or less socializing day in and day out would choose to live in such a secluded area.

I've decided, however, that Jarvis isn't really all that social an animal. By the end of the day, I think Jarvis has probably had just about all he can take of dealing with people.

In fact, I'm a little surprised he even lets his wife, Arlene, live here.

When Matthias lifted the huge brass knocker on the turquoise front door, Jarvis answered right away. Jarvis couldn't have been home very long. He was still wearing a navy blue suit with another version of the watercolor tie he'd had on yesterday. This one had a lot more splashes of turquoise in it.

I stared at the thing. Maybe Jarvis was starting to select his wardrobe to coordinate with his house.

"Why, Matthias, how nice to see you again!" Jarvis immediately said. His eyes, however, were saying something else. Something on the order of, what in hell are you doing all the way out here?

Jarvis's eyes then traveled to me. And narrowed a little. Obviously, Jarvis was still miffed about the front door to his office.

I gave him a quick smile.

Jarvis directed *his* smile at Matthias.

Oh, yes, indeedy, I'd say *this* was going to be a fun visit, all right.

Chapter 15

Jarvis may have said it was nice seeing Matthias again, but it was obvious that Arlene was the one who truly took the statement to heart. She came up behind Jarvis just as Jarvis spoke, and stared at Matthias wide-eyed, patting self-consciously at her shoulder-length, dark brown pageboy. "Hel-lo-o-o," Arlene said, making it sound like two words. "How wonderful to have you drop by!" Arlene's eyes were on Matthias. She was clearly *not* talking to me.

Stylishly thin, impeccably groomed, always looking as if she'd just that minute applied her makeup, Arlene is one of those women who could be any age.

Once, of course, you eliminated the twenties.

Arlene could be in her thirties, her forties, or even her fifties—if she'd recently had a face-lift. She's not about to tell you, however, if she's ever had one. Just like she's not about to give you any hints whatsoever about how old she really is. In fact, a good way to get Arlene to leave a room is to bring up the subject of age. Or birthdays. Or where you were when JFK was shot. Anything that might possibly pin down her age.

A good inch taller than her husband—which, of course, is not saying a lot—Arlene usually increased the distance by wearing five-inch stiletto heels. I've often wondered if she didn't do this just to intimidate Jarvis.

Today Arlene was wearing a red silk, short-sleeved camp shirt, designer jeans that looked as if maybe she'd ironed them before she put them on, and the ever-present stilettos. I noticed, as she stared at Matthias, she wet her lips. Like a carnivore getting ready for a big meal.

Evidently, she couldn't wait to be introduced. "I'm

Arlene Arndoerfer," she said, extending a crimson-tipped hand. "Call me Arlene. I'm so-o-o *glad* to meet you."

For a second there, I actually thought Arlene was going to curtsy.

While Arlene was in the act of giving Matthias a wide, toothy smile, she must've remembered that there had been a recent death in his family, and that perhaps giddy smiles might not be entirely appropriate. She immediately tried to abort midsmile, but only succeeded in looking as if she were grimacing. "I—I was so-o-o sorry to hear about your father," Arlene quickly added. "So-o-o *sorry*."

With Arlene grimacing like that, Jarvis must've decided she needed rescue. He brushed invisible hair off his forehead and boomed, "Well, well, what are we doing, all standing out here on the porch? Come in, come in, right this way!" Jarvis was using his patented, overly hearty "I'm-Your-Best-Friend" voice. It's a voice that, no doubt, has made old ladies beam at him, children crawl into his lap, and, yes, prospects sign on the dotted line.

We were led down a long hall to the family room on the main level. There's another family room on the lower level, too, but the one we were headed for, I knew, was the most impressive. It has a floor-to-ceiling creekstone fireplace. Which has never been used. As Arlene has told me many times, an actual fire would "dirty the fireplace all up."

You can't argue with that kind of logic.

"Would you like something to drink? Tea? Coffee?" Arlene asked the split-second Matthias and I sat down on the turquoise plaid sectional sofa. Her eyes were clearly glued to Matthias, but this time I decided I'd gone without long enough.

"Do you have any Coke?" I said. "I'd love a glass."

Arlene's eyes flickered toward me in a look of faint annoyance, but when Matthias said, "That sounds good to me, too," she apparently underwent a sudden change of heart.

"Oh, we *certainly* have Coke! I'd be glad to get it for

you! *Glad* to!" She turned toward the door, but before she left, she added, her eyes still on Matthias, "Be-e-e right back!" With that, Arlene headed out of the room with the sort of speed you might expect from someone intent on setting a world's record.

As soon as Arlene disappeared, Matthias turned to Jarvis and once again wasted no time at all on small talk. "We just got out of Addison Glassner's office," Matthias said, "and—"

I didn't want to sit through another demonstration of Matthias's remarkable talent for tact and diplomacy. This was my boss, for God's sake. I mean, I may have been an independent contractor and all that, but Jarvis *was* the guy I worked for. And, barring unforeseen circumstances, I wanted to continue to work for him.

Arndoerfer Realty may not have been the perfect place to work, but it sure beat a lot of the competition. Jarvis didn't make me go door-to-door trying to drum up business, he didn't make me wear a dumb uniform, and he didn't make me hand out potholders with the company name on it. All of which, in my book, put Jarvis way ahead of a lot of real estate brokers.

Assuming, of course, that the unforeseen circumstance I just mentioned did not include a homicide.

Assuming *that,* if it were possible to get through this little talk without totally alienating Jarvis, I was determined to do it.

So I cut Matthias off. "Jarvis," I said, "Matthias asked me to accompany him to Addison Glassner's this morning to go over some of his father's real estate papers with him. Just to acquaint him with the details, that sort of thing—"

Jarvis had been looking at me in a less than friendly way—obviously, he had no intention of forgiving me for that broken window any time soon—but when I mentioned the words "real estate papers," Jarvis's eyes no longer looked merely hostile. They actually looked *wary.*

I hurried on. "Anyway, when I was glancing through the papers on the sale of the Cross apartment building— the one, I believe, you handled?" I paused here, and looked at Jarvis questioningly. I tried to keep my eyes very wide, my face expressionless.

This is the look I always go for when I'm pulled over for speeding.

Wide-eyed innocence.

And blank-faced stupidity.

I hate to admit it, but I can pull this one off on a fairly regular basis. I have yet to get a speeding ticket.

Jarvis, like several policemen before him, seemed to be buying it. He actually seemed to believe that all I was doing was asking out of curiosity. Nothing more. "That's right, I did handle it," he said, giving me a quick nod.

"Well, you know, I noticed the funniest thing," I said. "The commission on the sale had been waived." I shook my head as if this had to be one of the strangest puzzles I'd ever come across. "And Matthias here wanted to know why." I shrugged my shoulders. "Well, I certainly didn't have an answer." I smiled at Jarvis. Engagingly, I hoped. "But I told Matthias, why, we'll just head right on over to Jarvis's, and I'm sure that he'll be glad to tell you all about it."

I think I *might* have overdone the dumb-but-curious act a little. Matthias was now staring at me with ill-concealed impatience. And even less concealed amazement.

I think I *definitely* had overestimated how glad Jarvis was to tell Matthias "all about it." Jarvis's eyes had started doing that flickering thing they'd done back at the office. Jarvis blinked a couple times, brushed more invisible hair off his forehead, cleared his throat, and then finally gave both Matthias and me a wide, magnanimous smile.

I've seen Jarvis smile this way when he's trying to explain to prospective buyers why what he'd described over the phone as "quiet neighbors next door" turned out to be a cemetery.

"Well," Jarvis said, "waiving my commission was something I *wanted* to do. Because, you see, there *was* a small problem with the listing."

The "small problem," according to Jarvis, who contin-

ued to give Matthias his cemetery-smile the entire time
he was talking, was that Ephraim Cross had threatened
to sue him if Jarvis had not relinquished his fee.

Correct me if I'm wrong, but this appeared to be a
problem that was not all that small.

"You see," Jarvis went on, spreading his hands in a
gesture as magnanimous as his smile, "your father's
apartment building was located in Old Louisville, and
I'd advertised it as being available for Historic Register
funds and a lower mortgage interest rate—which, I'm
certain even to this day, that your father did tell me it
qualified for—" Jarvis shrugged, and his cemetery-smile
grew even wider. "However, after the newspaper ad
started running, Ephraim phoned me to say that this was
not, in fact, the way it was, and that he'd simply mentioned it to me as a *possibility*. So that I myself could
check it out. Before, of course, I put it in the ad."

I stared at Jarvis. What he was describing was obviously a case of false advertising. For which both
Ephraim Cross and Jarvis himself could've been sued by
prospective buyers of the property. It was also obvious
to me that somebody with Jarvis's real estate experience—he'd been in the business for over twenty-five
years, mind you—would never have put this kind of
thing in print had his client not made it very clear that
the funds were definitely available.

So, the way I saw it, Jarvis had been set up.

Ephraim Cross had, in all probability, purposely
worked this little deal to put Jarvis in a terribly vulnera-
ble position. Cross had arranged it so that Jarvis had no
choice but to work for him for free. Because Jarvis certainly could not have a prominent citizen like Ephraim
Cross suing him. If Jarvis thought that a news article
describing how his office door had been damaged was
bad for business, what would he have thought of the
publicity involved in having Ephraim Cross haul him
into court?

Jarvis was still smiling, but his smile didn't quite ex-
tend to his eyes. Which, I couldn't help but notice, continued to flicker a little. "It was all just a simple
misunderstanding," Jarvis said.

A misunderstanding that had cost him twenty-one thousand dollars.

No wonder the file folder on the sale of the Cross building had been almost empty. I was now almost certain that Jarvis had purposely tossed the final settlement statement himself. So that there would be no painful reminders of how he'd been had.

And so that none of the rest of us would find out about it.

It had to have been a terrible blow to Jarvis's considerable pride to have Cross play him for a fool.

Could wounded pride be a motive for murder?

"I was *glad* to waive my commission in the interest of building goodwill," Jarvis was now saying.

Right, and if I believed that, Jarvis would probably want to talk to me about buying the Second Street bridge in downtown Louisville.

Matthias apparently wasn't interested in purchasing a bridge, either. Arlene returned with our Cokes right about then, and as he took his, Matthias asked—with, I might add, all the subtlety of a train wreck—"Do you two remember where you were last Wednesday night?"

It was a good thing Matthias had already taken his Coke. Arlene's hand jerked involuntarily, and some of the Coke she was handing me splashed on my skirt.

I watched the damp circle widen on my black linen skirt. Good thing, too, the skirt was a dark color. Even after the stain dried, it probably wouldn't show. Much.

No doubt Arlene had reached the same conclusion because she didn't even bother to say she was sorry. Or offer to clean my skirt. Or anything.

Of course, her eyes were more or less riveted on Matthias's face at that moment.

I took a long sip of my Coke and stared at the Arndoerfers.

Arlene and Jarvis at that moment looked almost like twins, the way both their eyes were showing the whites all around, and both their mouths were making an almost perfect O. Evidently, they were both identically shocked that Matthias would even ask such a question.

"Wednesday night we were right here," Jarvis said.

He sounded hurt. Apparently, if people were not immediately won over by his cemetery-smile and his best-friend voice, Jarvis took it personally. "We were here all night from about six o'clock on. Weren't we, honey?"

This, I believe, was the first time I'd ever heard Jarvis call Arlene by a term of endearment. It might've been the first time for Arlene, too. She gave Jarvis a quick look before she answered, as if checking to make sure he really was talking to her. "That's right," Arlene gave her pageboy another nervous pat. "We never left. Not even to go to the grocery. Or anything."

That seemed to cover all the possibilities nicely. In other words, Jarvis and Arlene were each other's alibi.

I can't say I was impressed.

Matthias didn't look particularly impressed, either, but he moved on to another topic. "Did you ever see my dad talking to anybody in particular at the office?"

Jarvis looked positively relieved that Matthias had moved on. Jarvis leaned forward, his best-friend voice even heartier than usual, "To tell you the truth, I believe Barbi Lundergan walked by and said hello the day Ephraim came by the office to sign the final listing papers—"

This, of course, meant nothing. If Barbi had not made an effort to say hello to someone of Ephraim Cross's stature, *that* would've been suspicious.

"—and, I believe, Charlotte Ackersen typed the revised settlement statement. But," Jarvis added, "neither woman was formally introduced."

This, I believed. As I mentioned earlier, Jarvis was not about to share a newfound client of Cross's social prominence with any other listing agent.

"Then you never saw my father with *any* of the women at Arndoerfer Realty?"

Jarvis was shaking his head at this when I happened to glance over at Arlene. She had yet to sit down. And she was wearing those stiletto heels. As a matter of fact, while Jarvis was insisting that no women in his office knew Ephraim Cross personally, Arlene was looking as if she would very much like to turn on her stiletto heels and run from the room.

I decided I'd help her out.

"Arlene," I said, "this Coke is a little flat. Could I have another one, please?"

Far from looking annoyed this time, Arlene gave me the kind of smile she'd been reserving for Matthias up until then. "Sure thing," Arlene said. In one smooth motion, she took the glass out of my hand and almost ran toward the kitchen.

I followed her. As if maybe I was under the impression that Arlene might need some help pouring me another Coke.

A job like that *could* get complicated.

Arlene apparently didn't realize I'd followed her. She dumped my Coke in the sink—a waste of perfectly good refreshment, I might add—turned, and was just opening the refrigerator door when I spoke. "Arlene?"

Arlene jumped. "Yes?" Her voice shook a little as she turned around to face me, the two-liter Coke bottle in her hand.

"I wanted to talk to you," I said. "Alone." I was acting on a hunch here, but judging from how uneasy Arlene had acted in the living room while Matthias was questioning Jarvis, I was fairly certain my hunch was right on target. "Matthias and I have been told that *you* were seen with his father."

Arlene's eyes widened, and for a second she actually looked as if she were going to cry. "I—I only went out to lunch with him once," she protested, putting the Coke bottle down on the counter. "That's all. Only once." Arlene turned, picked up the bottle again, and started pouring my drink. Her hands were now shaking so bad, I wondered if she might need some help pouring my drink, after all. "The only reason I went to lunch with Ephraim," Arlene said, "was to convince him not to sue Jarvis."

Arlene finished pouring my Coke, nearly spilling it down the side of the glass several times, took a deep breath, and turned back around. "Obviously, I didn't do very well convincing him," she said, handing me the glass. "He kept threatening to take Jarvis to court if Jarvis didn't waive his commission."

I took the glass, staring at her. Something seemed to be happening to Arlene's mouth. It was twisting. As if an invisible hand were wringing it out. "Ephraim could be such an asshole," Arlene said through her teeth. "You could tell he was *enjoying* himself, humiliating Jarvis like that."

Apparently, Arlene had said more than she meant to. She put one perfectly manicured hand to her crimson mouth, blinked, and then added, her voice a whisper, "Look, Schuyler, Jarvis doesn't know anything about my meeting with Ephraim. I—I didn't tell him. I knew Jarvis would think I was just interfering."

I continued to stare. Arlene had said she'd met Cross only for lunch and only for business reasons, and yet, she referred to him by his first name. Exactly how well had she really known him?

Then again, I could be jumping to conclusions here. That first-name thing might mean absolutely nothing. The Arndoerfers probably would be calling the *President* by his first name two seconds after they met him.

On the other hand, it might also mean that Arlene had been having an affair with Cross. The man she now so fondly referred to as an "asshole." Could Arlene have killed Ephraim Cross and now be trying to frame me for it? Arlene *had* been in the realty office on Friday last week. She could have stolen my willpower photo.

The only trouble with the Arlene-did-it theory, however, was—if Addison Glassner had been telling the truth and the will was genuine—this theory didn't exactly explain why Ephraim Cross had ended up leaving *me* a great deal of money.

"You're not going to tell Jarvis what I did, are you?" Arlene said. "I—I only did it to help him out."

It took me a second to realize that Arlene was talking about her accompanying Cross to lunch. Not anything else. I took a long sip of Coke. "Arlene," I said, "he won't find out from me."

He might find out from the police, though. If I ever came up with anything more than just a theory that didn't make sense.

Chapter 16

It was almost eleven-thirty when Arlene and I headed back into the living room, but neither Arlene nor Jarvis suggested that Matthias and I stay to lunch. You'd think a social climber like Jarvis would've leaped at the chance to break bread with Matthias, but this wasn't the case. In fact, after our little conversations, you could actually get the idea that Jarvis and his wife felt that continuing to have Matthias and me around might spoil their appetites.

You could also get the idea that both Arlene and Jarvis would not be all that heartbroken to see Matthias and me go. Like—*immediately*. Maybe it was the way Arlene continued to stand even after she and I got back to the living room. Or the way Jarvis got to his feet the second Arlene and I entered the room so that I didn't even have a chance to resume my seat on the sofa.

"Well, I only wish I could've been more help to you," Jarvis said, extending his hand toward Matthias. It appeared that if Matthias did not start heading toward the front door, Jarvis was going to drag him bodily toward it. "I'm truly sorry I didn't have more to tell you."

Jarvis didn't sound truly sorry. He sounded truly *happy* that Matthias was indeed taking the hint and starting to move out of the room.

I stood there in front of the turquoise plaid sofa, glass in hand, watching them go. Evidently, Jarvis and Arlene were not going to give me the chance to even finish my Coke. I took as big a gulp as I could, set the glass down on the coffee table—if Arlene didn't care about putting Coke stains on *my* linen skirt, I wasn't going to worry about leaving rings on *her* table—and I followed Matthias and the Arndoerfers down the hall toward the front door.

Matthias and I took our leave to a chorus of "—if there's anything else you need to know, just give us a call. We're only too glad to help. So glad you dropped by—" Lord. If I'd thought that Matthias's words as we'd left Glassner's office earlier had lacked conviction, I'd seen nothing yet. Jarvis and Arlene could teach Matthias a thing or two.

Actually, it was just as well that the Arndoerfers hadn't asked us to lunch. I was so eager to tell Matthias what I'd just learned from Arlene that I blurted it out the second Matthias got behind the wheel of the Mouse Hilton.

I was not, mind you, breaking my promise to Arlene. What I'd told her—and I thought I'd made it very clear—was that I wouldn't tell *Jarvis* anything. Matthias, on the other hand, I don't believe I mentioned at all.

Matthias had been about to put his key into the ignition, but as soon as I started talking, he stopped in mid-action and turned toward me. "How in the world did you get her to tell you all this?"

I shrugged. "I just told her somebody actually *saw* her with your dad."

Matthias stared at me. "But you were lying?"

His green eyes suddenly looked awfully intense. Uh-oh. Was this a trick question? If I admitted I'd lied to Arlene, would Matthias assume that I'd lied about other things? Little, insignificant things, like, oh, say, murdering his father, for instance? I smoothed a nonexistent wrinkle in my black linen skirt. "Well, yes," I admitted with some reluctance, "I guess you could say I did lie to Arlene. Strictly speaking. But I lied to find out the truth. That cancels out the lie, doesn't it?"

Lord. I sounded just like Daniel and Nathan, right after I'd caught them spending their grocery money on concert tickets. They'd told me they'd lied to me because they were worried about my health. It seems they hadn't wanted to upset me for fear it would give me ulcers.

Oh yes. We Ridgways were slippery-tongued devils, all right.

Matthias, oddly enough, did not look admiring. As a matter of fact, he didn't look anything. Not angry, not disgusted, not anything. I believe I've seen more animated expressions on a mannequin. "So," Matthias asked, his tone almost casual, but not quite, "what exactly tipped you off that Arlene was hiding something?"

I just looked at him. If I'd known I was in for an inquisition, I wouldn't have brought this subject up. My goodness, I was only trying to help, for God's sake. The next time Matthias could ask his own questions, and see how far it got him. No doubt, Arlene would *leap* at the chance to tell Ephraim Cross's son precisely how big an asshole she thought his father had been.

I shifted uneasily in the Mouse Hilton's front seat. It took me a couple seconds of uneasy shifting to think back and decide exactly what it was that had made me start wondering about Arlene.

Then it came to me.

"Her shoes."

"Her shoes?"

That did it. Matthias's face no longer looked like a mannequin's. The expression on his face now, though, was hardly an improvement. He was staring at me as if picturing me in one of those jackets with the extremely long sleeves that wrap around a few times and tie in the back.

"Her shoes," I repeated emphatically.

It was true. Arlene's shoes *had* been the tip-off. The last time I myself had worn stiletto heels like Arlene's had been over six months ago, but the entire evening unfortunately was still as clear in my mind as if it had been yesterday. I'd worn a black ruffled dress and black patent leather five-inch stilettos to a very posh, very crowded cocktail party held at a condo on Willow Avenue not far from where I live. At this very posh, very crowded party, every chair had been taken, and very nearly every inch of space had been filled. With either people or furniture. Or both.

There was not a doubt in my mind that the reason I remembered this particular evening so well was that about halfway through it, having spent all that time standing, I'd started doing a fairly convincing impression of Chester on the old *Gunsmoke* reruns. A couple of times I believe I did a pretty fair imitation of Grampa McCoy on *The Real McCoys*. Toward the end of the party, fearing that my parting impression would be one of *Ironside,* I'd perched myself on the corner of an end table in the foyer of the condo. I'd even had to move a lamp onto the floor to make room to sit down, but I'd done it, anyway. I was that desperate to get off my feet.

I didn't tell all this to Matthias, though. I'd already had to tell him about my willpower photo and admit that I was at present lugging around an extra ten pounds. I wasn't about to tell him that I'd actually spent an entire evening, limping painfully around on a couple of spikes. Oh no, all I said to Matthias was, "Those heels of Arlene's were practically *stilts,* which can't be all that comfortable to wear"—here I thought, *believe me, I know,* but I didn't say it—"and yet, with perfectly good chairs all around her, Arlene kept right on standing. So I knew she had to be awfully distracted about something. To be able to ignore her *feet.*"

For a second Matthias just looked at me. Then he gave me what I believe was his first truly genuine smile. It was a slow grin that crinkled the corners of his eyes. "I talked to Jarvis the whole time you were out in the kitchen with Arlene, and I didn't find out anything I didn't already know," Matthias said. His grin grew even wider. "You really are something."

I returned his smile. I couldn't be sure, but that had actually sounded like a compliment.

Matthias started the Mouse Hilton, and we headed away from the Arndoerfers.

Turning back toward I-71, Matthias said, "You actually think my dad could've been having an affair with Arlene Arndoerfer?"

I just looked at him. It *was* difficult picturing Arlene having an affair with anybody. I wasn't sure she'd be willing to do anything that might possibly mess up her makeup. And yet, it could be that I didn't know Arlene any better than I knew Jarvis. "I really don't know," I finally admitted.

Matthias ran his hand through his shaggy hair. "Could Arlene Arndoerfer have been seeing my dad, and Jarvis Arndoerfer have killed him out of jealousy? Or do you think the Arndoerfers could have been in it together?"

I blinked at that. Hearing Jarvis's name and the word "killed" in the same sentence was a little jarring. As I mentioned before, Jarvis *was* my boss. And, while all this was a terrible thing to suggest about anybody, it was a particularly terrible thing to suggest about your own boss. Loyalty aside, I do believe that if Jarvis ever heard me even *hinting* such a thing, I probably couldn't count on him to ever give me a good reference.

Of course, if Jarvis ended up in prison for murder, I probably wouldn't list him on my résumé, anyway.

I took a deep breath. "Actually, Matthias, I don't have any idea. All I'm telling you is what Arlene told me—"

Matthias had finished running his hand through his hair, and was now just shaking his head. "You really think it's possible that my father and *Arlene Arndoerfer—*"

Matthias said this in the exact same tone I've heard people say, "Frank Sinatra and *Nancy Reagan*?"

I continued to stare at him. What exactly was his point?

Matthias frowned and directed his gaze at the road. "Arlene's pretty skinny, isn't she?"

I stared at him some more. This was not sounding good. Was Matthias under the impression that there was some kind of a weight requirement for infidelity?

A requirement that *I* evidently met, but that Arlene did not?

Maybe I was being a bit oversensitive here, but I was starting to feel that this conversation was taking a definite downturn.

Matthias must've noticed the way the muscle in the side of my left jaw had, no doubt, hardened into rock, because he added, suddenly talking very fast, "What I mean to say is that my dad has always been something of a ladies' man, but that didn't mean that he always liked every woman he saw. In fact, he was pretty particular. Even back in college, from what I gather from his friends, Dad had a reputation for dating only women who were very shapely and stunningly good-looking. That, of course, includes my mother."

Well now. I could feel my jaw muscles relaxing. Let me see. According to Matthias, *everybody* knew that Ephraim Cross only went out with shapely, stunning women, and yet so far, nobody had laughed out loud at the notion that his latest girlfriend could possibly have been *me*?

My goodness, was it possible that being suspected of murder could actually turn out to be a boost to the old ego?

I guess giving Matthias someone else besides me to suspect of murder, and then being indirectly called "stunningly good-looking" must've gone to my head. Or maybe the strain of the last few days had finally taken its toll. Whatever the reason, when we pulled up in front of my house, before I could stop it, my mouth actually started asking Matthias to come in and let me make him lunch.

It had to be momentary insanity.

Or maybe those damn green eyes of his.

I never ask anybody to lunch. For one thing, given my cooking expertise, I've always thought it would come under the heading of cruel and unusual punishment. For both my guest *and* me.

I believe I've mentioned earlier just how much I enjoy cooking. In fact, there is every possibility if I ever have a house custom-built, I'll ask the builder to leave the kitchen out. Maybe make that room into another closet. Something I could really use.

My entire custom kitchen could easily consist of no more than a shelf holding a microwave, another shelf holding one of those tiny apartment-size refrigerators, and a final shelf holding a stack of discount coupons for every restaurant within a ten-mile radius. The whole thing could fit into a cupboard.

Having opened my big mouth, however, and actually asked Matthias to do the unthinkable, I had no choice but to actually head toward The Room-I-Never-Use. The trip took me right past the basket of laundry that was still sitting on the floor beside the Queen Anne chair next to the fireplace. I'd meant to put those clothes away right after I finished talking with the Bad Cops.

Being accused of murder, evidently, makes things slip your mind.

Matthias, at least, had the decency not to give me the sort of disapproving look that Reed had given me. Matthias just stepped neatly past the basket and followed me into the kitchen. Where I fixed us what I know how to fix best.

You guessed it, another couple of Cokes.

After I took a long sip, my head must've cleared enough for me to realize that the only thing I know how to cook without referring more than once to a cookbook is Tuna Noodle Casserole. Or Microwaved Hot Dogs. Not exactly the sort of fare to offer somebody who has just practically told you to your face that you're stunningly good-looking. On the other hand, I didn't particularly want to drag out five or six cookbooks, and start poring over them right in front of Matthias, trying to find something quick and simple to fix that both he and I could stomach.

Maybe Matthias picked up on the dazed and bewildered look on my face. Or maybe the gods had decided that being accused of murder was about all I could stand this week. After Matthias took a sip of *his* Coke, he actually said, "Why don't you let me do the cooking, okay?"

I rather hoped that I didn't look as wildly relieved as I felt. "Do you really want to?" I asked. If he said no, I seriously considered begging.

Matthias nodded. "I love to cook."

I stared at him. Obviously, the man was deranged, but who was I to argue? For a fleeting moment, I was tempted to kiss his feet.

Matthias turned out to be one of those cooks who completely amaze me. The kind that can open up a refrigerator and some cabinet doors, pull out this and that, and in about twenty minutes, actually have something bubbling on the stove that you didn't have the slightest idea you had the necessary ingredients for.

Matthias also actually found spices in the back of two of my kitchen cabinets. What's more, he *used* them.

I admit it, I was impressed. Even though I basically had no idea what in the world Matthias was making. All I knew was that it had some cream in it, some leftover cheddar cheese, some deli chicken slices, and part of a green pepper, and that after it bubbled for a while, Matthias poured it over toast.

I also knew that it was almost fun, surprisingly enough, helping Matthias make whatever it was. Finding him a wooden spoon (it was under my dish towels), making the toast (I forgot—*this* is another thing I can make without a cookbook), and just watching Matthias move expertly around my kitchen (he was wearing a very snug pair of Levi's).

There was, in fact, only one bad moment. It was right after Matthias and I had taken our plates into my dining room, and I'd tasted his mystery dish and pronounced it delicious. Matthias immediately grinned at me and said, "I guess you know who taught me how to cook."

I just looked at him, fork still in the air.

"My dad," Matthias said quietly. "He was a born cook."

Matthias was seated directly across the table from me, and even though he looked down at his plate immediately, I could still see very clearly the pain that suddenly appeared in his eyes.

I probably would've spent a little more time feeling sorry for him, except that almost immediately a worry began to nag at me. Had that been another trick question? Had Matthias really expected me to *know* that his father had been a good cook, too? Did Matthias still suspect that I'd known his dad, after all?

That, as I said, was the only bad moment. The rest of the time, you might've thought we were long-lost friends, the way Matthias and I jabbered away all through lunch. I found out that Matthias had been divorced for almost eight years. That he had one child, a girl named Emily, who was now eighteen and had just completed her freshman year at Boston College.

"My daughter is two years *older* than my sister, Tiffany," Matthias said. "Sometimes that's even a surprise to *me*."

I just smiled at him, but I couldn't help thinking that it probably hadn't just been a surprise to Matthias. Tiffany would've been born when Ephraim Cross was forty-eight. Which didn't exactly sound like a planned pregnancy to me.

According to Matthias, his daughter Emily lived with his ex-wife Barbara in Boston, but spent one month of every summer with him. "You'd think, with them being so close in age, that Tiffany and Emily would be good friends, but they've never hit it off."

I had a feeling that there was probably more to this story, but I didn't press it. I just ate my Whatever-It-Was and listened.

"Emily and Barbara both came down for Dad's memorial service," Matthias told me, "but they had to get right back. Barb owns a boutique up there, which evidently doesn't run very well without her. And Emily's taking a class in summer school."

I took another bite, and gave Matthias a weak smile. I have to admire anybody who can get a kid to stay in college.

I also have to admire a man who doesn't spend a whole lot of time telling you how rotten his first wife was. As a single woman, you can get a little tired of listening to the litany of horrors a first wife is capable of. It's like hearing the same awful song time and time again, only sung by different—but equally angry—voices. The only hint that Matthias dropped that perhaps his relationship with Barbara had been something less than marital bliss was when he told me that she'd married another man two days after their divorce.

Unless the woman believed in love at first sight, I think I could probably assume that Barbara had been running around on Matthias.

Which, seated across from him at my dining-room table, was hard to believe. Barbara, no doubt, needed to have her eyes checked.

I decided old Barbara probably also needed psychiatric care when, right after I'd taken my last bite of Whatever-It-Was, Matthias pushed back his chair and started clearing the table.

Actually picking up his dishes, taking them out into the kitchen, and loading them into the dishwasher. All by himself. Without my even asking him to.

Then, believe it or not, Matthias started running water in the sink. Really. And cleaning the frying pan that he'd cooked his mystery dish in.

Matthias even acted as if this were a perfectly natural thing to do. In fact, the entire time he was doing this, he was continuing to talk about his daughter, and his work, and this and that. As if he weren't really paying any attention to what he was doing.

It was a real effort to keep from gaping at this point. Ed, I was certain, would not to this day be able to tell you where his own dishwasher was located.

And he lived alone.

I had, of course, dated men who'd cooked for me before. In fact, one of them had actually told me, "Honey, the best chefs are always men." This guy had apparently, however, also thought that the best dishwashers are always women, because he'd left every pan and utensil he'd used scattered all over my kitchen for me to clean up.

Matthias was now scrubbing down the top of my stove, still talking away. I was, of course, still trying not to stare. I picked up my own dishes, joined Matthias in the kitchen, loaded my dishes into the dishwasher, and in general, tried to help him clean up. I also tried to concentrate on what all Matthias was saying, but to tell you the truth, there was one thing that kept going through my head that seemed to blot everything else out.

Barbara, Barbara, Barbara, you *had* to have rocks in your head.

Something else also went through *my* head. I couldn't help wondering what it would be like to kiss a man with a beard. I never have had the opportunity. Up to now, I believe I'd always been a little afraid that it could possibly be like kissing King Kong, only smaller. Now, watching Matthias do the dishes, I changed my mind.

Maybe it would be like kissing a cuddly puppy. You know, furry and warm?

By the time the dishes were done, the kitchen was clean, and my dining-room table wiped off, I'd found myself telling Matthias all about Daniel and Nathan and how I ended up being a real estate agent. I'd even showed considerable restraint in telling him about Ed. If Matthias wasn't going to bad-mouth Barbara, I wasn't going to bad-mouth Ed.

At least, I was going to try not to. I was doing pretty well right up until Matthias and I freshened our Cokes, and carried them out into the living room. By that time all I'd really said was that Ed and I were "incompatible." What I'd meant, of course, was that nice people like me and jerks like Ed don't get along any too well, but I hadn't actually voiced this aloud.

Once we were settled on my Ethan Allen couch, Matthias, however, made the mistake of asking me straight out, "Just how incompatible *were* you and your husband?"

So, naturally, I had to tell him. All about Ed's Girlfriend-of-the-Month Club. "I guess that was pretty much the crux of our incompatibility," I said. "Ed wanted to see a lot of other women, and I didn't want him to."

I was smiling when I said this, but Matthias didn't smile back. If anything, he actually looked a little angry. "Well," he said, "I probably shouldn't say this, but in my opinion, your husband was a—"

I think I probably would've enjoyed hearing Matthias finish that sentence, but as it turned out, he didn't get the chance. At that moment, my front door was flung open with enough force to send it banging against the wall.

This is not the kind of thing you need to hear within twenty-four hours of being shot at.

I jumped so high, a couple of ice cubes bounced out of my Coke and rattled onto the floor. Next, I probably would've flung myself prone on the carpet in front of my couch with my arms shielding my head. Except for one thing. It took me only one quick glance to immediately recognize the person now standing in my foyer.

It was Matthias's mother.

And what she was holding in her hand was clearly a small gray clutch purse.

Not a gun.

Thank goodness.

As I've said before, Harriet Schackelford Cross is a very beautiful woman. At least, she is during those times when her eyes aren't bugging out. And when her face isn't turning purple. And, oh yes, when the arteries in her neck aren't standing out like gigantic twisted cords.

This, however, was not one of those times.

Chapter 17

It was one of those moments that, in retrospect, appear to be frozen in your mind. Like a single frame lifted out of a movie. For what seemed like an eternity, Harriet Cross stood motionless in my foyer, her tall, slender figure framed by the arched doorway leading into my living room, her large gray eyes wild and glaring.

As on Monday in Glassner's office, Harriet was once again dressed in gray. Charcoal gray linen sheath, transparent gray hose, and simple but elegant charcoal gray pumps. In spite of her obvious agitation, not a strand of her upswept silver hair was out of place.

You had to kind of admire that.

Across the room, to complete the tableau, Matthias and I sat side by side on my couch, knees almost touching, Cokes in hand, our heads turned toward Harriet, our faces registering identical openmouthed surprise.

And, oh yes, our feet nearly touching two ice cubes already beginning to melt into my carpet.

I know it was crass of me at an emotionally charged, frozen moment like this one to even notice such a thing, but from where I sat, it looked to me as if the watch Harriet was wearing was a Rolex.

All right, let's face it, I *am* shallow. As soon as I noticed the watch, the next thing I thought of was that there was every chance that what Matthias's mother was presently wearing out in my foyer probably cost more than all the furniture in my house put together. And that included the Ethan Allen couch I was sitting on. At its regular price. Which I didn't pay.

The frozen moment seemed suddenly to have thawed. Matthias abruptly got to his feet. "Mother—"

I glanced over at Matthias. *Mother?* Matthias referred to Ephraim Cross as *Dad,* and yet, Harriet he called *Mother?* This was hardly a surprise. Harriet Cross looked like the type who would insist that her children address her formally at all times.

Even at times like these.

"—what brings you over here?" Matthias's tone might've made you think that he was delighted to have his mom drop by.

Harriet didn't look convinced. The minute Matthias spoke, she started breathing so loud through her nose that the sound carried all the way across the room to where I was now bending over, picking up the two ice cubes off the floor. I put them in the blue ceramic ashtray I keep on my end table.

"*I* could ask you the same thing," Harriet said. "I—I just can't believe it! What in the world do you think you're doing?"

At this point, I wasn't quite sure to whom Harriet was directing her question. Her eyes were so wild it was hard to tell whom she was looking at—me or Matthias? I swallowed uneasily. Her eyes did seem focused in my direction. Sort of. Should I start telling her that I was just picking up the ice cubes I spilled? And yet, surely Harriet hadn't come storming in here to ask about *that.*

Matthias, thank heavens, must've been a lot more accustomed to seeing his mother in this kind of mood, because he seemed to know exactly who Harriet was talking to. Before I could make up my mind whether or not to answer, Matthias jumped right in with: "Now, now, Mother, Schuyler and I were just—"

"Just *what?*" Harriet now looked as if she might be inclined to use the gray clutch purse she was holding as some kind of missile. She drew it closer to her chest as if gathering strength for the throw.

Just to be on the safe side, I got ready to duck.

Matthias tried once more to finish his sentence. "We were just—"

It was apparently hopeless. "Well, I won't have it," Harriet interrupted Matthias again. "Do you hear me? I will *not* have it!"

Harriet was not making a lot of sense, but I didn't think it necessary to point this out to anybody. Particularly while Harriet was still gripping that purse like a football.

"Mother—" Matthias said again, beginning now to move toward her. Very slowly. The way you might move toward an animal that's baring its teeth.

At Matthias's approach, Harriet took a couple of steps backward, now holding her clutch purse out in front of her as if it were some kind of shield.

"When Addison phoned me, I didn't believe it," she said. "I really didn't believe it! I *had* to come over here and see for myself." Turning away from Matthias, she actually started pacing my foyer. There's not a lot of room out there for extensive pacing, but Harriet was evidently doing the best she could. "But it's *true*," she went on, her tone horrified. "Every word Addison said was *true!*"

I sat there, watching Harriet pace and wondering exactly what words Glassner had said to her, when Harriet thoughtfully decided to go into more detail. She stopped pacing, moved around Matthias—who was by now standing in the entrance to my living room—so that her view of my face was unobstructed. "You're trying to bewitch my son just like you bewitched my husband! You're—you're nothing but a *SLUT!*"

One thing about it. I was now not at all confused as to whom Harriet was directing her comments. My goodness. This did clear things up a lot. Thanks so much, Harriet.

"Now, just a minute—" I began, getting to my feet.

At the same time Matthias was saying, "Mother! For God's sake—" Matthias was obviously trying to cut his mother off, but Harriet was on a roll.

"You're a tramp! A—a—harlot! A common *prostitute*—"

As much as I admired Harriet's ability to come up with all these names without the aid of a thesaurus, enough was enough. "Look, Mrs. Cross—"

Harriet, however, was not any more willing to listen to *me* than she had been to listen to Matthias. "I've already *looked*," she said, tossing her silver head. "And I think I've seen all I care to see!"

Harriet's eyes at this point were such teeny-tiny slits, it was a wonder she could see anything.

Matthias reached out to touch his mother's shoulder, but you might've thought he'd hit her. Flinching, Harriet shrugged off Matthias's hand and wheeled on him. Pointing her clutch purse dangerously close to his nose, Harriet all but spat out, "You're a damn *fool*, Matthias. You know it? A damn fool!"

Matthias tried for a conciliatory tone. "Mother, now calm down. You're—"

Calming down was definitely not on Harriet's list of Things to Do Today. "I won't stand for this," she said. Her voice now sounded as if she were close to tears. "I mean it! I will not put up with this!"

I would've liked for Harriet to hang around a little while longer and perhaps elaborate on exactly what "not putting up with this" entailed, but Harriet was already heading out my front door.

She stomped off down my sidewalk, and out to the gray, late model BMW she'd parked at my curb. Leaving my front door standing wide open.

I've got a single clump of violets growing at the end of my sidewalk right next to the curb. I didn't plant them myself, of course, but they've come up every year I've lived here. Before Harriet got into her Beemer, she gave my little clump of violets a vicious kick.

It did not do them any good.

I stood there in front of the double windows in the middle of my living room, watching Harriet pull away. Other than possibly charging Harriet with violets-abuse, I felt totally at a loss for what to do—or say—next.

I do believe even Emily Post herself might've been a little perplexed in a situation like this.

Particularly if, like me, she'd glanced over at Matthias—who at that moment was standing at my open front door—and saw how embarrassed he looked.

I tried for a light tone. "Well," I said, "how nice to see your mother again."

Matthias did not smile. "Look, Schuyler," he said, "I can't tell you how sorry I am."

Now what do you say to *that*? Oh, that's okay. Don't mind a bit. Any time your mom wants to drop by and call me a few names, she's more than welcome.

Instead, I said, "I know your mother is terribly upset. She probably didn't even realize what she was saying—"

Which, of course, I didn't believe for an instant. There wasn't a doubt in my mind that Harriet knew precisely what she was saying. The words she used weren't all that obscure. Let me see. Slut. Tramp. Harlot. Prostitute. Oh yes, I'd say the definitions of those words were pretty much common knowledge.

Oddly enough, Matthias decided that this was a good time to leave. Maybe he was afraid that Harriet was just circling the block, and like Arnold Schwarzenegger in that *Terminator* movie, she'd "be back."

Before he left, though, Matthias took a deep breath and looked back over at me. "You know," he said quietly, "I think my mother is right. I *am* getting bewitched."

And then he turned and walked out.

Leaving me still standing there in the middle of my living room, listening to the Mouse Hilton start up, back out of my driveway, and head down the street.

With my neck blotching up again.

I must've stood there, unmoving, for a full minute. With about a hundred things going through my mind, all clamoring for attention at once.

The one, of course, that seemed to outdistance all the others was: My God, was Matthias serious? We had had a nice lunch, but was he now telling me that he was actually interested in *me*—the woman he'd suspected of killing his own father not three days ago?

That alone was neck-blotching enough. What, however, could without a doubt turn my neck into something close to red paisley was this little idea: Was it possible that I myself was growing more and more attracted to him, too?

Lord. Could it be that I was a sucker for anybody who'd help me with the dishes?

I blinked the thought away, went straight over to my front door, closed it and locked it. With the dead bolt.

Then, true to form, I picked up my glass, headed straight into my kitchen, made myself a fresh Coke—*very* heavy on the ice—and I drank almost half in a single swallow.

Lord. If my life didn't settle down soon, I was going to end up being a chain-drinker.

And a chain-burper.

I refilled my glass and took it with me when I went back into the living room. Where I finally picked up the offending basket of laundry, balanced it on one hip, and lugged it upstairs.

When I'm really upset, like I said before, I drink. Vast quantities of Coke. I also clean up things.

I don't know if I clean simply because I can't stand seeing anything in a mess when I'm upset. Or if my being upset just gives me a lot of excess energy to work off.

All I do know is that during the six months it took me and Ed to finalize our divorce, every room in my home could've been featured in *House Beautiful*.

It could also be that I clean because I'm instinctively trying to stay so busy that I can't possibly think about whatever is bothering me.

If my motive, however, was the last one, this time it wasn't working.

After changing into a short-sleeved white shirt, denim cut-offs, and no shoes—I always go barefoot in the house during the summertime—I dug in with a vengeance. All the time, however, that I was stuffing my underwear into my underwear drawer, and hanging up my blouses, and sorting my socks, my mind was going almost as fast as my hands.

What an unbelievable mess.

And I was not referring to my underwear drawer.

In less than a week, my world had turned upside down to the point where I had a strange woman showing up at my door, calling me names.

And *strange* was certainly the word for Harriet. I didn't want to criticize Matthias's mother, but Harriet's temper tantrum downstairs could certainly make you wonder if the woman could actually be capable of murder.

Just judging from the way her eyes bugged out, Harriet had *my* vote.

Was it possible—regardless of what Glassner had said to the contrary—that Harriet Cross *had* known about her husband's affair, and that she in her fury had decided to punish him on a pretty much permanent basis?

My God. Could Matthias's own mother have killed his father?

Which, of course, led me right into thinking about something else. The thing I really didn't want to think about. How exactly did I feel about Matthias?

At this point I started feverishly refolding my T-shirt drawer, making sure every one of them were stacked precisely on top of the other, but it didn't help. I couldn't put Matthias out of my mind.

I realized, of course, that I did without a doubt have an undeniable admiration for his green eyes, and something close to outright awe for his cooking ability, but was that all?

I had a sinking feeling it wasn't.

Back in high school, I'd made it a point never to like the guy all the other girls liked. It probably had a lot to do with how sure I was at the time that the guy voted "Most Handsome" was not going to be interested in the likes of *me,* but I think it also had something to do with my not wanting to be just one more face in the adoring crowd.

And yet, here I was. Seriously considering adding my voice to what already seemed to be a chorus of women who found Matthias attractive. Let me see, there was Barbi Lundergan and Flossy Fenwick. There was even Arlene Arndoerfer. Before Matthias had started inquiring about women in my office who'd been acquainted with his father, Arlene had looked mesmerized.

Lord. What was I doing? Planning on starting a fan club?

There was also the undeniable possibility that Matthias's admission earlier was all part of the Plan. The Plan by which Matthias intended to worm his way into my confidence, and ultimately, accumulate enough evidence against me to convict me of his father's murder. What had he said? He was getting "bewitched?"

Was he? Or was he trying to bewitch *me*? It could very well be that Matthias was playing Good Cop to the hilt, hoping I'd fall for him—and his damn green eyes.

All of the above is a fairly accurate representation of the way my thought processes went for the next couple of hours. Over and over and over again. Like a VCR programmed to play, rewind, and play again.

On the positive side, I did get my laundry put away—and by the end of the day, the drawers of the dresser and the bureau in my bedroom had never looked better.

At one point, I actually considered heading into work. When this occurred to me, it was not even four-thirty yet, so the office *was* still open. No doubt, if I were the Wonder Realtor that Jarvis had made me out to be, I would've gone in. And yet, ultimately I decided against it. After all that had happened, I just didn't have it in me to face Charlotte's curious questions.

In fact, the closest I came to going into work was going downstairs a little after five to check my answering machine.

Minutes later, I was standing there in my living room, actually feeling relieved that *both* prospects who'd shown an interest in the houses I'd had open on the weekend had apparently left messages while Matthias and I were at the Arndoerfers, saying that they wanted to look around some more. In my experience, this usually meant the sales were lost, but for once, I didn't even care.

These days losing a mere sale didn't seem all that bad.

I really intended to give my office a call right after that, just to check in with Charlotte—no extended conversation—but the minute I picked up the phone and started to dial, my front doorbell sounded.

My answering machine and phone are on a table in the corner of my living room farthest from the foyer. From where I was standing, you couldn't get a good look through the semisheers covering the narrow windows on either side of my front door.

Naturally, the first thing I thought of when I heard the doorbell was that Harriet the Horrible had returned. There was always the distinct possibility that she'd hurried home, flipped through her *Roget's,* and headed back here, armed with some really creative names to call me.

It was with some trepidation that I went over and peered through the narrow window to the left of my front door.

It was not Harriet.

Standing out there on my front porch was, however, just about the only member of the Cross family who hadn't yet dropped by to see me.

Tiffany, Matthias's sister.

At least, I *thought* it was Tiffany. The face looked pretty much the same, but everything else appeared to have undergone a major transformation since I'd last seen Tiffany, seated next to her mother in Glassner's office.

The Tiffany standing on my porch was hardly the meek woman-child I remembered. This one was chewing gum and dressed in black skin-tight bicycle shorts, a black T-shirt, black socks, and black Reeboks.

Also gone was the freshly scrubbed face I'd seen Monday. Today's Tiffany had apparently applied her makeup with a putty knife. Her brown eyes were outlined in black, her pouty mouth outlined in scarlet, and her cheeks smeared with what could only be described as red slashes. I believe I've seen war paint that was more subtle.

Tiffany's brown hair was once again pulled over to one side, but this time there was no barrette. This time her hair didn't look limp, either. What it looked like was that Tiffany, after pulling all of her hair over from the right side, had set off a small explosive charge just above her left ear, sending all her hair on that side hurtling skyward.

Over the course of my life, there have been several times when I've had the distinct impression that I've lived too long. One of those times was when I found out that rock stars had started biting the heads off chickens as part of their performance. Another was when people on TV actually began to refer to the New Kids on the Block as sex symbols. And then, of course, there was the moment I opened my front door, and got a good look at Tiffany's hair.

I couldn't help staring at it. I also couldn't help wondering, does your mother know you go out looking like this?

Of course, who was I to talk? The mother of a kid with bullet holes in his clothes. I have no doubt that people look at Daniel every day with the identical wide-eyed expression with which I now stared at Matthias's sister.

"Tiffany?" I said.

If this was the way Tiffany usually looked these days, no wonder she'd been walking with her head down in Glassner's office. No doubt, she'd been mortified wearing what Harriet obviously had insisted was appropriate for the occasion.

This certainly explained why that dress Tiffany had worn had looked so tight. Tiffany probably hadn't worn the thing in ages.

It also explained why Matthias's daughter, Emily, and Tiffany had not hit it off. It could very well be that Emily was normal.

Tiffany's opening line was original. "Man oh man, did you ever piss off Mother!"

Evidently, my having done such a thing had made Tiffany's day. She walked straight past me with a smile so big it looked as if it could wrap around her face a couple of times. "You should've seen her! Man oh man, I thought she was going to have a *stroke,* the way she was carrying on!"

Such an eventuality did not appear to upset Tiffany in the least. She was still grinning at me as she plopped herself down in the middle of my sofa, crossed one chubby leg over the other, and continued to chew her gum. Loudly. "Well," Tiffany said, "I just came over here to let you and Matthias know that I'm behind you one hundred percent!"

She'd lost me. "You're what?"

Tiffany cocked her exploded head in my direction. "Oh, I know you guys killed Dad." Here she actually shrugged, as if what she was saying was of no real consequence. "I just wanted you two to know how *glad* I am about it!"

At this point, judging from my behavior earlier, you might've thought that once again I would've been at a complete loss for words. This time, however, I believe I responded—without any hesitation at all—in exactly the same way that Emily Post herself would have if she'd ever been in a similar circumstance.

"Excuse me?" I said.

Chapter 18

Tiffany waved a plump hand in the air. "Oh, don't look so worried, Schuyler," she said. "I'm not going to tell anybody that you and Matthias killed Dad." Her brown eyes looked as carefree as a baby's. "I mean, it's perfectly cool with me!" Tiffany punctuated this last sentence by popping her gum.

I just stood there and stared at her. Let me get this straight. According to Tiffany, she was sure that Matthias and I were cold-blooded murderers, and yet, she was willing to overlook it?

How terribly openminded of her.

I took a deep breath. In light of what Tiffany had just said, I didn't feel at all inclined to sit. What I felt like doing was pacing, but, mind you, I *was* still barefoot. My luck, I'd step on something sharp. And believe me, I was feeling enough pain already just listening to what Tiffany had to say.

I forced myself, then, to take a seat next to Tiffany on my sofa. Moving very calmly, very casually. I also forced myself to resist telling Tiffany at the top of my lungs exactly what I thought of her little theory. No doubt, if I started screaming, Tiffany would only be more convinced that she was right on the money.

So I made my voice as even as I could. "Tiffany," I began, "I don't know how you could've gotten the idea that—"

Tiffany waved my words away. "Oh, you're *not* going to try to tell me that you and my brother didn't have anything to do with Dad's death, are you?" Her eyes rolled heavenward. "Man oh man," Tiffany said, her gum smacks punctuating just about every third word.

"*Next,* you'll be telling me you two didn't even know each other before Dad died!"

I blinked. Tiffany had apparently leaped to some truly appalling conclusions. What an adorable child.

Sitting this close to her, I could now see that what I'd at first taken to be delicate, antique silver drop earrings dangling from Tiffany's ears were something quite different—and that was putting it mildly. Each of Tiffany's earrings was, in actuality, a tiny, gray, pointy-nailed claw holding onto what looked to be a clear crystal marble.

Tiffany's necklace made a matching set. Suspended from the heavy silver chain around her neck was a somewhat larger dismembered gray claw, gripping a somewhat larger clear crystal marble.

I'd seen this kind of jewelry before. New Age jewelry, I think it's called. I couldn't help staring at it. Oh yes, it was a new age, all right. From a casual glance, you might easily come to the conclusion that Tiffany had constructed her earrings and necklace out of road kill.

How cute.

With some effort, I pulled my eyes away from Tiffany's ears and looked her straight in the eye. A woman-to-woman sort of look, I thought. "Tiffany," I began once again, this time with only the slightest edge to my voice, "now listen to me. I'm telling you the truth. I not only did *not* know your brother before Monday of this week, I didn't even know your *dad*—"

I couldn't have sounded more sincere if I'd been hooked up to a lie detector, but Tiffany's reaction was less than what I'd hoped for.

She hooted.

I think that's the most accurate way to describe the sound that came out of Tiffany's mouth.

"Are you kidding?" Tiffany slapped her meaty thigh. "Come on, Schuyler, you don't have to pretend with me! I'm not just some silly *child,* you know!"

I just looked at her. She was sporting road kill jewelry, exploded hair, and war paint, and yet, Tiffany actually thought that I might possibly consider her a silly child? My goodness, where in the world do kids get these crazy ideas?

Tiffany was hurrying on. "Look, I *know* it was you who lured Dad to that park so that Matthias could shoot him there. But it's cool. *Really*." She smacked her gum good-naturedly. "After running around on Mother all these years, Dad finally got what was coming to him!"

I believe I could assume here that Tiffany was not dressed in black out of any sense of grief.

I took another deep breath. I believe I was showing real restraint here. "Now, Tiffany," I said, "I'm sure you don't really mean any of—"

For an answer, Tiffany hooted again. "Are you kidding? I hated his guts!" she said. "Man oh man, *you* try living under that man's thumb all your life! Talk about an asshole!"

If I'd thought Tiffany was really serious, I probably would've told her right then that this was no way to talk about her own father. Deceased or otherwise.

But, to tell you the truth, I didn't put a whole lot of stock in what Tiffany was saying. She was, after all, a teenager. Something I myself—in spite of what my sons would, no doubt, say to the contrary—could clearly recall being. The way I remember it, *all* teenagers hate their parents. They may not really want to, but they have to. It's a teenager's job. It doesn't really mean anything. As a matter of fact, if I had a dollar for every time I'd called my mom and dad an asshole (not to their faces, of course, or there's a good chance I wouldn't still be here to tell about it), I probably wouldn't have to work today.

Then, too, there was every chance that Tiffany's anger was just her way of masking her own grief.

"My father was the biggest jerk that ever lived!" Tiffany was now saying. "He made my life a living *HELL*!"

Of course, I could be wrong.

"Here Dad was always telling *me* about the 'right way' to behave," Tiffany went on, "and always getting on *me* about the way I dress, *of all things*—"

I didn't even blink. Of all things. Was the man from the Victorian Age, or what?

"—and yet, look at him!"

I was missing Tiffany's point here. Did Ephraim Cross

wear road kill jewelry, too? It had to be that, because I think I would've remembered a photo of him with exploded hair.

Tiffany thoughtfully clarified her comments. "Dad was nothing but a damn hypocrite! He was telling *me* all this crap about 'proper behavior' while *he* was running around with every tramp in town!" Here Tiffany abruptly stopped, gave me a quick sideways glance, and put her hand over her mouth, as if she'd let something slip inadvertently. "Oh, I'm sorry, Schuyler. No offense."

"Oh, none taken," I said. "None *whatsoever.*"

My tone was about as sarcastic as I could make it, but it was completely lost on Tiffany. She chomped down on her gum with a loud pop. "I think Dad deserved what you and Matthias did to him! If anything, somebody should've done it sooner!"

Needless to say, I was getting very tired of hearing her say this. "Tiffany—"

Tiffany ignored me. "I mean, Mother knew for *years,*" she said, "but did she do anything? No, she just looked the other way, for the sake of appearances! She just—"

I sat up a little straighter, tucking one bare foot under me. Well now, *this* was interesting. Tiffany's version seemed to be distinctly different from what Glassner had told Matthias and me. Hadn't Glassner insisted that Harriet knew nothing of her husband's infidelity?

On the other hand, could you really trust the word of an angry teenager with road kill hanging from her ears?

"How exactly do you know," I said, "that your Mother knew your father was unfaithful?"

Tiffany looked at me as if I'd just asked how she knew water was wet. "How else?" she said with a shrug. "I asked her, and she told me!"

That did seem rather cut-and-dried.

Tiffany popped her gum again. "Mother said something real dumb after she told me, too. She said, 'We women sometimes have to take the bad with the good.' Can you *imagine*? Hell, Mother should've shot Dad a long time ago. In *my* opinion, you and Matthias did her a favor!"

I actually winced at that one. If Tiffany went around

repeating this little opinion of hers, I think I could rest assured that the Bad Cops would definitely not agree with her on the "favor" aspect. Nor would a jury of my peers. I held up my hand. "All right. Enough!" I said. "I mean it, Tiffany. Stop right there! You have *GOT* to believe me. Your brother and I didn't do anything to your dad—"

Tiffany now actually looked irritated. As if I'd taken a giant step down from asking her about water being wet. Now, she looked at me as if I were not only seriously questioning her intelligence, but also her sanity.

"Schuyler," Tiffany said, her voice unmistakably testy, "I *thought* I made it clear, you don't have to pretend around me." As she said this, Tiffany was pulling a folded sheet of paper out of her T-shirt pocket. "I'm not some crazy kid, you know. I've got proof. See? I know exactly how you two did it."

And with that, she handed me the paper.

As I unfolded it, Tiffany went on. "I found that note stuck in the pages of the owner's manual in my dad's glove compartment. Right after the authorities released his car back to Mother. Can you believe it? *I* found something the cops must've missed." Tiffany sounded proud of herself. "But, don't worry, Schuyler, I haven't shown that to anybody else. *Really.* I haven't."

The note was short, to the point, and printed in all capitals. Either the writer had the IQ of a preschooler, or else she'd been deliberately trying to disguise her handwriting: EPHRAIM—MEET YOU IN CHEROKEE PARK AT THE USUAL PLACE, THE USUAL TIME. LOVE AND KISSES—YOUR BUTTERCUP.

My stomach knotted.

Tiffany was now leaning against me, her eyes on the note. The sounds made by her gum chewing were like tiny explosions in my ear. "That's how you got him into the park on Wednesday night, isn't it?"

I leaned away from her. The note was undated, but Tiffany was probably right. This note probably *had* been the way Ephraim Cross had been lured to his death.

And *now,* since I hadn't had any idea what it was

before I let Tiffany hand it to me, this note had my fingerprints on it.

Terrific.

So it wasn't as if I could just hand the thing over to the police at this point. I could only imagine the overjoyed expressions on the faces of Reed and Constello if I ever gave them a note signed "Buttercup," with *my* prints all over it.

Thanks so much, Tiffany.

Which, of course, made something else occur to me.

I turned slowly to stare at the plump teenager sitting next to me. Was this some kind of setup? Could it be that Tiffany was faking her anger at her father, and that, in reality, she was determined to bring his murderer to justice? After listening to her mother, no doubt, say extremely flattering things about me, had Tiffany come over here to get conclusive evidence to incriminate me once and for all?

My eyes were probably looking a lot like saucers by the time all this flashed through my mind because Tiffany reached out and patted me on the arm. "Hey, Schuyler, don't look so upset. I'm going to keep quiet. I really am."

This little speech was broken up by more loud gum-smacking. It made you doubt that Tiffany ever kept quiet.

She gave me another one of her wraparound grins. "In fact, just to show you my heart's in the right place, I'm giving you this note so you can destroy it. Okay?" She patted my arm again. "I want you and Matthias to know for sure that I'm on your side. Trust me, I can keep my mouth shut."

I just looked at her. Right. You could probably trust Tiffany with your secrets with roughly the same confidence with which you could trust the *National Enquirer*.

My neck was blotching up again. I could feel it.

"Tiffany, I'm going to say this again." This time I spoke even more slowly so that Tiffany could not possibly have a problem following my every word. "And I want you to listen to me. I mean it. *LISTEN*. I did *not* know your dad. At all. None. Zip. Goose egg. And the first time I ever met your brother was on Monday in Addison Glassner's office. This is the *truth. DO YOU UNDERSTAND*?"

For an answer, Tiffany popped her gum just once and pointed under my chin. "Did you know that your neck's got all these big, red spots on it?"

I could feel my jaw tighten. I was beginning to believe what several of my middle-aged friends have told me. That teenagers should be locked in their rooms until they're thirty. "Tiffany," I said, "I know. My neck looks like this because I'm allergic to being accused of doing something I didn't do!" My voice was loud and not at all kind.

Tiffany blinked. For a brief moment, she actually looked just like a little kid being scolded. Tears sprang to her eyes. "Man oh man," she said, pouting. "All I'm trying to do is help, and here you are getting all mad and stuff!"

"Tiffany, you're wrong about Matthias and—"

Tiffany's eyes flashed. "I am not! It was you and Mathias, and I know it! Everybody always thinks I'm this dumb kid, but I tell you, I'm not! I know all about how Dad threatened to destroy the Kentucky School of Art! And how mad Matthias got about it!"

I sank back against my sofa cushions, staring at her. Almost wishing I could stop her before she told me the rest. But, of course, there was no stopping Tiffany, the girl who insisted she could be trusted to keep her mouth shut. It all poured out like water from a fountain. "I *heard* them the morning Dad died. Matthias was in Dad's den, shouting at him!"

According to Tiffany, Matthias wasn't the only one shouting. "Dad was real mad. He told Matthias that he was forty years old, and that it was high time Matthias stopped playing around and got serious!" Cross had gone on to demand that Matthias join him in the family business. Or else. The *else* being that Cross intended to use his considerable influence to see that the Kentucky School of Art lost all private funding.

Tiffany had my full attention now, and she knew it. She began to drag out every single sentence. She even chewed her gum more slowly. "I moved down the hall right after Dad said that stuff about taking away the funding so I could hear better. I positioned myself just outside the den door so I could hear every single word."

Tiffany stopped talking altogether at this point, and just sat there, idly fingering the gray claw on her necklace.

I, of course, idly clenched one of my hands to keep from idly slapping her silly. "Tiffany," I said, "what did Matthias and his father say after that?"

Tiffany dropped the claw, took her gum out of her mouth, looked at it, and put it back in again before she answered. She was obviously playing this one to the hilt. "Wel-l-l," she said, "I heard Matthias tell Dad then that the art school was almost totally supported by private donations, and that if Dad did what he was threatening to do, the school would be put out of business."

Tiffany paused here and just looked at me. "Guess what Dad said next?"

This time I considered not just slapping her, but maybe strangling her, too. "What, Tiffany?" I said evenly.

Tiffany responded with a grin and her loudest gum pop so far. "Dad said, 'Go to hell.' "

I blinked. *That* had probably gone over well.

Sure enough, according to Tiffany, Matthias had started shouting even louder. "Man oh man," Tiffany said, smacking her gum eagerly, "you didn't have to be standing outside the door anymore to hear Matthias. Man oh man, you probably could've heard him outside in the *yard*!"

I had to clear my throat before I could ask my next question. "So, what exactly did Matthias yell?"

Tiffany's grin had returned. "He said, 'I could kill you for this.' " Tiffany said these words in the same monotone that grade school children use to recite from memory. "*That's* what he said." The appalled look on my face must've been the reaction Tiffany was aiming for because her grin grew even wider. " 'I could *kill* you for this!' " she repeated. "I heard Matthias say those very words."

For a second I just sat there, staring at Tiffany. Okay, okay, all this didn't sound any too good. That was for sure. But, even though it sounded incriminating, the argument between Matthias and his father could've still been just your typical family spat.

Although offhand I couldn't remember ever threatening to actually *kill* either of my parents. Even through all those teen years when I'd thought I'd hated them.

It was important to remember, however, that I had only *Tiffany's* word that this scene even took place. She did look positively delighted to repeat it to me. This kid probably had a real career ahead of her, delivering the bad news to the next of kin of plane crash victims. I peered at her even more closely. Was it possible that Tiffany was making the whole thing up?

Matthias had certainly not mentioned anything about this. Of course, it wasn't exactly the sort of thing you would volunteer. I could just hear Matthias now. Oh, by the way, Schuyler, now that I think of it, I *did* happen to threaten to kill my father on the morning of the very day he was murdered. I would've told you sooner, but it must've slipped my mind.

Right.

I couldn't help remembering the feeling I'd had, on our way to Jarvis's, that Mathias was not exactly telling me the entire story. This certainly sounded like it could be the part he'd left out.

I fixed Tiffany with a look. "All right," I said, "so your brother *was* mad at your dad that day. That doesn't mean he killed him. It also doesn't mean that *I* had anything at all to do with it. I was not your father's girlfriend. *EVER.*"

Tiffany's eyes narrowed, and for a brief moment, I could see the resemblance to her mother. "You were, too! *Everybody* knows it." She flounced a little on the couch. Which had to be hard to do in a sitting position. "I don't know *why* you keep on lying about this, Schuyler. I already told you I'm not going to tell."

This was, as I mentioned before, not the sort of assurance I was willing to bet the rest of my life on. It didn't take a lot of imagination to figure out what could happen to me—not to mention, Matthias—if Tiffany decided to start spreading her little theory all over town.

It was with this powerful image in mind that for the next few minutes I tried my best to convince Tiffany that finding a note in her father's car and hearing her mother call me a few names—none of them "Buttercup," I might add—did not necessarily mean that Matthias and I were guilty of murder. It became abundantly clear, however, that Tiffany had already made up her mind. Nothing—not even the truth—was going to change it. This was particularly clear after Tiffany said, "Do you really expect me to believe that you and Matthias are *already* all lovey-dovey, and you two just met *this* week?"

Apparently, Harriet had embellished her story a little. Or else, once again, the other half of my split personality had been having the time of my life with Matthias on my couch, and I'd missed the entire thing.

I went with the more likely choice. "Tiffany, I don't care what your mother told you, Matthias and I are *not* lovey-dovey!" I felt stupid even saying the words. "He and I barely know each other. When your mother walked in, we were just talking."

"Uh-huh."

"I mean it, that's *all* that was going on!"

"Uh-huh."

It went on like this for a while. To everything I said, Tiffany replied, "Uh-huh." We sounded like a Diet Pepsi commercial.

Finally, I told her, "Look, Tiffany, if Matthias himself told you that he and I didn't even know each other before Monday—let alone, do all the other things you've decided we did—will you believe it?"

I must've caught Tiffany off guard. For a second, she just stared at me, smacking her gum. Then, giving one of her earrings a little flip, she finally said with a funny, little smile, "Wel-l-l, I *might*."

With that kind of definite commitment, I hurried upstairs, found my Keds, my car keys, my purse, and without even running a comb through my hair, I herded Tiffany out to my car.

Once out my front door, Tiffany actually started trying to herd *me* into her own car. Which, judging solely from the direction she started heading, had to be the black Trans Am parked on the opposite side of the street, directly in front of my house. "Let me drive," Tiffany said, pulling out her car keys.

If Tiffany drove the way she dressed, I didn't think my heart could stand the excitement.

"*I'll* drive," I said, heading for my Tercel, parked not five feet away in my driveway.

Tiffany shrugged and followed me, but you could tell she wasn't happy. Sitting on the passenger side of my Tercel, sullenly giving me directions, she sulked all the way to Matthias's apartment.

His apartment turned out to be surprisingly close to where I live. In fact, it was on the other side of Bardstown Road, on the first floor of a brownstone on the left-hand side of Douglass Boulevard, not even a mile away.

It was a good thing. If I'd had to drive for an extended length of time with a grouchy teenager pouting beside me, I might've started seriously reconsidering the trip.

Lined on both sides with huge maples, oaks, and elms that keep most of the street in shade almost all day long, a significant part of Douglass Boulevard runs parallel to Harvard Drive. But where Harvard is narrow and winding and has a roller-coaster dip at one end, Douglass is wide and gently curving and fairly flat. This is, no doubt, why Douglass rates the designation "Boulevard," and Harvard is just a lowly "Drive."

Unfortunately, it was still afternoon rush hour when Tiffany and I left my house. At this time of day, it doesn't matter how wide Douglass Boulevard is. We crept along for almost ten minutes before we finally pulled into what looked to be the only empty parking space anywhere near Matthias's brownstone—at least ten car lengths down the road.

I'd been concentrating on looking for a parking space, or else I probably would've noticed a couple of things even before Tiffany and I got out of my car and started walking back toward Matthias's apartment building.

As it was, I noticed these things when we were almost

ready to turn onto the cobbled walk leading toward the brownstone's heavy oak front door.

The first thing would've been hard to miss on foot. It was a shiny, bright red Corvette parked directly in front of the cobbled walk. Its license plate fairly screamed at me. TRU LUV.

Uh-oh.

For a second I couldn't take my eyes off that plate. When I finally did, though, the very next thing I focused on was the large flower bed in the side yard of the duplex right across the street. A bright patch of yellow, it was filled with buttercups.

Double uh-oh.

Chapter 19

I would've liked to have said that it was just seeing all those buttercups that rattled me so much. And yet, if I were being totally honest, I'd have to admit that suddenly finding out that there were a lot of yellow flowers right across the street from his apartment—that Matthias could easily get his hands on if he wanted to—probably wasn't quite enough all by itself to make my heart pound the way it was pounding.

Of course, having just heard Tiffany's account of Matthias's fight with their father, I certainly couldn't say that the buttercups didn't bother me at all. But I did immediately realize that the flowers in Matthias's neighbor's yard could just be a coincidence.

Not to mention, having easy access to a certain yellow flower wasn't, by itself, conclusive proof that a person had committed murder. If it was, the Bad Cops would've arrested every florist in Louisville by now.

No, what really rattled me, no doubt about it, was recognizing Barbi Lundergan's Corvette parked conspicuously out in front of Matthias's apartment.

I believe I could assume that Barbi had probably not dropped by to point out the advantages of owning rather than renting.

With Tiffany at my heels, I'd been moving briskly up the walk. When I saw Barbi's car, however, I stopped so short, Tiffany almost ran into me.

"Hey—" Tiffany said. Judging from her tone, I'd say Tiffany's mood had not improved during the ride over here.

Standing there stock-still, making no move whatsoever to step onto the cobbled walk leading to Matthias's apartment, I swallowed once before I spoke. "Tiffany, it looks like your brother has company. So this probably isn't a good time to drop in on him, after all."

My eyes must've been glued to Barbi's license plate because Tiffany's eyes immediately traveled in that direction, too.

Tiffany's eyes narrowed. "Is this somebody you know?" she asked, indicating the Corvette with a jerk of her head. The exploded part of her hair wobbled precariously.

I nodded. "As a matter of fact, it's a woman I work with, so I really think we should—"

"A pretty woman?"

I was probably not the one to ask. Ever since Barbi had started suffering from Pit-Bull Syndrome, she'd started looking extremely unattractive to me. "Well, yes, I suppose, she's kind of—"

Tiffany was headed up the cobbled walk before I'd even finished. "Come on," she said, her eyes dancing with excitement. "You said we're going to talk to Matthias, and that's *exactly* what we're gonna do!"

Obviously, the kid loved drama.

Of course, this was something I should've guessed about her the second I got a good look at her jewelry.

Tiffany moved toward Matthias's apartment with all the eagerness of somebody expecting to witness firsthand a scene from her favorite soap opera.

I took a weary breath. There didn't seem to be anything else to do but follow Tiffany. I certainly couldn't have the girl charging into Matthias's apartment and accusing him and me of murder right in front of Barbi.

I followed Tiffany up the cobbled walk, through the brownstone's entrance door, and on up to the first door on the left. All the time telling Tiffany, "Look, remember what you said about how good you are at keeping your mouth shut? Let *me* tell Matthias why we came by. When nobody else is listening. Okay?"

As it turned out, I needn't have bothered telling Tiffany anything. The second Matthias came to his door, all thoughts of making any immediate accusations of *murder* were apparently erased from Tiffany's mind.

She was too anxious to accuse him of something else.

Matthias opened his door, still wearing the jeans and blue acid-washed knit shirt he'd had on earlier in the day. He was now, however, wearing a little something that, as I recall, he'd *not* been wearing earlier.

A smear of red lipstick ran across his mouth, trailing off into his beard.

Tiffany took one look, turned, and actually beamed at me. "Man oh man, Schuyler, I think you're right. This really *could* be a bad time to drop in! At least, for *you,* it is!"

Tiffany seemed to take particular delight in delivering this news. Either she really did not care for me at all. Or else, she just adored being a part of this kind of drama.

Hell. It sure beat the movies.

In back of Matthias, I could see Barbi getting to her feet. She'd apparently been seated on a blue couch to the right of the front door. From the expression on Barbi's face, I'd say Barbi definitely agreed with Tiffany. This was a bad time to visit.

Apparently, before paying Matthias a visit, Barbi had taken particular care with her wardrobe. She was wearing skin-tight blue jeans, high-heeled white cowboy boots, and an off-the-shoulder, ruffled red gingham blouse. All in all, an outfit entirely appropriate for appearing as one of the barnyard girls on *Hee Haw*. This, I guessed, was Country Girl Barbi determined to make Matthias her Country Guy Ken.

How quaint.

After having spent a good part of the last hour, however, trying to convince Tiffany that there was nothing romantic going on between her brother and me, I couldn't very well now let Tiffany think that seeing Matthias with somebody else's lipstick on his face bothered me in the least.

Although, I guess you already know, it did.

Perhaps I was being a little oversensitive, but wasn't this the same guy who'd just told me that he was getting "bewitched?"

For Matthias, the chance to "bewitch" him must be

an equal-opportunity thing. Apparently, he was willing to give every woman he knew an equal shot at it.

I put a smile on my face that probably looked about as natural as those you sometimes see on the harried faces behind the counter at McDonald's.

Matthias, smooth as you please, returned my smile. "Schuyler! And Tiffany! This isn't a bad time for you to come by. Not at all," he said. "Come on in."

Matthias was evidently accustomed to seeing his sister with an exploded hairdo and road kill jewelry because he barely gave Tiffany a glance as she went by. His eyes were fixed on me. "Barbi Lundergan and I were just talking," Matthias actually had the nerve to say.

Barbi's reaction to Matthias inviting Tiffany and me in was predictable. Her face fell.

Tiffany's reaction to Matthias's last sentence was also predictable. She hooted. Maybe even louder than she'd hooted back at my house. "Just *talking,* huh?" Tiffany said, going over to Matthias's couch and plopping herself down in the middle of it much as she'd done in my living room earlier.

Matthias's apartment looked fairly typical for bachelor quarters. Wall-to-wall clutter. There were magazines spilling off his battered coffee table, a pair of socks in one corner of his living room, shirts and blue jeans thrown across both chairs. There was also a half-eaten pizza on an end table, and a Coke sitting on the floor next to the couch.

This certainly explained why Matthias had just stepped coolly around the basket of laundry in my own living room. He'd probably just thought that we had the same interior decorator.

Tiffany was still grinning at her big brother. "Don't look now, Matthias, but your *talk* has gotten smeared all over your mouth!"

Matthias immediately touched his hand to his mouth and stared at it, but I didn't pay much attention. My eyes were back on Barbi. As soon as Tiffany spoke, Barbi's chin went up a little. As if she were actually proud that every one in the room seemed to have noticed that *talking* had been the least of what she and Matthias had been doing.

Barbi gave me a tiny, victorious smile. Then, picking up her purse, she started toward the door. "Well," Barbi said, "my goodness, I guess I'd better be running along now."

I was still standing just inside the door. When Barbi got up to me, she waved. "Hi, Schuyler," she said. Passing me, Barbi added, "Bye, Schuyler." At this point, she actually giggled, as if what she'd just said should maybe appear in a skit on *Saturday Night Live*.

I gave her another McSmile.

Matthias was standing in back of me, and when Barbi started to go past him, she drew up short. Leaning close enough to crumple her gingham ruffles, she stared into his eyes.

The green ones. *You* remember.

"Now, you call me," Barbi said. Her asthma was as bad as I'd ever heard it. "I'll be waiting."

Matthias at that particular moment looked as if the thing *he* was waiting for was Barbi to leave. Evidently, so that he could excuse himself and disappear into the bathroom. Because that's what he did the second Barbi was out the door.

When Matthias reappeared, his mouth no longer looked lipstick-red. It looked, instead, scrubbed-raw red.

Strangely enough.

Tiffany, in the meantime, had evidently contracted a bad case of tennis eyes because she couldn't seem to decide which one of us to look at. Me or Matthias. Her eyes darted back and forth between us. While, of course, she continued to pop her gum rhythmically.

That gum-popping was getting on my nerves.

As was the entire Cross family.

And a certain Cross family member, in particular—with green eyes, mind you—who'd been apparently trying to play me for a total fool.

What really frosted my cake was that he'd almost succeeded. If I hadn't come over here and seen Barbi—and, of course, the memento of her visit all over Matthias's mouth—I might still be back home, trying to decide just how much I was truly attracted to him.

Well, now I knew.

Not at all.

In fact, it would be all right with me if I never saw Matthias or his charming family *ever* again.

After, of course, Matthias took care of one tiny, little matter.

Matthias, not surprisingly, seemed every bit as anxious as I to convince his sister that he and I were not—I repeat, *not*—the reincarnated Bonnie and Clyde. Matthias's face noticeably paled when Tiffany showed him the note that she'd found in her father's car. He looked even more alarmed when she blithely explained the conclusions she'd drawn after finding it. "Oh, for God's sake, Tiffany," Matthias burst out, "how could you even *think* such an absurd thing!"

Tiffany, as usual, popped her gum before she answered. "It was easy," she said.

It also appeared to be easy, oddly enough, for Matthias to convince Tiffany that she was mistaken. You could actually get the idea that the girl valued Matthias's word a lot more than she did mine.

Matthias did do a pretty convincing job. The only thing that marred his story was that all the time he was assuring Tiffany that he and I meant nothing whatsoever to each other, his eyes kept traveling over to me worriedly. Just the way a guilty boyfriend's might, if he'd been caught carrying on with another woman.

It was an expression I was all too familiar with. I'd seen it enough times on Ed's face.

"Okay, okay," Tiffany said after Matthias had talked to her for no more than five minutes. "So I was wrong. So I jumped to a few conclusions. So sue me!"

As I said before, what an adorable child.

Apparently, expecting Tiffany to offer an apology for doing something so insignificant as making a murder accusation was too much to hope for.

Matthias may have convinced Tiffany, but ironically, as I listened to him, *I* was beginning to wonder. Maybe

Tiffany had been *almost* right. Maybe, instead of it being Matthias and me, it had been Matthias and *Barbi.*

Maybe Barbi had only been *pretending* to meet Matthias for the first time at Arndoerfer Realty this week. Maybe she knew him quite well. Enough to help him with a little problem.

If Tiffany's version of the argument with his father was accurate, Matthias did have one terrific motive. And, let's face it, Barbi would do anything to latch onto somebody with money. Or somebody who was *going* to have money, once his parents were no longer with us. Maybe it had been Barbi who'd seduced Ephraim Cross, and once she'd gained the older man's trust, lured him to Cherokee Park. Where his own son had shot him.

I felt cold even thinking such a thing.

And yet, Lord, it *could* all fit. Matthias's apartment *was* even closer to Cherokee Park than my own house. *And,* if Barbi had known in advance that her and Cross's relationship was destined to end in murder, Barbi could have given Ephraim Cross an assumed name right from the beginning. An assumed name like, oh, say, *Schuyler Ridgway.*

The name had a certain ring to it.

According to Glassner, whoever Buttercup was, she'd only known Cross a scant three weeks before his death. Barbi could easily have fooled Cross for that short a length of time.

Then, too, Barbi would've had access to my personnel file. Jarvis didn't keep his office files locked up or anything. Barbi could've easily looked up my Social Security number and given it to Cross when he'd asked. She could also have stolen my willpower photo out of my wallet last Friday. And then lied to me about ever seeing it.

My hand went to my throat. There was no getting around it. It could very well be that Matthias and Barbi had planned to implicate me from the start.

Until all this went through my mind, I don't think I had any idea how much I already cared about Matthias. But, sitting there in his cluttered living room, watching him talk to Tiffany, I knew suddenly that I'd been fooling myself. It was not, after all, a matter of my deciding *if* I cared about him. I obviously cared. Because now, suspecting Matthias of all this was almost physically painful. I actually felt sick.

I didn't want to believe any of it, and yet the inescapable fact was, Barbi wasn't smart enough to plan something like this on her own. She would definitely have needed the help of someone like Matthias. Lord, it might even have been *Matthias* himself who'd printed the note that Tiffany had just handed over to him.

"I'm going to give this note you found to the police, Tiffany," Matthias was now saying.

That got my attention. My head went up as I gave Matthias a quick, startled look.

And then, of course, I realized that he had to be lying. All the time he'd been talking to Tiffany, Matthias had been making no effort to handle the note only by its edges. And now, he was actually saying that he intended to hand it over to the authorities?

With his *own* fingerprints on it?

Fat chance.

Matthias was now refolding the note and putting it in the back pocket of his jeans. "Let me handle this from now on, okay?" Matthias told Tiffany. "I don't want you getting involved in something dangerous, understand?"

Matthias was giving a fairly believable performance as the older brother mainly concerned about protecting his young sister. And yet, I wondered. Could Matthias just be protecting himself?

Besides, if Matthias was truly concerned about Tiffany, he'd be rushing her to a new beautician.

And a more conservative jeweler.

I didn't hang around once Matthias finished talking to Tiffany. In fact, if somebody had been clocking us, I'd bet that I would've set the world's record for exiting an apartment building.

People probably haven't left apartment buildings that were on *fire* quite as fast as I left Matthias's.

I said, "Well, thanks, that's all we came by for." And I was out of there.

On the way back, Tiffany said, "It's a good thing we

went over there. Because I believe you two now. I really do. Matthias sure convinced me."

It was when she said it more than once that it began to bother me.

It also bothered me when Tiffany said just as we were pulling into my driveway, "Schuyler, I mean it, you and Matthias don't have to worry anymore. Because I know now that I was way off base."

I just looked at her. Maybe Matthias hadn't done such a good job, after all. Maybe Tiffany had agreed a little too easily. I could be wrong. In fact, I hoped I *was* wrong, but it looked to me as if it were only a matter of time before Tiffany decided to tell somebody about the note she'd found. Somebody like, oh, say, *anybody* who'd listen.

And then, Matthias and I were going to be in big trouble for withholding evidence.

If not worse.

I stood there on my front porch and watched Tiffany pull away in her Trans Am. Actually, what Tiffany did was a little more than just pull away. She left two long strips of black rubber in front of my house as she went from 0 to 60 in about half a second. She also made a screech that brought Mrs. Pettigrew next door and Mrs. Alta across the street out on their front porches.

It was enough to make me feel very glad *I'd* done the driving over to Matthias's.

Going as fast as Tiffany was going on a road as narrow and winding as Harvard is about as stupid as you can get.

I believe, glancing around at the horrified looks on Mrs. Pettigrew's and Mrs. Alta's faces, that my neighbors agreed.

Watching Tiffany careen down Harvard, I probably should've been more worried about her safety. What I was mainly thinking, however, was: *Thank God, there goes the last member of the Cross family I'm going to see today.*

As it turned out, I was being slightly optimistic.

No sooner had Tiffany's black Trans Am disappeared over the roller-coaster dip at the end of Harvard than the Mouse Hilton pulled into my driveway.

As Mrs. Pettigrew and Mrs. Alta openly stared, Matthias got out and walked quickly toward me.

Chapter 20

Matthias started talking before he even got to my porch. "Look, Schuyler, I came over to tell you that I have no intention of giving the police that note Tiffany found. Okay? I just told Tiffany I was going to do that so that she'd hand the note over to me. I didn't want her keeping it. There was no telling who she'd show it to."

Mrs. Pettigrew next door and Mrs. Alta across the street were continuing to stare. Apparently, my life had gotten more interesting than the six o'clock news.

I turned quickly to unlock my front door. "You didn't have to come over here to tell me that," I said. "I already knew you were a *liar*."

I hadn't meant to, but I guess it certainly sounded as if I'd intentionally put a little extra emphasis on that last word.

Matthias winced as if he'd been stung. He evidently decided not to discuss *that* one, however, because he just ran his hand through his shaggy hair and said, "I wanted to make sure that you didn't still think that I considered *you* a suspect in my father's death."

Matthias's voice was fairly low when he said this. I couldn't help but wonder how well his voice carried, though. I also couldn't help but take a quick peek next door. It looked to me as if Mrs. Pettigrew was leaning conspicuously this way. If she'd been a dog, her ears would've been pricked up.

The woman obviously needed a hobby.

I got my front door open, and turned to face Matthias. With Mrs. Alta and Mrs. Pettigrew looking on, this was hardly the time to discuss anything. Besides, how did I

know that Matthias was even telling me the truth? Did
he *really* no longer suspect me? Or was this more of his
"bewitching?" "Okay," I said, doing my best to emulate
Ice Breath, "you told me."

I stood there, my hand on my door, obviously waiting
for him to go.

Maybe it wasn't as obvious as I thought. Matthias
didn't budge. Instead, he said, "I realize now that you
could never do anything like that."

I just looked at him. I only wished I could say the
same of *him*.

Mathias was now taking a deep breath. "I also wanted
to explain about Barbi—"

I started shaking my head the second the words were
out of Matthias's mouth. "Unh-uh. No. You don't have
to explain to *me*. It's really not any of my business."

I had my door open, and was starting to move inside
even as I spoke. I couldn't help but notice that both Mrs.
Pettigrew and Mrs. Alta looked visibly disappointed that
I was moving out of view.

Matthias, however, was moving, too. His hand shot
out to stop me from closing the door right in his face.
For a long moment, we both stood there on either side
of my door, with me trying to push my front door shut,
and Matthias trying to keep it open.

I could almost feel the intensity of Mrs. Alta's and
Mrs. Pettigrew's stares. Lord. I was now not only beating
out the news, but I probably stood a good chance of
outdoing *Hard Copy*.

I gave up on my door, and let Matthias follow me
inside. "Schuyler, come on," he said, "you and I both
know I need to explain." He took a deep breath and
ran his hand through his hair again. "Look, I'm making
it your business, understand?"

Now what do you say to that? If you're as quick-
witted as I am, you just stand there in your foyer, like
maybe you've been struck dumb, and stare.

Matthias started talking fast. "Barbi just showed up
on my doorstep this evening, no phone call or anything.
She said she had some information she wanted to give
me about Dad's death." He shrugged. "As it turned out,

she didn't have anything new to tell me. Once she was inside, she admitted that all she really wanted to do was come over, and get better acquainted."

Really? What a surprise.

"Well, I guess you two were certainly doing *that*—" I began, and then I abruptly stopped. Lord. I sounded just like a jealous wife. And Matthias and I hadn't even gone out on a *date*, for God's sake.

I held up my hand. This was starting to feel too much like a scene I'd played far too many times with Ed. A scene I'd told myself I would never, *never, NEVER* play again. "Wait a minute, Matthias. There's absolutely no reason to tell me all this. You and Barbi have my blessing, okay?"

Matthias winced again. "Schuyler, I'm not interested in Barbi. Not at all."

What exactly was he interested in, then? Her lipstick?

"Right," I said, "and I suppose you're going to tell me that Barbi had suddenly fainted, and you were giving her mouth-to-mouth resuscitation?"

Ed had actually used this one on me once. What's worse, I'd actually believed it at the time. I think if I ever write a book about Ed's and my marriage, that little episode would appear in the chapter entitled, "How Dumb Can You Be When You're Only in Your Twenties."

What would appear in the chapter, "How Dumb Can You Be If Your Name is Ed Ridgway," would be how many times after that Ed actually tried to pull the same scam *again*.

Matthias now looked every bit as angry at *me* as I was at him. "Schuyler, it was Barbi who kissed *me*," he said. "One minute we were just sitting there on my couch, talking, and the next minute, she was all over me. And the minute after *that*, you and Tiffany were knocking at my front door!"

Oh yes, and I'm sure Matthias was beating Barbi off with a stick. Or—remembering the outfit she'd been wearing—a lariat.

At this point, I didn't care if what Matthias was saying was true or not, I just wanted him out of my sight.

"All right, I believe you," I lied. "Is there anything else you wanted to tell me, because it *is* getting late—"

This, of course, was a totally ridiculous thing to say. It had to be all of six-fifteen, tops, but to hear me talk, you'd have thought that any minute now, the local stations would be signing off with the national anthem.

Matthias just looked at me. In the puzzled way you might actually look at somebody who was talking about it being *late* when it was still light outside.

Undaunted, I stared back at him. "Is there anything else—"

For an answer, Matthias kissed me. So quickly that I didn't see it coming, or else I would've ducked.

At least, I think I would've.

Of course, this might be a little hard to believe considering how long I let that kiss go on. And how much, to a casual onlooker, it might've appeared that I was actually enjoying it.

Kissing a bearded man was not at all like kissing a small King Kong. Or a cuddly puppy. Of course, I couldn't speak for *all* bearded men, but kissing Matthias was dizzying. And warm. And wonderful.

Okay. Okay. I admit it. It did take me a little while, but I think what counts is that, after only a few brief moments, I came to my senses.

If I hadn't been so distracted, no doubt, quite a few things would've occurred to me sooner. Things like, for example, while it *was* true that my standards had changed considerably since high school—and that I no longer expected the man in my life to be outrageously handsome like Robert Redford or to have a build comparable to Arnold Schwarzenegger—I did still expect him not to have murdered anybody lately.

Call me picky.

And, hadn't it been less than a half hour ago at Matthias's apartment that I'd actually been wondering if Matthias and Barbi had jointly killed his father? Given that, wasn't it possible that Matthias could just be doing this to convince me once and for all that there was nothing between him and Barbi? What exactly was this kiss supposed to be? Exhibit A in the presentation of his case?

Even if Matthias weren't guilty of murder, what made me think that this kiss wasn't just one more step in the Plan by which he wormed his sneaky way next to me, won my love-starved confidence, and *then* tried to find out enough to turn me in to the police?

At forty-one, I was a little old to make a fool of myself over some man.

Even if he did have green eyes. And could certainly kiss.

Besides, Matthias hadn't exactly offered to give *me* Tiffany's note, had he? Or, for that matter, to give me back my willpower photo.

I put both my hands on his chest and pushed.

"Get out," I said. I would've liked to have said it with a lot more force. As it was, the words came out weak and shaky.

They had the desired effect, though.

Matthias looked as if I'd slapped him. He turned and headed out my front door without a word.

And I, of course, went over, locked the door, and headed straight into my kitchen. Where I got out the biggest glass I could, and filled it to the brim with Coke. Extra-heavy on the ice.

Maybe it was ingesting all that caffeine that made it impossible for me to sleep that night. At two a.m., I was still lying in bed, wide awake, staring at the ceiling.

Of course, it might not have been the caffeine. It might've been all the worries clamoring for attention in my mind.

Let me see. Worry #1 was that if Tiffany mentioned that note to anybody, I could probably count on getting a private tour of Louisville's police station.

And it was probably about as sure as the sun coming up tomorrow that Tiffany couldn't keep something like that quiet for long.

Worry #1 was probably enough all by itself to keep my eyes open for a good part of the night. For the next two hours, I kept turning over, plumping my pillow, and fidgeting with my covers.

Maybe what I should do is just tell Matthias to give the note to the police, and take my chances.

Although, let's face it, my chances didn't look good.

Worry #2 had all the eye-opening power of Worry #1. Worry #2 was, of course, Matthias. Lord, could a man I was attracted to really have killed his own father? Was I that poor a judge of character?

Of course, my marriage to Ed, of bed-hopping fame, was not exactly a testament to my character-judging ability.

Once I had gone over Worry #1 and Worry #2 about a hundred times, I'd say all my worries after that, #3 through #5, started with the letter B. Barbi, buttercups, and birthday presents. Could Barbi really have been an accessory before the fact? Could *she* have been Ephraim's buttercup?

I turned over and plumped my pillow for what had to be the millionth time. What was it again that Ephraim Cross had told Glassner? That his legacy of $107,560 was supposed to be for all the birthday presents he wouldn't be there to buy? Barbi would certainly have appreciated Cross's taste in presents, that was for certain.

I must've tossed and turned all night. Toward morning it occurred to me that $107,560 was really a weird sum of money to leave somebody. I mean, don't people generally leave a nice round number, like a hundred thousand? Or a hundred and *ten* thousand? You might even believe that somebody might leave a bequest of a hundred and *seven* thousand dollars. But a *hundred and seven thousand, five hundred and sixty*?

It *was* strange.

How on earth had Cross come up with such a number? I fell asleep finally, still turning over that question again and again in my mind.

Five hours later, I discovered an amazing thing. That article I'd read in *Psychology Today* about how your subconscious continues to busily work on problems while you're snoring away had been absolute fact.

At six-thirty, when my alarm clock went off, I reached over, shut the alarm off, and started to stretch.

And then it hit me.

And I sat bolt upright in bed.

My God. Was it possible? Could the answer I was looking for really be this simple? If I was right, it would only take a quick check of Arndoerfer Realty's personnel files to find out.

I ran downstairs for a glass of eye-popping Coke, and then I hurried back upstairs to get dressed. I moved as fast as I could because I wanted to make sure that I'd arrive at the office before anybody else and be able to do my checking without anybody looking over my shoulder.

I dressed quickly in a navy blue jacket, navy slacks, and a red silk shell. I may have been in a hurry, but I chose what I was going to wear carefully. My reasoning here might've been a little silly, but I wasn't taking any chances. You know how in every mystery and horror movie you see, the victims always seem to be dressed in white? Or a light color? I suppose they do this so that the bloodstains will show up extremely well on screen. Whatever the reason, today I was determined not to dress like a possible victim. Particularly if there was somebody still out there with a gun. If possible, I'd have worn a red jumpsuit, but I didn't have one.

It took me only ten minutes after I unlocked the Arndoerfer Realty front door to find out that what I suspected was indeed true. By that time I'd only checked two personnel files, but that didn't matter. There it was, in only the second file I looked into. Clearly written in black and white. The birthday—October seventh, nineteen fifty six. 10–7–56. Add a zero, and you had one hundred and seven thousand, five hundred and sixty.

Surely this couldn't be a coincidence.

Could it?

And yet, staring at the name on the personnel folder, I wasn't so sure. Could she really be the right person?

Could *Charlotte Ackersen* really be Buttercup?

I stood there, with that folder in my hand, remembering the way Addison Glassner had spoken of Buttercup's "appetites." Somehow, the idea of meek Charlotte as a wild woman in bed seemed awfully farfetched.

I mean, Charlotte wore Alice in Wonderland dresses,

for God's sake. *And* the last time I checked, femme fatales didn't generally have voices like Minnie Mouse.

Even more farfetched was this little idea: Could a meek, Minnie Mouse-voiced, Alice in Wonderland actually have murdered Ephraim Cross?

For all my doubts, however, I was still a little afraid to just get in my car and blithely head for the address listed on Charlotte's personnel folder without letting somebody know where I was going. I couldn't picture myself as being in any real danger—actually, the thought was just about as unbelievable as the idea of Charlotte being the acrobatic equivalent of a Flying Wallenda in bed—but just in case, I thought I'd give my sons a call.

Just to let them know my last-known whereabouts.

Even thinking to do such a thing made me smile at my own idiocy.

I particularly began to feel like an idiot when Nathan picked up the phone. Sounding as if I'd just awakened him from a deep sleep, he barely let me say hello before he started in. "Mom? Why are you calling so early?" Nathan must not have been all that interested in my answer, because he went right on, "Well, I'm sure glad you called because I've been meaning to call you myself. Listen, is it true what Daniel's been telling me? That you're going to give him ninety dollars for running shoes?"

I was in no mood to discuss shoes at this point. "Nathan," I said, "I called to tell you that—"

For a kid who was sleepy, Nathan could still interrupt pretty fast. "Because it isn't fair, you know. If you spend ninety dollars on Daniel, I think you should spend ninety dollars on me, too."

I couldn't believe it. How old was Nathan now? Twenty? I was fairly certain we'd had a similar conversation when he was five. Only back then it hadn't been about shoes. It had been about a Fisher-Price toy airport that I'd bought Daniel for his birthday. Had I ended up buying Nathan a compensatory present back then? From the way he was talking, it sounded as if I actually might have.

It also sounded as if this could be another episode in

the "How Dumb Can You Be" chapter of my autobiography.

"You don't have to bother actually *buying* me anything, though," Nathan was saying. "Because I don't really need running shoes like Daniel. I'll just take the cash."

I gritted my teeth. I was on my way to meet a possible murderer, and if the worst should happen, I might very well spend my final moments remembering that the last conversation I'd had with my youngest son, he'd been hitting me up for money.

"Nathan," I said. "We'll talk about all this some other time, okay? Right now I want to tell you that—"

"But, Mom, if Daniel gets—"

"Nathan, *shut up* and listen." So much for having a memorable last talk. Now Nathan was going to remember that my last words to *him* had included: *Shut up.*

I took a deep breath, and told Nathan as fast as I could exactly who I was going to see and what her address was.

Nathan was obviously hanging on my every word. "Sure, Mom, I got it, but—"

I started to disconnect right then. But then, just in case the unthinkable *should* happen, I paused. "I love you, Nathan," I said. "I'll talk to you later, hon."

Nathan's final words to me were not exactly the sort of thing that makes for nostalgic reminiscing on Mother's Day.

"You know, Mom, it doesn't necessarily have to be cash. I'd take a check, too."

That kind of sentiment certainly brings a tear to a mother's eye.

Chapter 21

Charlotte Ackersen's house looked a lot like Charlotte herself—trim, neat, unassuming. A frame Cape Cod, painted a noncommittal beige, set on a well-manicured square of lawn, with beige shutters, a beige roof, and a beige front door. If the place were for sale and I were its listing agent, I would've added the words, "Do not curb appraise," to the newspaper ad. In all caps.

I might've also put it on the yard sign.

In a fairly well-to-do subdivision—all its neighbors being in the $100,000 to $125,000 range—the Ackersen home was located in Jeffersontown, a fast-growing suburb of Louisville some twenty minutes from Arndoerfer Realty. Which meant I had some time to think before I got there.

By the time I pulled up in front of Charlotte's home, I'd almost decided not to go in. What I was dealing with here was, after all, a possible *murderer*. A person who killed people. *People* being a group among which I believe I could definitely be included. So, let's face it, it would no doubt be safer just to tell the Bad Cops what I'd found out, and let them take it from there.

If, of course, they put any stock whatsoever in what I had to say. It *would* be a little humiliating to tell them all this, and have them laugh right in my face. Was it possible that it might sound as if I were scraping the bottom of the barrel to clear my name? Lord. Would they think that it had finally come down to my dragging in people's *birthdays,* of all things, as evidence? Or, even worse, would they think that *I* had lied to Ephraim Cross in the first place, giving him Charlotte's birth date instead of mine, in order to divert suspicion right from the start?

Then again, there was always the possibility that Charlotte's birth date really was nothing more than a coincidence. It didn't seem like a very likely coincidence, but that didn't necessarily mean it couldn't be one.

I also really hated to turn over all this information to the police without even so much as giving Charlotte a chance to defend herself. After all, she was supposed to be a friend of mine, wasn't she?

A friend who, let us not forget, might've pointed a gun at a man she was having an affair with and coldly pulled the trigger.

Like I said, by the time I pulled up in front of Charlotte's house, I'd almost decided not to go in, after all. What finally made up my mind was getting a good look into Charlotte's dining room. The chandelier over her dining-room table illuminated everything in the room, and from where I was parked, I could plainly see Charlotte's two children, Donnie and Marie, sitting there at the table, eating their breakfast cereal. Charlotte herself was standing in back of Marie, pouring the little girl a glass of milk.

It was the sort of idyllic scene you see every day on TV commercials. The pretty young mother lovingly attending a towheaded little boy about eight and a chubby-cheeked little girl about six.

I sat there in my car, watching the three of them— and, yes, breathing a sigh of relief. Charlotte Ackersen— a murderer? The idea was absurd. I mean, the woman had named her kids after the *Osmonds,* for God's sake.

I got out of my Tercel, and headed toward the front door. Besides, even if Charlotte *were* guilty, surely, she wouldn't blow me away in front of her kids.

I think the second she opened the door, Charlotte might've had an idea why I'd come. She was already dressed for work, wearing a pale blue jumper and a pale blue paisley blouse, her shoulder-length blond hair neatly pulled back with a pale blue ribbon. She had not yet put on any makeup, though, and at first, I thought maybe that was why she looked so pale.

Until she spoke.

"Why, Schuyler," Charlotte said, "what brings you here so early in the morning?"

Charlotte was obviously trying for a casual tone, but her voice probably wouldn't have shook *that* badly if we'd been in the middle of an earthquake.

Charlotte's face paled even more when I told her what I'd found out. "Can you believe it?" I finished. "The numbers of *your* birth date exactly match the sum of money that was left to me."

I had to hand it to her. Charlotte tried to brazen it out. Opening her blue eyes very wide, Charlotte said, "Why, that *is* an odd coincidence, isn't it? But, Schuyler, that's all it is. It certainly doesn't mean—"

I just looked at her. Would you believe it? Charlotte was actually doing my dumb-and-innocent routine—the one I mentioned earlier that I always do when I'm pulled over for speeding.

I cleared my throat. You should never try to kid a kidder. I was tired of playing games. I had not had a good week. *And,* if this birth date deal really didn't mean anything, as Charlotte insisted, then why did Charlotte sound as if we were in the middle of something that might register a seven or better on the Richter scale? "Come off it, Charlotte," I said. Not at all gently, I might add. "You and I both know *exactly* what it means. Do I need to spell it out for you?"

The only reaction I got to that was a widening of Charlotte's already wide eyes.

"Better still," I added, "do I need to spell it out for the police?"

Charlotte's eyes actually bugged out a little at that one. She gave a hasty glance over her shoulder toward the dining room, stepped aside, and silently motioned me toward her living room.

Charlotte's living room was clearly one of those living rooms that are for viewing purposes only. In fact, this room looked as if perhaps, right up until a few seconds ago, it had been hermetically sealed. I couldn't find so much as a speck of lint marring Charlotte's off-white velvet loveseat, her matching off-white Queen Anne chairs, or her off-white plush carpeting. There were only three magazines—*House Beautiful, Country Living,* and *Vogue*—on top of Charlotte's French Provincial coffee table, and they were all lying exactly parallel to one another, each angled to precisely the same degree. Charlotte's white silk lampshades looked to be dust-free, too, her French Provincial end tables gleamed with polish, and her carpet still showed vacuum cleaner tracks.

I paused in the doorway and stared. This room made you want to trip and spill something. A pizza, maybe.

Charlotte followed me, but only after she'd put her head into the dining room across the way, and said, "Mommy needs to talk to this nice lady for a minute, okay? I'll be right back." After which, she closed the dining-room door behind her. Very firmly.

In the living room, Charlotte did not sit down. She stood directly opposite me, twisting her hands, while she admitted, "All right, Schuyler, I guess I'm going to have to be frank with you—"

Frankness was not quite what I was hoping for. *Spilling her guts* was more what I had in mind. Hoping that Charlotte was making a major understatement here, I tried not to look too eager.

"Yes, Charlotte?" I said coaxingly.

If Charlotte wasn't sitting down, it didn't seem polite for me to. I continued to stand in the middle of that pristine living room, while I listened to what possibly might have been the first real dirt Charlotte had ever allowed into her life.

"I—I *was* having an affair with Ephraim," Charlotte blurted, looking at her feet. Minnie Mouse sounded contrite.

As I mentioned earlier, I had certainly been thinking along these lines, but actually hearing it said aloud was something else again. It was an effort to keep from gasping.

"But I didn't kill him," Charlotte was hurrying on. "You've got to believe me about that—"

Actually, now that Charlotte mentioned it, that was what I preferred to believe. Particularly since she and

I were alone in this room, and I had not frisked her for weapons.

As Charlotte spoke, I did find my eyes wandering to the pockets on her jumper. They looked too small to conceal anything lethal. Not to mention, surely Charlotte didn't make it a habit of carrying around a spare gun while she was pouring Rice Krispies for Donnie and Marie.

Charlotte's voice was still shaking. "There was no reason for me to kill Ephraim. I certainly wasn't in love with him, and I had no intention whatsoever of marrying him—

I just looked at her. Charlotte said this as if it were a point in her favor. Evidently, she might consent to having an affair with a married man, but she drew the line at being a home wrecker.

"Our affair was really nothing more than a series of one-night stands," Charlotte said, waving her hand in the air as if she were discussing something trivial. "It meant nothing. It was, well, just *fun,* that's all. I never had any intention of taking Ephraim away from his wife and family."

Charlotte was getting a little color in her face as she said this. It was a noticeable improvement. This was probably, however, not the sort of beauty tip you'll find in any of those beauty manuals you see all the time in bookstores. Just travel around to your friends and confess a few infidelities—you'll save a fortune on blush. No, that one probably won't appear in print any time soon.

Charlotte was staring at me now, almost defiantly. "You've been divorced, Schuyler—you know how it is. Right after your marriage is over, your ego's shot to pieces, and you need somebody to make you feel good for a while. Ephraim did that for me. We were very, very good friends."

I didn't even blink. From what Glassner had told me, Charlotte and Ephraim had certainly been that. In fact, they'd sounded extremely friendly. *Pals,* you might say.

According to Charlotte, she'd met Ephraim Cross at a Burger King, of all places, after seeing him just once at the Arndoerfer real estate office. "I was just so surprised to see *Ephraim Cross* in a place like that." Charlotte said his name the way a country music fan might say Garth Brooks. "I mean, a man with *his* money, just eating an ordinary hamburger!"

Charlotte must've been under the impression that the rich only eat caviar.

Charlotte was now actually smiling a little, remembering. "And Ephraim was so funny, and so easy to talk to, and so witty. He walked right up to me and said, 'What's a nice girl like you doing in a place like this?'"

Charlotte actually said this as if she thought it was one of the cleverest things she'd ever heard. Once again, I didn't blink. This woman obviously needed to get out more.

"*Naturally,* I'd wanted to go out with him," Charlotte said.

Naturally. With an original approach like that, how could any woman resist?

Charlotte had now returned to staring at her shoes. "You see, Schuyler, other than Leonard, I'd never, ever—um—that is, I'd never—" Charlotte was obviously searching for a good euphemism at this point. It took her a second to come up with a bad one. "I'd—um—never, ever *dated* anyone else. As you know, Leonard and I started going out in high school, and then we got married, and so I'd never, um, ever *dated* any other man. Was it so bad of me to want to *date* somebody else besides Leonard?"

Charlotte put a little extra emphasis on the word *date* every time she said it. I was definitely getting her drift. I could also see her point about Leonard. In fact, the very idea of *dating* Leonard, with his nonstop fidgeting, was enough to give me the willies.

I nodded, and tried to look sympathetic. Charlotte, however, must've mistook my sympathetic look for one of disapproval because she started frowning. Jabbing her finger in my direction, she burst out, "Well, you needn't stand there, looking so sanctimonious, Schuyler!" Minnie Mouse sounded angry now. "I'm sure I haven't done anything *you* haven't!"

Naturally I couldn't help once again recalling Addison Glassner's remark about "appetites." It seemed to me that there was a distinct possibility that I really might not have done some of the things Charlotte had done, but I didn't feel like going into a play-by-play. I just looked at her without saying a word.

"I mean," Charlotte went on, "you've been divorced for *years*, haven't you? You've probably *dated* hundreds of men!"

Wait a second now. If I was reading her euphemisms right, I believe I could assume here that Charlotte was not talking about how many dinner invitations I'd accepted since Ed and I split up. If I didn't know better, in fact, I'd say Charlotte seemed to be implying that my name and phone number were probably written on the walls of every men's locker room in Louisville. And that maybe *I* myself had done the writing. I held up my hand. "Whoa, Charlotte," I said. "Just a minute now. I wouldn't say I've dated hundreds. *And* I certainly wouldn't say that I've dated every man I've gone out with!"

It was at this point, of course, that I mentally played back what I'd just said. And realized I was now making no sense whatsoever.

Charlotte, nevertheless, seemed to get my meaning. She shrugged. "Anyway," she said, "I knew dating Ephraim was going to be tricky."

I didn't say a word, I didn't even crack a smile.

"I was afraid Leonard would find out all about it, and since Leonard has reminded me over and over that we're only *separated*—that, technically, we're still married— well, I didn't want Leonard calling me awful names in court and maybe, getting custody of the kids—" Charlotte took a deep breath at this point, and then said the rest very quickly. "—so, *of course,* I couldn't tell Ephraim my real name."

Of course.

I just stared at her. Deadpan. Okay, Charlotte, don't help me now, let me *guess* whose name you used.

"So-o-o," I said evenly, "you told Ephraim Cross that your name was Schuyler Ridgway."

What a great idea. My goodness, that did solve everything, didn't it? I must not have looked as if I were all that admiring of her ingenuity because Charlotte began to talk faster than ever. "I—I didn't have a choice, Schuyler! I didn't!" Evidently, after Charlotte had blithely told Ephraim Cross that she was *me,* she'd continued the pretense every time Cross had asked for more details. Supplying him, of course, with information she'd gleaned from *my* personnel file. She'd given him my Social Security number, my address—

"In fact," Charlotte said, "the *only* thing I told Ephraim that was the truth about me was my own birth date." Here Charlotte looked straight at me, her blue eyes as guileless as a child's. "I guess you already know why. Because Ephraim certainly wouldn't ever *believe* that I was as old as you!"

That did it. While it *was* true that Charlotte was somewhat younger than me, she was making it sound as if I should have a walker. This, from the woman who'd been carrying on with a guy in his *sixties,* for Pete's sake. I took a deep breath. "Look, Charlotte," I said, my tone irritated. "Didn't it occur to you that all this could possibly cause me a few problems?"

Charlotte's Minnie Mouse voice got even higher. "It shouldn't have caused you any problems at all!" Charlotte's tone implied that none of this was her fault. "Schuyler, I'm not dumb, you know. I knew from the start that I wouldn't be able to fool Ephraim forever. He was bound to find out the truth sooner or later. But, well, I thought by the time he found out, my divorce would be final. And then it wouldn't matter."

Apparently, Charlotte had not planned on Cross being final first.

Charlotte was now practically glaring at me. "It was the only way, Schuyler. Like I said, I really didn't have a choice!"

I shifted my weight from one foot to the other, trying to control my anger. Wait a second now. Hold the phone. It appeared to me that there *had* been an alternative that Charlotte had overlooked. A fairly simple alternative at that. How about putting off having the affair until *after* the divorce? Charlotte was acting as if Ephraim Cross had made her a limited time offer that she'd had to accept immediately, or else lose out forever. What did she think—that he was going out of business?

Somehow, I suspected that Cross would've made good on his offer just about any time Charlotte wanted to take him up on it.

"Everything would've been fine if he hadn't died!" Charlotte now burst out.

That one brought me up short. I stared back at her and thought sarcastic thoughts. Like, how *inconsiderate* of Cross to let himself get murdered like that. How *rude*. What poor *planning*. But that was before I noticed the tears shining in Charlotte's eyes.

"I—I never thought that Ephraim would end up—that he'd be—" Charlotte evidently couldn't bring herself to say it.

It was hard to believe that a woman who couldn't even *voice* the words aloud could have actually done the deed. The way I saw it, Charlotte was looking more and more innocent. Either that, or there were some Academy Award winners Charlotte could give lessons to.

I cleared my throat. "I don't suppose, once Ephraim was found dead, that 'you even considered coming forward?"

I knew, of course, it was a stupid question.

Charlotte looked at me as if she thought the question was moronic. She began to pace her words, as if going over the whole thing very, very slowly would make dull-witted me understand.

According to Charlotte, the day she found out that Ephraim had been murdered, she'd panicked. Particularly after reading in the *Courier* about the flower that had been left in his car. It was obvious that the police were going to want to talk to the woman who'd been Ephraim's buttercup. "So," Charlotte said, her Minnie Mouse voice now almost a whine, "I had to think of *something*."

The *something* she came up with was, in actuality, quite a few things. Things like, planting Cross's note in my car last Friday and absconding with my willpower photo. And over the weekend, using the duplicate key to Cross's office that Cross had given her, to go in and plant my photo in the top drawer of Cross's desk where Matthias would find it.

I let Charlotte go on without interrupting, but inwardly, I was fuming, just listening to her tell about it.

Charlotte must've picked up on how heavy my breathing had become—or maybe the way my eyes had narrowed—because she speeded up again. "I'm really sorry, Schuyler. I really am. But I couldn't let Leonard take my babies away!"

On Tuesday when she'd found out that I had been left $107,560, Charlotte had known immediately, of course, that the money was really hers. "I also knew that if I tried to claim it, Leonard would begin custody proceedings. I knew it! So my only choice was to keep everybody believing that *you* were the one who'd been involved with Ephraim."

"Charlotte, they don't just think I was involved with him. They think *I* killed him."

Charlotte shrugged as if what I'd just said was ridiculous. "Nonsense. *I* didn't kill him, so why would anybody think *you* did? Oh sure, I knew the police would want to *talk* to you, but they couldn't possibly really suspect you, not—"

I interrupted her. "Believe me, Charlotte, the police really do think I could've killed Ephraim. In fact, a *lot* of people think it. The police, Ephraim's family, his attorney—" Here I got even angrier as something else occurred to me. "Why do you think somebody took a shot at me? Don't you think it could possibly mean that somebody thinks Ephraim Cross's buttercup actually *murdered* him? And that, whoever this particular somebody is, he's not in all that great a mood about it?"

Charlotte blinked. "But, Schuyler, how could anybody believe such a thing? I didn't love Ephraim, I wasn't going to marry him, and Ephraim had never even told me that he was leaving me anything in his will," Charlotte said. "So I didn't even have a motive!"

I just stared at her. Charlotte certainly sounded as if she were telling the truth. And yet, Flossy Fenwick and

Glassner had both insisted that Ephraim Cross had told them that he'd made his intentions clear to his girlfriend. Was it possible Cross had just said that to shut everybody up? Because, from what Glassner had said, Glassner *had* been trying to talk Cross out of leaving his buttercup the money. Could Cross have simply lied about already having told his girlfriend about the bequest just to make it sound as if it were already a done deal? So Glassner would get off his back and let him do what he wanted to do?

I wondered.

I also wondered if Charlotte was telling the whopper of her life.

Charlotte had begun to pace across her impeccable carpet, leaving soft footprints in its virgin surface. "I mean," she said, "who would've ever believed that Ephraim wasn't lying to me!"

I stayed right where I was. "Excuse me?"

Charlotte turned to face me. "I'm *not* some naive schoolgirl, Schuyler," she said, hands on her hips.

I didn't blink this time either.

"I *know* how men are," Charlotte said. "Sure, I may not have known a lot of men in my life, but I've watched *Days of Our Lives*, you know."

Oh yes. I'd say *that* particular show was certainly an accurate representation of real life. My goodness, yes, watching *Days of Our Lives* was practically just like reading the *newspaper*.

"I'd heard all the rumors about Ephraim and his women," Charlotte went on. "Who would've ever thought that all the times he told me he loved me, he was actually telling me the truth? I mean, Ephraim *was* supposed to be this big womanizer, wasn't he?" Charlotte took a deep breath. "*Naturally*, I thought Ephraim considered our affair as lightly as I did."

Naturally.

Charlotte started pacing again. "I find it hard to believe even now. Although I'm *sure* Ephraim would've changed his tune, don't you think, when he found out that I had two children? Ephraim couldn't possibly have been the *least* bit interested in me once he found out that he would've been expected to be a stepfather to two kids. I'm *sure* of that, all right. I really am."

I couldn't decide, listening to her, if Charlotte really *was* sure, or if she was just trying to convince herself so that her loss wouldn't be so painful.

The sad fact was, nobody knew just how much Ephraim Cross truly had loved Charlotte. Or how he would've reacted to finding out about her children. And now, nobody would ever know.

The whole thing made me feel sad—and tired. I was particularly getting tired of standing by this time. To hell with it, furniture was made for sitting, wasn't it? I went over and sat down in the middle of Charlotte's off-white loveseat.

Charlotte was blinking back tears and starting now to recall, in a halting voice, what had happened the day Ephraim had died. I don't think she even noticed that I was no longer on my feet.

According to Charlotte, she and Ephraim had fallen into a pattern of meeting on Wednesdays and Fridays. So, on the Wednesday Cross died, she'd come home from the office expecting to have a message on her answering machine, setting up a place to meet.

"At first," Charlotte said, "I'd sent little notes to his office, arranging a meeting place—"

I just looked at her. One of the messages that Charlotte had sent must've been the one that Tiffany found in her father's car.

"—but later I'd started waiting for Ephraim to call me." Charlotte sighed here, and glanced my way. "I didn't want it to look like I was chasing him, you know."

My own eyes widened at that. The woman actually sounded as if she might still be back in high school.

Charlotte paused, taking deep shaky breaths. For a second, I was afraid she was going to break down and cry on me. Charlotte may not have loved Ephraim Cross, but clearly, she *had* cared about him.

"Go on, Charlotte," I said gently.

Stopping every once in a while to take more deep breaths, Charlotte eventually managed to get out that, fearing that someone might recognize Ephraim's voice, she'd asked Ephraim not to call her at the office, but just to leave a message on her answering machine at her home. Ephraim's messages had always been something like: Buttercup, meet me tonight at such and such place and at such and such time. I can't wait to see you, darling." Charlotte sighed again. "Ephraim was always *so* romantic. He was always speaking French—"

I didn't even blink. Like, for example, raison d'être, that sort of thing?

"—and he was always bringing me flowers—"

I bet I could guess what kind.

"—and he was always writing me little love notes."

Such as the one she'd hidden in my glove compartment, by any chance?

"He was the sweetest man," Charlotte went on. "Ephraim always made me feel as if I were the most important woman in his life."

I cleared my throat. Charlotte probably *was*. If, of course, you didn't count his wife and daughter.

Last Wednesday, however, there had been no message when Charlotte got home from work. Nothing. And the very next morning, she'd read in the paper about his death.

Charlotte had stopped pacing and was now standing motionless on the other side of the coffee table, directly across from me. "Ephraim and I had met more than once in Cherokee Park, but Schuyler, I can't understand how *anybody* could've known about our meeting place."

I just stared at her. From what she'd just told me, I could make a guess.

I shifted position uneasily on Charlotte's couch, no doubt putting the very first wrinkles in its off-white surface. "Tell me, Charlotte, is this answering machine of yours the kind where you can get your message remotely, by calling your own phone number and dialing a code?"

Charlotte nodded, her eyes getting very round.

"By any chance, does it erase messages the same way?"

As Charlotte nodded again, I decided it would probably be a terrific idea for her and me to go take a quick look at her machine.

Kept on the nightstand beside her bed, Charlotte's answering machine turned out to be—just as I suspected—similar to the one I myself had at home. Just like mine, the security code was printed just under the lid.

So that all anyone had to do was lift the thing to read it.

I stood there, next to Charlotte's neatly made bed, and stared at that code.

My mouth was starting to get very dry.

Chapter 22

Charlotte's bedroom was almost as pristine as her living room, with eyelet curtains and a lace-trimmed coverlet as white as those you see in detergent commercials. I barely gave the room a glance, though. All my attention was focused on the three-digit security code printed just under the lid of her answering machine. It was four-eight-eight.

Not exactly a difficult number to remember. Once you got a look at it.

Ephraim Cross's murderer, then, could have easily called up Charlotte's machine, listened to Charlotte's message from Ephraim that Wednesday, telling her to, no doubt, meet him in Cherokee Park. And then the murderer could've erased the message. All from a phone miles away.

Which, of course, brought yet another question to mind. "Charlotte, who's visited you since you've had this thing?"

Charlotte looked at me as if I'd asked her to recite the phone book. "Schuyler, I've had this answering machine for a little over five months now. So it's kind of difficult to remember every single person who's come by."

I wasn't about to be put off. "Charlotte, you've stolen my name, my Social Security number, a picture out of my wallet, and God knows what else. Why don't you *try* as hard as you can to remember? For *me*?"

I had meant that to sound as if I were just making a suggestion, nothing more, but like I said before, I'd had a bad week. It was entirely possible I could've sounded more threatening than I intended.

Charlotte blinked and took a step away from me.

"Um, I do remember that Jarvis came by once," she said, "to pick up a Multiple Listing book that I'd taken home by mistake."

Well, well. *This* was interesting. "Jarvis came in here?"

"Into my bedroom? My goodness, no!" Charlotte sounded appalled.

I had to agree with her. The idea of Jarvis in your bedroom *was* an appalling thought. I sat down.

"Jarvis certainly didn't come in *here*." Charlotte hurried on. She frowned, obviously thinking back, and added, "In fact, as I recall, Jarvis never went into any room other than the dining room. I'd left the Multiple Listing book out on the table in there, so I just got it for him, and Jarvis was on his way."

"Then Jarvis was never out of your sight?"

Charlotte shook her head, her Alice in Wonderland hair whispering across her shoulders. "*Never,*" she said.

If Charlotte was remembering correctly, that would certainly seem to eliminate Jarvis as a suspect.

"Come to think of it," Charlotte was now saying. "*Barbi* also came by a couple times, to borrow jewelry and return it." Charlotte indicated the jewelry box sitting on the dresser across from her bed.

"Was she ever in here alone?"

Charlotte nodded. "She could've been. I mean, I might've had to leave to get something for the kids. It would only have been for a second, though."

A second would've been all Barbi needed.

I tried not to react. I just sat there on that virgin couch, unmoving, as if maybe what Charlotte was telling me was nothing more than a plot to a movie she'd seen. Not real. Not people I knew.

Yet, listening to her, I was starting to feel a little sick.

Barbi could've looked at the code, and given it to Matthias. And, together, they could've checked Charlotte's messages.

I had to swallow once before I trusted my voice enough to ask, "How about Leonard?" I was thinking, of course, that Charlotte's husband could also have read the code. Moreover, if he'd actually listened to any of those messages, he would, no doubt, have instantly acquired a terrific motive for killing Cross.

Charlotte, however, sounded even more shocked than
she'd sounded about Jarvis. "Oh, my God, no! Leonard
has never been inside this house for a second when I
wasn't with him. And he certainly has *not* set foot in my
bedroom since our separation."

Charlotte sounded aghast that I would even think such
a thing. Apparently, Charlotte might admit that she'd
been sleeping with another woman's husband, but the
very idea that she might have also slept with her own
was revolting.

Charlotte was still shaking her blond head. "Leonard
only comes and picks up the kids, that's *all*."

I just stared at Charlotte for a long moment.

Once you eliminated Jarvis and Leonard, that left only
the Barbi/Matthias team.

My mouth had gotten unbelievably dry. What I
needed was a Coke. Bad. It would, however, probably
be bad form at this point to ask Charlotte if she had any.

Her last statement apparently reminded her of something. Checking her watch, Charlotte said, "Oh dear.
Um, Schuyler? Leonard is due any minute now to pick
up the kids. He's taken a day off work to take them to
the zoo." Here Charlotte blinked a couple of times, took
a deep breath, and said very fast, "You're, um, not going
to mention any of this to him, are you?" Minnie Mouse
sounded as if, once again, she were in the middle of
an earthquake.

I took a breath as deep as the one she'd taken. I was
not going to lie to her. "Charlotte, I'm not going to
mention any of this to Leonard," I said. "I am, however,
going to tell everything I know to the police."

Charlotte, I would say, did not take that little bit of
news well. "No-o-o!" she wailed. "You can't! I'll lose
my kids! For God's sake, Schuyler, I thought that if I
just explained everything to you, you'd understand.
Come on, Schuyler, you *can't*—"

I was on my feet by then. Staring at her in disbelief,
of course. Had Charlotte actually thought that all she
had to do was tell me what she'd told me, and I would

just go away? Did she really think it was going to be that simple?

I took another deep breath and interrupted her. "Charlotte, listen to me, you won't lose your kids. They don't take custody away from a mother these days just because she starts dating some guy while she's separated—"

"Are you *kidding*?" Charlotte said. "It happens all the time on *Days of Our Lives,* and *The Young and the Restless,* and—and—"

I had turned and started to head toward her front door, but when Charlotte began naming off *soap operas* of all things, I stopped and wheeled around to face her.

It seemed pointless to start explaining the difference between TV-life and real-life. Instead I said, "Charlotte, I mean it. *Listen* to me." My voice was very calm. In fact, I do believe I was demonstrating vast quantities of patience here. "A man is *dead*. Understand? And a *murderer* is walking around loose. Have you got that? We have to tell the police what we know, or else they might never catch whoever did this!"

I did not add—Oh, yes, and there's every possibility that the police just might end up catching *me*—but I thought it, all right.

I turned then and had taken a couple more steps toward her front door when Charlotte caught up with me. "Schuyler, *please,* can't you just keep my name out of this?"

I shook my head. And—no doubt, it was heartless of me—I said the first thing that came to my mind. "Couldn't you just have kept *my* name out of this?"

I fully intended to head for the police station right that minute, but one small thing made me come to an abrupt halt on Charlotte's front porch.

The Mouse Hilton was pulling up right behind my Tercel.

My heart started doing a drum solo.

At that moment I believe I can say with certainty that my heart was pounding just from fear alone. And not from anything else.

I would've walked right by Matthias and gotten into

my car, without even speaking to him, except that he grabbed my arm. "Schuyler," he said, "I tried to get in touch with you at your home *and* at your office, and I finally ended up calling your sons to find out where you were." His grip tightened on my arm. "Look—I don't care what you say—after last night, we *need* to talk."

I shook off his hand. "No, we don't."

Charlotte was standing on her porch, watching us. I think she might've followed me out to my car, still begging me to keep my mouth shut, except that she didn't want to say such things in front of Matthias.

Matthias's eyes had now traveled to Charlotte. "Will you at least tell me what you just found out from *her*?"

I thought my answer to that was succinct. "Nope," I said.

Matthias grabbed my arm again, his eyes deepening to an emerald green. Was it anger that made his eyes darken that way? "Schuyler, listen to me—"

Did Matthias's voice now actually sound threatening?

I stared at him, feeling suddenly chilled, just as Leonard Ackersen pulled his Camry into Charlotte's driveway.

I've seen long-lost relatives finally reunited on *Unsolved Mysteries* greet each other with a lot less enthusiasm than I greeted Leonard. "Leonard!" I said. "How great to see you again!"

Leonard was definitely *not* looking at me as if I were a long-lost relative. He was looking at me as if I were a mental case. "Uh, hi," he said uncertainly, giving Matthias an uneasy glance.

I took Leonard's arm. This was a little difficult to do since the second he got out of his car, Leonard had, of course, started fidgeting like he always does, pulling at his cuffs, smoothing his shirtfront, and running his hand through his hair, all in a whirl of motion. I was determined, though. I grabbed an elbow and hung on. "You know," I said brightly, "I think I'll go back inside with you, okay?" I gave him an insincere smile. "I was just talking to Charlotte, and I believe I forgot to ask her something."

Something on the order of, say, how quickly can you call the police?

Leonard was giving me the kind of look you'd give somebody wearing their underwear on the outside of their clothes, but he continued to let me hold onto his arm as we headed toward the house. I think my weight slowed him down some, too, because on the way, he didn't fidget once.

Once Leonard and I started moving, I told Matthias over my shoulder, "I'll call you later, okay?"

Matthias didn't even blink. He also didn't leave. He just stepped in behind me and Leonard, and followed us, saying, "Well, actually, Schuyler, I'll just wait, okay? I'd really like to talk to you as soon as you finish up here—"

I gave him a weak smile. Getting rid of Matthias was going to be harder than I thought. Did he suspect something? Did he somehow sense that what I fully intended to finish was an extended conversation with the cops?

Inside, both of the Ackersen kids had evidently finished their Rice Krispies and from the splashing sounds coming from the top of the stairs, they'd gone up to the bathroom to wash their hands and get ready to leave with their father.

I stood for a long moment at the bottom of the stairs, scrambling around in my mind for something to ask Charlotte. "Uh, Charlotte, I came back inside to ask you something that I meant to ask you before, but, uh—"

Charlotte, no doubt, thought she was helping me out. She glanced at both men uncertainly, ran her hand nervously through her blond hair, and said, "Was it, um, something about the answering machine?"

Leonard, at that moment, did a noticeable intake of breath. "What about the answering machine?" he asked. Amazingly enough, he did not fidget this time either, as he asked the question.

I stared at him. On the upside, Leonard was no longer looking at me as if I were a nut. On the downside, however, he was now looking at me as if I might be something to be squashed on the bottom of his shoe.

Even Leonard's ears looked angry.

Charlotte must've seen this look on Leonard's face

before. Her already wide eyes managed to enlarge about three times their normal size, and she actually began to babble. "Oh, um, Leonard, it's nothing, really. Schuyler and I were, um, just talking about how my answering machine worked. That's all."

Leonard's face went a little paler than Charlotte's. His eyes narrowed to slits, as he continued to stare at me. I returned his stare, remembering now, a tiny bit too late, something that Charlotte had told me months ago.

It had been *Leonard* who'd given the answering machine to Charlotte in the first place.

Oh God.

Had I just been walking arm in arm with a murderer?

It stood to reason that, possessive husband that he was, in all likelihood, Leonard would've memorized the security code *before* he gave the machine to Charlotte. In fact, this was probably why old Leonard had suddenly gotten so generous and outfitted Charlotte's office in the first place. He couldn't have just given her the machine all by itself. Charlotte might've caught on that he was only giving it to her to keep track of her. And to find out if she was seeing anybody else.

Standing there, still listening to Donnie and Marie brushing their teeth a floor away, I remembered something else. Just before Matthias and I were shot at, we'd talked to Leonard and told him that we were investigating the murder.

My heart sounded like a drum *quartet* now. Leonard had had plenty of time that afternoon. After he'd taken Charlotte to get her driver's license renewed—and had taken her home—he could easily have returned to try to scare the living daylights out of Matthias and me.

Or—maybe he hadn't been just trying to scare us. Maybe old Leonard here was just a lousy shot. Maybe he'd really been trying to kill us both.

The drum quartet was doing it up big as Leonard reached into his suit coat pocket and pulled out a gun. "You've figured it out, haven't you?" he said.

For a man with too much nervous energy, Leonard held that gun amazingly steady.

I shrugged my shoulders. "Well, no," I said, "I really haven't thought much more about anything—"

At that moment, Matthias apparently didn't put a whole lot of thought into what he was doing, either. He lunged for Leonard's gun.

And Leonard shot him.

Matthias might've screamed as he went down, grabbing his leg, but if he did, I didn't hear him. It was completely drowned out by all the screaming Charlotte and I were doing at the exact same time.

It was also drowned out by Charlotte and Leonard's son screaming at the top of the stairs.

Little Donnie might have a career ahead of him just like that of his namesake. The kid had quite a set of lungs for an eight-year-old.

Leonard's head jerked in his son's direction, and when he did, I brought my extremely expensive Dooney & Bourke purse—the one, I believe, that I've already mentioned has made me so paranoid, I never put it down—crashing down on his wrist.

It was the first time in my life I'd ever been glad that I carry so much makeup around with me. That purse had to weigh at least twenty pounds.

It was also the first time I'd ever felt that maybe what I'd spent for that Dooney & Bourke had been totally worth it.

When my purse connected with Leonard's wrist, his gun hit the hardwood floor with a thunk and slid into the dining room under a chair.

And then, Charlotte and Leonard and I all went for it.

I believe I could've beaten out Leonard. The gun had landed farther away from him than from me.

Charlotte, however, was another story. She'd been standing several inches closer to the dining room door when I'd Dooney & Bourke'd Leonard's wrist.

This was, obviously, why Charlotte beat me to the gun. I really don't think it had anything whatsoever to do with her being younger than me.

When Charlotte picked up the revolver, the drum quartet began to sound in my chest all over again.

Chapter 23

For a crazy moment, right after Charlotte grabbed the gun, it was as if we'd all been playing Frozen Catchers, and Charlotte had just caught Leonard and me. Up until then, Leonard and I had both been on our hands and knees, scrambling toward the gun. Once the gun was in Charlotte's hands, though, we stopped in midaction right where we were. Motionless, Leonard and I stared at Charlotte as she got to her feet and turned to face us.

Matthias was staring at Charlotte, too, but he was not playing by the rules. In fact, poor Matthias was far from frozen. He was writhing on the floor, holding his leg. It made my stomach wrench to look at him.

"Charlotte—" I began. I was going to point out to her that Matthias needed help—and that he needed help *quickly*—but Leonard drowned me out.

"Charlotte!" Leonard shouted. "Give me that gun! *NOW!"* The man was apparently accustomed to telling Charlotte what to do. Leonard didn't even seem to question whether or not Charlotte would obey him. Would you believe, he was actually *smiling* as he put his hand out for the weapon.

Charlotte, for her part, looked dazed. She stared first at Leonard, then at me, and finally at the gun in her hand, as if almost surprised to find it there.

Slowly, her hand began to move.

In Leonard's direction.

Oh, God. Was she just going to hand it over to him? "Charlotte, *NO!"* I said. "For God's sake—"

That was about all I had time to say before Leonard jumped to his feet, yelling, "Shut up, *BITCH!"*

Leonard's eyes were focused on the gun in Charlotte's

hand, but there was no question that Leonard's comments were clearly directed at me. From Charlotte's reaction, though, you might've thought he'd yelled at *her*. She gave a little shudder, and her mouth went very white.

Leonard took a quick step toward Charlotte, his hand still extended. "Charlotte!" As he spoke, Leonard bounced nervously on the balls of his feet. I swallowed, watching him. Was he getting ready to make a grab for the gun?

Leonard was still bouncing. "Charlotte, I mean it—" Leonard's voice shook with fury. "—give me the damn gun *THIS MINUTE*!"

Charlotte blinked.

Then she took a quick step of her own. A step backward. Raising the gun, she pointed it steadily at her husband's chest.

"Leonard," Charlotte said, "*SHUT UP.*"

Minnie Mouse sounded very irritated.

Leonard's eyes got very round.

And me, I took what felt like the first breath I'd taken since Charlotte had picked up the gun.

I was starting to get to my feet, and feeling a vast wave of relief, when I got a good look at Charlotte's eyes.

Uh-oh.

That wave of relief might've been a little premature.

There on the floor, staring up at her, I could almost see what Charlotte was thinking. Holding that gun on her husband, she was remembering what Leonard had done to Ephraim Cross.

The man who'd loved her.

"Uh, Charlotte—" I said. I made my voice sound as casual as I could, given the circumstances. "Charlotte, now, you don't want to do anything you'd regret—"

I'm not sure Charlotte even heard me.

Almost immediately, however, she did seem to hear something else.

All the noise still being generated at the top of the stairs.

Her son, Donnie, was now not only demonstrating re-

markable lung capacity but a truly talented ability to
hold a note. Little Marie had joined her brother in the
chorus: "Mommy! Mommy! *MOMMMM-MEEEEE!*"

Charlotte blinked again, took a firmer grip on the gun,
and then drew a long, tremulous breath. "It's okay,
kids!" she yelled. "Just stay right where you are. Everything's fine! I'll be up there in a little while!"

I took another long breath myself. I'd been right.
Charlotte was not going to shoot anybody in front of
her kids.

Especially not their own father.

Even though he richly deserved it.

Charlotte was now looking straight at me. "Call the
police, Schuyler," she said. "And call an ambulance,
too. Quick!"

Which just goes to show you. Give a meek woman a
loaded gun, and it gives her a world of self-confidence.

Charlotte once again demonstrated her newfound self-
confidence when the ambulance arrived for Matthias. By
that time, I was on my knees by his side. Matthias was
going in and out of consciousness, and I was holding a
towel I'd gotten out of the kitchen against Matthias's
leg, trying to stop the bleeding. Seeing all that blood had
all but rendered *me* mute—and not a little dizzy—but
Charlotte was amazing. She actually started yelling at
the paramedics the second they pulled up outside.

"Hey! Hurry up, for crying out loud!" she shouted.
"A man's been shot in here! *Move!*" The police had not
yet arrived, so Charlotte yelled this, all the while she
was still holding the gun on Leonard.

Don't ever let anybody tell you that Minnie Mouse
was not a hell of a woman.

Of course, I imagine it's helped Charlotte's confidence
level quite a bit just to have Leonard out of her life.
Leonard, no surprise, is spending his time these days
behind bars.

Matthias, on the other hand, is spending his time these
days in the hospital. According to the doctors, the bullet
went right through the thigh muscle of his left leg, On
the way the bullet didn't do any permanent damage, but
Matthias is going to be immobile for a while.

Which is not altogether a bad thing. It's giving us a lot of time to talk. And to get better acquainted.

While Matthias and I are getting better acquainted, Charlotte actually seems to be getting more and more assertive. It's been three weeks since all this happened, and yesterday, when a client started yelling at her over the phone because his mortgage hadn't been approved, Charlotte actually yelled back. "Look, Buster," she said, "it's not *my* fault you can't afford the house you want!"

And she hung up on him.

Charlotte's also gotten a lot more open about hers and Leonard's relationship. Far from being the loving husband he purported to be, Leonard was evidently so jealous and possessive, he rarely let poor Charlotte out of his sight the entire time they were married.

While he wasn't exactly physically abusive, Leonard *was* emotionally abusive, beating Charlotte down until she felt as if she could never possibly fend for herself. Having moved from her parents' home to Leonard's home without ever holding more than a summer job, Charlotte had never learned any better. In fact, all her life she'd had somebody else taking care of her.

I realize now that it had taken real courage for Charlotte to finally leave Leonard. Because even after she left—from what she now tells me—she was always wondering if she could go it alone. It didn't help to have old Leonard undermining every independent step Charlotte took. Even his driving her all over town had been one more way he was showing her that she really wasn't capable of ever being independent. "Hell," Charlotte told me just yesterday, "if I couldn't even be trusted to drive myself somewhere, how the hell did I ever think I could make a living for myself and Donnie and Marie?"

Oh yes. Charlotte says "hell" and sometimes, even "damn" these days. She's getting to be a wild woman.

Of course, I guess Ephraim Cross, God rest his soul, had already found *that* out.

Today, with Leonard in jail, Charlotte seems to be finding out just exactly how strong she really is. She also seems to be realizing how much her children need her now. Although Donnie and Marie seem to be doing better than anybody could've guessed. I don't think it was any accident that the only person those two ever yelled for that day was "Mommy!" According to Charlotte, Leonard had always been too busy being in charge to have time to be a loving parent. So far, the children, if anything, actually seem happier without Leonard in the picture.

Then again, I guess it also helps Charlotte to have a spare $100,000 or so to ease her financial problems. Charlotte and I have reached an agreement on this. Even though I knew very well that I shouldn't get any of the money—Cross definitely didn't leave it to *me*— Charlotte insisted on giving me the equivalent of my real estate commission—7 percent. I guess you'd call it hazard pay.

What could I say? Except, Thanks so much, I'll take it.

Having listened to Charlotte's story, I also came up with a few things of my own to say to Daniel and Nathan. Maybe it's very true that if you always have somebody taking care of you, you'll always remain a child. Right after Charlotte started telling me about hers and Leonard's marriage, I told Daniel and Nathan that I could not be counted on any longer to do any more bailing out of their boat. In fact, I flatly refused to give them any more money for groceries, or running shoes, or anything else.

Their wails could probably be heard as far away as Tennessee.

I guess you could say I've just enrolled my sons in the School of Hard Knocks. I'm certainly hoping they graduate.

I've also been doing a little hoping about something else.

Me and Matthias.

I've been spending quite a bit of my spare time visiting him. Of course, I try to time my visits to those hours when his mother isn't dropping by.

Particularly after what happened that first week.

I'd arrived at the hospital to visit Matthias, and as it turned out, Harriet was getting off the elevator just as I was getting on. Judging from the look she gave me, and from the way she stiffened all over, I believe the woman was not a bit moved by the concern I was showing for her son.

As a matter of fact, Harriet first coldly stared at me and then at the balloons I was holding—I'd brought a dozen multicolored helium balloons that all said "Get Well Soon!" Harriet moved on to coldly stare at the brightly wrapped package I was carrying—I'd bought Matthias some books and magazines to read. And then, after that, Harriet's eyes didn't do any more staring. Mainly because her eyes had become very tiny slits.

I tried to ignore all of the above. While the lines between Harriet's eyebrows and at the corners of her mouth deepened into caverns, I gave her as bright a smile as I could muster. "Why, Mrs. Cross, how nice to see you again," I lied.

Harriet didn't say a word. In fact, she swept past me without so much as a nod in my direction.

I believe I could assume that if Harriet had a pin, my balloons would've been history.

Harriet, evidently, is *still* unconvinced that I was not the one having an affair with her late husband. Can you believe that? Harriet appears to have me confused with that woman Glenn Close played in *Fatal Attraction*.

I guess, once you get an idea in your mind, it's hard to let go.

Although Matthias, unlike his mom, seems very eager to let go of one of his. Over these last three weeks, he's told me several times, looking at me tenderly, "You know, Schuyler, I never really suspected you for a second."

So far, I've resisted the impulse to remind him what his first words to me were.

Besides, I'm telling him the same thing. How I never suspected him, either. Not for a second. Not for a millisecond.

I think we both know we're lying.

I also think we both know that something special is happening between us.

These days when I'm not visiting Matthias, and when I'm not working, I'm once again exercising to my Jane

Fonda tape. While Jane puts me through my paces, however, I'm not thinking of ways to bump her off anymore. I've decided that murder is too awful a thing even to joke around about.

No, what I'm thinking about, while I twist and turn and bounce sweatily to Jane's barked instructions, is something entirely different.

The doctors have said that Matthias won't be released from the hospital for at least another two weeks, and even after that, he's going to have to undergo some physical therapy. The way I see it, that should give me enough time to drop ten pounds.

So that, just in case Matthias and I do end up *dating*—in, I'm shameless to say, *every* sense of the word—I will look exactly like I do in my willpower photo. Which, incidentally, Matthias has never returned.

So, you see, I'm certainly not plotting murder, anymore.

But I *am* plotting.

Don't miss the next mystery to feature Schuyler Ridgway, *Closing Statement*.

It was only nine a.m. on a beautiful September Wednesday, and already I was not having a good day. In fact, the only way my day could've gotten any worse was if, when I showed up for work, Mike Wallace from *60 Minutes* was waiting for me, microphone in hand, camera crew at the ready.

As it was, instead of Mike Wallace, I had Jarvis Arndoerfer—the man some people might call my boss—waiting for me just inside the front door of Arndoerfer Realty.

The front door of the real estate office is always kept standing wide open during the day in order to encourage walk-ins, so I spotted Jarvis through the storm door the second I turned off Taylorsville Road into the Arndoerfer Realty parking lot.

In his late fifties, with a good-sized gut hanging over his belt, extra-thick lips, and a nose reminiscent of W. C. Fields, Jarvis is not exactly the sort of thing you want to lay eyes on first thing in the morning.

I've often wondered how his wife can stand it.

And, technically speaking, no matter what anybody might call him, Jarvis is not my boss. Jarvis does happen to be co-owner—along with his wife—of the firm I work out of, but as a real estate agent, I'm supposed to be an independent contractor. Who, for all intents and purposes, works for herself. Sans boss.

What this means, I do believe, is that I actually get to make my own decisions. It also means that, while Jarvis does take a percentage of all the commissions I earn, he does not have any kind of final authority over me. I needed to remind myself of this as I walked in and immediately noticed that Jarvis had planted himself directly in my path—and that two of the veins in Jarvis's forehead looked close to bursting.

I also needed to remind myself that I was a forty-two-year-old grownup, and *not* a six-year-old first grader about to be reprimanded by her teacher.

Since the front door of Arndoerfer Realty opens into one huge room with four metal desks, one in each corner, you can see at a glance exactly who is there at any given moment. At this particular moment, for example, I could plainly see that there were two other real estate agents present—Barbi Lundergan and Charlotte Ackersen.

Neither of these women, however, even glanced my way. In fact, it looked as if both were trying their best to look totally absorbed in whatever happened to be on top of their respective desks. Barbi, for example, appeared to be mesmerized by a large, cut-glass ashtray.

I turned back to Jarvis. "Good morning," I said cheerily. I already knew, of course, that the morning wasn't good, but, hey, I thought I'd give it a shot.

"Schuyler," Jarvis said, "thank God! *There* you are! I've been trying to phone you at home!"

Apparently, a "Good morning" in return was out of the question.

"Something awful has happened!" Jarvis hurried on. *"SOMETHING AWFUL HAS HAPPENED!"* Lately, whenever Jarvis gets excited, he repeats himself. The second time Jarvis says something is always quite a bit louder than the first. It's like watching an instant replay with the volume turned up a little.

I'm not sure why Jarvis started doing this. I do know this past year Jarvis became terribly absorbed in the NBA and NFL playoffs. Maybe all that time in front of the tube affected his mind. Maybe he became convinced that every exciting moment in his life has to be replayed at least once.

It must be doing wonders for his love life.

"It's terrible, Schuyler! *IT'S TERRIBLE!*"

During the first play and the replay of "It's terrible," Jarvis had started waving in my face what looked to be an entire newspaper section. Even though he'd wrinkled it badly, clutching it that tightly in his fist, I knew exactly what newspaper it had to be. Yesterday's *Courier-*

Journal. I even knew what section it was. Section B—
the Metro Section.

Call me psychic.

"Have you read this?" Jarvis was now saying. *"HAVE
YOU READ THIS?"*

I opened my eyes very wide, stared for a long moment
at the newspaper, and then finally shook my head.
"Have I read the entire paper? No, Jarvis, as a matter
of fact, I don't believe I have."

I was being deliberately obtuse. I've always thought
one of the advantages of being a woman is that, if you
want to, you can act incredibly stupid, and sure enough,
some man will actually believe you're really that dumb.

One of the veins in Jarvis's forehead now appeared to
be doing a pretty good imitation of Mt. Vesuvius just
before that Pompeii incident. "No, *not* the *ENTIRE*
paper!" Jarvis said. "Have you read the article about
this firm?"

Actually, it wasn't exactly an article *about* Arndoerfer
Realty, but I could see how Jarvis might look at it that
way.

I shrugged, trying to look as if he were talking about
something inconsequential. "Oh, that," I said.

"That? *THAT?*" Jarvis really needed to do something
about those veins. Siphon them off. Have them removed.
Something. "I got home very late last night, after writing
and rewriting a contract on one of my listings, so I didn't
read yesterday's paper until this morning," he said. "I
was eating breakfast when I saw it. God, I almost
choked. *I ALMOST CHOKED!*"

I was tempted to say, "No kidding. *NO KIDDING!*"
But I resisted.

Jarvis's eyes were now bulging out a little more than
his veins. "Your mess is splattered all over the paper for
the entire *WORLD* to see!"

I just looked at him. Was Jarvis actually suggesting
that at this very moment there were people in *Bosnia*
perusing the Louisville *Courier-Journal?* Somehow, I
doubted it.

Jarvis might also give you the impression that "my
mess," as he called it, had made front page news.

This was far from the truth. The article to which Jarvis
was referring was in the second section of the paper, on

page B5, toward the bottom of the page, and it couldn't have been more than four inches long.

It didn't even rate a picture.

Under the headline LAWYER SUES REAL ESTATE AGENT, there were a few extremely brief words that detailed how a local real estate agent by the name of Schuyler Ridgway—that's me—was being sued by a local attorney by the name of Edward Bartlett—that's slime—to whom the agent had sold a house a couple of months earlier. The article also mentioned that Bartlett alleged that the aforementioned Schuyler Ridgway of Arndoerfer Realty had known about several defects in the house she sold him, *and* that she'd knowingly and deliberately not told Bartlett about the defects before the sale had been closed.

That was just about all the article said. Other than, toward the end, where whoever wrote the article had thought to mention that lawsuits only tell one side of a case.

When I'd read the article last night, it had distressed me a little that the *Courier* hadn't even called me up for my reaction before they'd printed the thing.

It was probably just as well, though. I probably would've called Bartlett "a lying weasel" at the top of my lungs. Which would've been a big mistake.

Not, of course, because this was an inaccurate assessment. Bartlett *was* a lying weasel. Make no mistake about that.

Inaccurate assessment or not, however, in a couple of days, there would've been, no doubt, yet another article detailing how local real estate agent, Schuyler Ridgway, was once again being sued by local attorney, Edward Bartlett. This time, for slander.

I suspect one reason the *Courier* didn't call me was that they didn't want to waste any more time reporting this thing than they absolutely had to. Because it was obvious, if you glanced over the entire page on which my little article appeared, that even the people at the *Courier* realized it made for pretty boring reading. They'd put it right next to a news item headlined UTILITY POLE REPLACED. The utility pole headline was in significantly larger type than mine.

I cleared my throat. "look, Jarvis, this thing is not exactly splattered all over the—"

Jarvis interrupted me. This is something Jarvis does a

lot. Standing 5'5" in his stocking feet—and that's only when he wears very thick socks—poor Jarvis has been suffering from SMD, Short Man's Disease, for as long as I've known him. One of the symptoms of this affliction is that its sufferers feel compelled to dominate every conversation. They also labor under the delusion that they know everything there is to know about everything, and they feel as if they must demonstrate it. Frequently.

Jarvis was obviously in the throes of a relapse. "This thing could end up costing a small fortune! *A SMALL FORTUNE!*"

I just looked at him. To hear Jarvis talk, you might've thought the money would be coming out of his own pocket. The truth was, everybody at Arndoerfer Realty carries insurance for just this sort of thing. It's called E and O insurance, which stands for Errors and Omissions, and it's supposed to cover us in case some client ends up doing exactly what Bartlett was doing—taking us to court over some error or omission that he thinks occurred during the sale of his property.

E and O insurance is not in the least bit cheap, and this is yet another way in which it's a lot like the malpractice insurance doctors carry. "Jarvis," I said, trying to be patient, "I believe our insurance would—"

Jarvis interrupted me again. Hardly a surprise. "Even if it didn't cost anybody a dime personally, it's the worst kind of publicity!"

Jarvis is not only short in stature, he's also a little short in the hair department. He only has this furry brown border left just above his ears and around the back of his head. I have to hand it to Jarvis, though. At least, he doesn't do what a lot of bald guys do—let his hair grow very long on one side, and comb it across. What Jarvis does do, however, is constantly swipe at his forehead as if there's this great mass of hair there that he's brushing out of his eyes. He was brushing nonexistent hair out of his eyes now, as he did his replay. *"IT'S THE WORST KIND OF PUBLICITY!"*

I tried for a placating tone. "Now, Jarvis, some people say that any kind of publicity is Okay as long as they spell your name correctly."

This was evidently not the best thing in the world I could've chosen to say. Jarvis did not seem the least bit placated. In fact, his eyes and his veins suddenly seemed to be engaged in bulging contest.

"Well, now, Schuyler, they certainly spelled my name correctly, didn't they?" Jarvis punctuated this by waving the *Courier* in my face all over again.

What Jarvis was referring to here was one other tiny detail that the newspaper article had also mentioned. This particular tiny detail had been mentioned in the very last sentence, and there was every chance that most people didn't even read that far.

Still, to give Jarvis his due, I have to admit that what few people did happen to read that far would find out that, since he was the broker I represented, Jarvis had been named as co-defendant in Bartlett's lawsuit.

This was not exactly news to me. As a matter of fact, I'd been meaning to tell Jarvis about it myself. I'd been meaning to tell him ever since yesterday morning when some guy from the sheriff's office had dropped by Arndoerfer Reality to serve papers on me.

If Jarvis had been in the office, the guy would've served papers on him, too. As luck would have it, however, I had been the only one in the office at the time.

Like I said, I'd been meaning to let Jarvis know. I'd just been waiting for the most opportune time, that's all. Like, for example, a time when I felt particularly in the mood to poke a tiger.

Of course, if I'd known this article was going to appear in yesterday's paper, I certainly would've gotten into a tiger-poking mood right away.

Jarvis's voice had reached the peak of its crescendo. *"OH YEAH, SCHUYLER, I'D SAY THEY SPELLED MY NAME CORRECTLY, ALL RIGHT! YESSIRREE—"*

I took a deep breath. "Look, Jarvis, I'm sorry about this, I really—"

Jarvis brushed nonexistent hair out of his eyes. Again. And interrupted me. Again. "You're sorry? *You're* sorry? Well, *I'm* sorry, too! I'm sorry you didn't do what I told you to do!" Jarvis had gone back to waving the *Courier* again. *"I'M SORRY YOU DIDN'T SETTLE THIS DAMN THING OUT OF COURT!"*

Jarvis, as much as I hated to admit it, did have a point. Last night, as I sat reading that horrid little article in the comfort of my living room, I'd realized that settling out of court probably would've been the prudent thing to do.

Actually, I probably would have settled—just as Jarvis had suggested—except for one thing. "Jarvis, how many times do I have to tell you? Settling out of court is *exactly* what Bartlett wants us to do! It would be playing right into his hands!"

Indeed, settling was what Edward Bartlett himself had been telling me to do ever since he first threatened to file a lawsuit.l For months now, the little weasel had been phoning me off and on to remind me that he had a witness who was prepared to testify in court that I'd mentioned in her presence that I was well aware that the basement of Bartlett's new house leaked, that the plumbing in the bathroom was faulty, and that the fireplace in the living room was not usable. Moreover, according to Bartlett, I'd said all this to his alleged witness before we'd even written up a contract.

It had taken Bartlett almost a month before he'd finally told me who his witness was. Gloria Thurman, his girlfriend.

Uh huh.

That was believable. Bartlett's own girlfriend certainly wouldn't lie for him. Oh no. Not a chance. What a ridiculous idea.

Once I found out who his witness was, I had trouble believing that *anybody* would take Bartlett's accusations seriously. Why on earth would I admit to Bartlett's girlfriend, of all people, that I intended to deceive Bartlett? Were we supposed to be sharing girlish secrets or what?

Not to mention, sharing anything with Gloria Thurman would've been a little difficult, since I'd never even met her, for God's sake.

I took another deep breath. "Jarvis," I said, "Bartlett is trying to pull a scam, and I, for one, am not going to let him get away with it."

Actually, I'd had my doubts about Bartlett the second he'd walked into Arndoerfer Realty. I'd taken in the cheap polyester suit, the two pinkie rings, and the way Bartlett's tiny brown eyes never quite met mine, and I'd thought, this guy is a weasel. No joke. That had been my first thought.

My second thought, unfortunately, had been, So what? Even weasels need to buy and sell their houses every once in a while.

I should've known better.

I should've realized that weasels need to stick with their own kind.

The entire time I was showing Bartlett houses, he'd kept grumbling about the 7 percent commission he had to pay me to sell the house he presently owned. More than once, he'd whined, "That sure is a lot of moolah just for herding a few folks through a house." Bartlett had made it sound as if my job could easily be confused with an episode of that old sixties television show *Rawhide*.

Now there wasn't a doubt in my mind that the slimy little jerk had decided to take me to court to recoup the commission he'd paid. Not to mention, to get his new house repaired for free—if, indeed, repairs really did need to be made, a thing I questioned as much as everything else.

"Jarvis, if I settle out of court, it would be the same as admitting that I'd done something wrong when I sold Bartlett his house," I said. "Well, I didn't do anything wrong, and I won't say I did!"

Jarvis's eye-bulging, vein-bulging contest looked to be a dead heat. *"Instead,"* he said, "you let this Bartlett guy drag this firm's name through the mud! This article makes us all sound like a bunch of crooks!"

"Nonsense. *He's* the one that's a crook. Bartlett's not only a crook, he's a lying, cheating, little weasel that deserves to be hit by a truck!"

"I don't care if he's a woodchuck!" Jarvis said.

It was at this point that a muffled sound reminded me that there were other people in the room. I glanced in the direction of the noise. Over at her desk, Barbi Lundergan was snickering into her hand. Charlotte Ackersen, at *her* desk, immediately turned away, but not before I saw the smile twitching at the corners of her mouth.

Jarvis didn't seem to care who heard him. "You need to settle this thing!" he was going on. "And you need to settle it *FAST!*"

I took still another deep breath. I was on the verge of telling Jarvis that I was about as likely to do that as

I was to go bungee jumping. Then it occurred to me that, given the choice, I was a *lot* more likely to plunge headfirst off a very high platform, head screaming toward the ground while most of my internal organs headed toward my throat, and then be snatched from certain death by a thin elastic cord that bounced me around until my eyes rattled in my head like marbles, than it was to give in to Bartlett.

What's more, now that I really thought it over, there was no actual choice about it. "Jarvis," I began, "I would sooner—"

At that moment, I was interrupted. By someone other than Jarvis, believe it or not. Walking through the storm door in back of me was a young couple in their early twenties. I couldn't help staring.

The two of them looked exactly the way I pictured the Bobbsey twins looking, once they'd grown to young adulthood. That's the younger set of Bobbseys I'm talking about—Freddy and Flossy, the ones always described in the Bobbsey twin books as having "fair, round faces, light-blue eyes, and fluffy, golden hair."

The young woman and young man walking into Arndoerfer Realty had fair, round faces, all right. They also had light-blue eyes, and short, wavy blond hair that could easily be described as both "fluffy" and "golden."

The younger Bobbseys in the Bobbsey twin series were also always described as "plump," and while neither the young woman nor the young man walking into Arndoerfer Realty even came close to meeting this particular description, the young woman *was* nicely rounded. I gave her a quick, envious glance.

By letting Jane Fonda—through the magic of videotape, of course—torture me three times a week, I had managed to finally get down to 128 pounds. At 5'6", I probably would not be confused any time soon with the Goodyear blimp. The young woman, in front of me, however, looked as if she not only didn't have to worry about having the word *Goodyear* stenciled on her side, she probably didn't even know what the word *cellulite* meant.

The young man probably didn't either. In fact, both of these two looked as if they spent a significant part of their lives in a gym somewhere.

Of course, since in all those books I read as a child, the Bobbsey twins really didn't seem to do anything but play, spending a large part of their young adult lives in a gym was, no doubt, exactly what the Bobbseys themselves would do.

The young man and woman in front of me were even dressed the way you might dress boy and girl twins. The woman was wearing a white short-sleeve polo shirt and a khaki-colored skirt that ended just above her knees, and her companion had on an identical white short-sleeve polo shirt and khaki-colored shorts. Both were wearing white Nike Airs and no socks, and both had identical golden tans.

I blinked again. If I hadn't already had a pretty good idea who they were, I would've taken them for, if not fraternal twins, then at least brother and sister.

Last night, however, a woman by the name of Amy Hollander had phoned me at home and had started off the conversation by telling me that she'd just picked my name out of the Yellow Pages. A first, I do believe. Up to that moment, I'd been under the impression that I paid to have my name listed in the Yellow Pages just because all the other real estate agents in Louisville seemed to list theirs in there, and I didn't want to be the only real estate agent in town who didn't.

Last night, Amy had asked if I'd show her and her fiancé, Jack Lockwood, a few listings in the immediate area, and we'd agreed to meet at Arndoerfer Realty around nine.

Well, it was around nine. Freddy and Flossy here had to be jack and Amy.

Sometimes, I suspect Jarvis can smell a new client. His bulbous nose actually started quivering a little the moment the Bobbsey twins walked in, and Jarvis's manner immediately underwent an abrupt transformation. Jarvis's veins even stopped pulsing. "Why, hello," he said, taking a quick step forward and extending his hand toward the young man. Jarvis's voice could've been mixed with vinegar and poured on a salad. "May I help you?"

The young man shook Jarvis's hand, but he was looking directly at me. "We're here to see Schuyler Ridgway?"

Jarvis's face fell.

I smiled.